To Joyce

With love

Anya Paris

Brenda

Brenda Parker

1

Brenda Parker's early career as a Production Assistant with a London ITV company was significant in providing close involvement with script-writing and creative thought. Then marriage and second career in catering took over. Now retired, this is her second work of historical fiction, and reflects an enduring affection for Northumberland, where she spent the early years of her marriage. She presently lives near Yeovil in Somerset.

CHAPTER ONE

History has an uncanny way of repeating itself. Events come and go, and just as they are all but forgotten, reappear in a different form. The disguise is subtle - familiar enough to evoke a sense of déjà vu without quite conveying a warning of the consequences. Were it not so, Florence thought, her family would never have embarked on some hare-brained scheme to rescue them from their financial straits. They would simply have sold land, pictures, whatever it took to raise funds to repair the roof of Foxsteads. Had things been different, then 1959 would not have been the watershed it was, with Florence in her ninety-fifth year forced to admit that there was nothing new under the sun. But then of course history also has an uncanny way of being wise after the event.

But on this particular day history had yet to be written - and Florence's thoughts were focussed on less vexing matters. Shuffling deeper into her wicker chair, tugging at the tartan rug over her knees, she raised her face to the sun and grinned benignly. It was spring, and she had made it through the coldest and most prolonged winter she could remember. An achievement in itself.

This was the first time the wicker chair had been brought onto the terrace, and as the men of the household had already gone about their business, it had fallen to her niece-in-law to mountaineer into the attic to retrieve it. Florence did not entertain the least pang of guilt. Implacably she had watched Katherine struggling down the stairs with it, wondering how anyone not yet seventy could make such heavy weather of the task. Then she had had Katherine running in and out of the house on the least pretext ever since. Florence rather enjoyed being a nuisance. At ninety-four she reckoned she had earned the right to be demanding.

She leant back and gazed upwards through the pink starred tendrils of the overhanging clematis. Rising through it she could see the grey stones of the old house warmed by the sunshine, and at the top the just discernible crenulations of the pele tower, cutting a jagged pattern against the sky. A pair of swallows swooped low over her head then soared away out of sight. Florence smiled to herself. Her eyesight was no longer good, but so familiar was this corner and so well loved the sight, that in her way she could make out every line and detail of it. Even the swallows might have been the self-same birds she had watched here as a small girl, clinging to her nanny's hand. They still nested in the same crevices. For years she had entered the date of their arrival in her diary. But alas, the diary was no longer kept. It was a pity, Florence thought. To have lived in one place for nearly a century was quite something for the record.

Florence's memories were undeniably a colourful page of history. Hers had been a Victorian childhood of endless summers, when the house had worn an air of opulence, echoing an opulent age. In those days Foxsteads had presided over an expansive social scene –when lavish entertaining was simply part of a way of life. She remembered as a child standing tiptoe on this very spot, eagerly awaiting the arrival of carriages, seeing the gravel of the drive painstakingly raked into shell-shaped patterns, only to be scattered by the first equipage – then afterwards hiding behind the curtains on the landing to watch guests mingling below. It had been so splendid to see her mother dressed in rustling blue taffeta – almost always blue, Florence recalled, perhaps because of the sapphires she liked to wear – and her dear father, towering above everyone, quite the handsomest man in the whole world. Memories to take the breath away. Florence, who could not always remember the day before yesterday with any clarity, held every detail of her childhood safely tucked away in the deepest corner of her mind.

But inevitably all that had changed. Of course the Chevenings were still a handsome lot - no doubt of that - but the airs and graces had long since vanished, along with the plentiful servants and the appetite for high living. Even the sapphires had had to go. It was all such a pity. But it had also been a century of seismic change and unimagined social upheaval, a century scarred by war and rocked by revolution.

Many were the telegrams that had blighted lives at Foxsteads. Somehow there could be little glory in a victory that had extinguished the lives of the men she loved best – darling Freddie, her beloved brother who had volunteered in 1914 against all advice, only to be lost when the war was all but won – Cousin Jamie killed in South Africa - and many years earlier, but most poignant of all, Robert Westbury, the young man she should have married, had some foray in India not precipitated his untimely death from an unspeakable disease. Somehow the loss of others in the family had just seemed painfully inevitable after that. She sighed. Between them they had left a gap that contained an entire ocean of might-have-beens.

But of course all that was in the distant past. The world had continued to turn. Life had moved on. And living out the role of the classic spinster aunt – a drama queen, bound by tragic circumstance to the Old Queen herself (she liked to think) - she had established a place for herself at the very heart of the family. In a curious way she had become something of a matriarch after all.

Florence emitted an audible breath of satisfaction, warmed by the spring sunshine and the thought of the family gathered about her. They were all of them bound inextricably to this small corner of Northumberland, with Foxsteads at its heart, round which all other lives moved in wider but fainter concentric circles. Just like the swallows we are, Florence thought gazing upwards, and she smiled to herself as she closed her eyes against the glare. Moments later she was gently snoring.

* * *

Meanwhile, her great nephew Matthew had ridden high onto the fell behind the house and was surveying the landscape with a farmer's eye. It seemed that at long last spring had arrived, finally committing the hardest winter in living memory to history. Today gentle breezes were sweeping down from the Pennines, turning the last vestiges of snow from the gullies into swift little streams cascading through the heather. All about him lusty green spears were thrusting upwards through the decay of winter, each individual shoot shimmering as if to assert its own achievement. Spring at last. Matthew permitted himself the luxury of crossing one small problem from his seemingly endless list.

The old bay gelding had covered the last couple miles or so at a brisk canter, mane flying, damp sods of turf spraying from his hooves. Now reined back to a leisurely pace, his head was turned towards Foxsteads Crag. Matthew leant forward in the saddle and slapped his neck. 'Well done, Bramble. Now walk on old fellow.' He felt the slackening of tension in his shoulders - an unexpected sense of pleasure. It was why he liked to ride to the summit of this mighty landmark when things became tiresome at home – and things had never been more tiresome than they were at this moment.

But for once it had nothing to do with the family – not even his overbearing great aunt Florence - and in fairness neither was it entirely because of the portrait. Truth was that from the moment he had taken over the reins of running things at Foxsteads, following his father's untimely accident back in the winter, things had gone badly downhill. Of course he could not shoulder all the blame. It was scarcely his fault that the weather had turned out to be the direst since records began, making the struggle to run the farm and stud practically impossible. And the worst possible luck that just as this was all but over, yet another bombshell had dispelled any embryonic seeds of optimism. The discovery of extensive dry rot in the roof timbers of the house itself, needing urgent and unaffordable repairs, was quite simply the final straw.

On the other hand he supposed he was entirely culpable when it came to the matter of the portrait. With finances already stretched to breaking point, he knew he should have known better than to listen to his brother Giles with his crazy schemes. But of course at its conception, fuelled by a good bottle of wine and atmosphere of bonhomie, the idea of commissioning a family portrait had seemed irresistible. Besides, at that time nobody could have predicted such a winter, or guessed that the house was about to fall into terminal decay. It was all down to the worst possible timing.

Curiously Matthew no longer remembered exactly how it had come about – even whether the idea had introduced the artist, or the artist the idea - only that any scheme concerning his brother inevitably involved some kind of ambiguity. It was simply the way Giles was.

The plan had been hatched in the dark days of winter as their father struggled to recover from the crashing fall that had ended his career in the saddle and almost cost him his life. Late into the night, still surrounded by the debris of an excellent Boxing Day dinner, they had sat in conference about the dining table at Foxsteads - he and his brothers and sister – together with his daughter, Dorothy, who at eighteen counted herself as one of them. Hers was the opening gambit. 'What are we going to do about Grandfather's big birthday? Isn't reaching seventy something a bit special?'

In the ensuing silence, as they exchanged looks of agreement, Giles's gaze swept round the dining room and out of the blue he said, 'A portrait. That's what we should do. Commission a portrait.'

There was a sceptical silence. Then everyone began to talk at once.

'What an extraordinary idea.'

'Could even be the answer I suppose.'

'Whatever inspired that?'

Again Giles looked about him – at the dining room's gallery of portraits, mostly of family, where William Chevening's image was conspicuously absent. 'It suddenly seems rather obvious, that's all.'

'But it would cost a small fortune – *if* we could find the right person to paint it.'

Giles eyed them sagely. 'But you see I already *know* the right person,' he replied looking curiously smug. 'Her name is Anya Paris.'

So the seed was sown. She was, Giles told them, a new talent well thought of in informed circles. This also had to be taken with a pretty large pinch of salt of course, coming from one who would have them believe that his life in London was poised on the brink of entrée into these so-called informed circles - which sad reality did not bear out. Giles had struggled to succeed as an author for almost twenty years, and his buoyant air of self-belief no longer fooled any of them – least of all Matthew himself. But he said kindly, 'Okay then. Tell us more.'

So Giles had nurtured his seed. It appeared that by profession Anya Paris was a historian, a restorer of art - by inclination an artist. Portraits and animal studies were what she did best. She was young. She was probably hard up. And she was unknown.

Fuelled by these promising facts, it had fallen upon Matthew to contact the young artist. Today she was driving down to London having completed a mission to some stately pile north of the border, and had agreed to meet him in the White Hart in Fallowfell – neutral ground as she put it. She would be easy to recognise, she assured him. Red hair - driving a red MG - and probably wearing a green duffle coat. He had smiled wryly and not argued with the choice. Besides, better at this stage to keep the older members of the family out of things. He had merely excused himself from lunch muttering something about seeing a man about a horse – euphemism for don't-bother-to-ask, which was received without comment. Nobody remarked upon his unusually groomed appearance – tweed hacking Jacket, polished boots, his thatch of fair hair brushed into a rare semblance of control. It was just as well. Although still unsure whether this was the chicken or egg of the situation, the irony was pretty clear, as he prepared to consider commissioning another work of art to grace the dining room at Foxsteads, even while its roof fell into decay overhead.

He urged the horse into motion. There was little need. The old gelding very well knew the rutted track that led upwards, and spontaneously paused at the summit, knowing what was expected of him. Oh, that human beings were as tractable!

Matthew paused and looked about him. Today the air was clear as far as the eye could see, and from this height the horizon was a great distance away. To the west heather-strewn expanses of moorland peppered with hardy sheep rose steeply to the foothills of the Pennines. To the east were rolling pastures and tracts of woodland, where in the distance a grey cluster of cottages wreathed in wood smoke marked the village of Fallowfell. Beyond that the river was a silver shard. Matthew's focus changed and he traced the road along its convolute route to the house where he had been born and his father and grandfather before him.

Foxsteads. He saw a fine old house, sprawling haphazardly beneath a lichen-covered roof, dominated by the crenulated bulk of a pele tower. It was a place deeply rooted in the soil of Northumberland, its mellow walls seemingly engendered by the landscape itself, a one-time battleground of border reivers and Jacobite warriors. It was hard to accept that a threat of terminal decay hung over the future of such a house. Well aware of its place in family history and the importance of passing it on intact, Matthew's thoughts deepened as he began his descent from the crag, and he wondered just why he had agreed to the day's trivial mission when faced with such facts.

Gradually the land levelled, the pace quickened and he let the gelding have his head. This too was expected. The horse needed no encouragement, covering the distance at full stretch, finally clearing the boundary hedge into Friar's Meadow with consummate ease. It was good galloping country, prime pasture, bordered on one side by an urgent little stream and on the other by a rutted lane. But Matthew reined back as he reached the gateway and paused for a moment to allow a noisy tractor to trundle past. Bramble side-stepped and turned in an agitated circle. Although capable of galloping flat out all day over the roughest terrain, taking stone-walls in his stride, he was inclined to be unreliable and easily spooked in traffic. One tractor spewing out noise and fumes was all it took. Even from the safety of the gateway he was beginning to dance and side-step in protest. A pity, Matthew thought, for it was a bad fault in an otherwise faultless mount.

The tractor rounded the curve of the lane. Mathew unlatched the gate and guided the animal through. As he struggled to quieten him and refasten the latch, there came another violent sound. This time it was the sudden roar of an engine, followed by the blast of a horn and the screeching of tyres. Then without warning a little red sports car shot into view, skidding on the muddy road, finally embedding itself on the opposite verge amidst a shower of mud and flying turf. The horse panicked, sliding and cavorting on the slippery ground. Then wildly he rose on his hind legs. Matthew could do nothing to save himself. He slid into the mud with a squelching thud.

To his anguish he saw a young woman hastily clambering from the little red car and crossing the lane. Moments later he was looking up into a small face that might have materialised from a Titian canvas. It was framed by an unruly halo of bright amber hair. 'I could have killed you!' she gasped.

Still hanging onto the reins, he scrambled to his feet, struggling to quieten the horse and recover his dignity. He was covered in mud, and incandescent with rage. 'You could have killed us both,' he said. 'What on earth possessed you to drive like a maniac on a road like this?'

'I'm afraid I'm just horribly lost. Then this tractor appeared from nowhere.'

'Lost. Where are you supposed to be going then on a track like this?'

'I'm looking for a pub and some clown I'm supposed to be meeting for lunch.'

'I see,' he slowly said in a dry tone, suddenly aware of just how he must appear in this humiliating situation. 'Then perhaps I can assist you – since very probably I'm the clown you're looking for.'

For a moment she stared in disbelief, slowly summing up the situation. Then all at once her face lit up and a pair of disarmingly direct green eyes filled with mirth. 'Well I'm blessed - what a stroke of luck. How do you do?'

'How do I do?' he exclaimed. 'Bloody badly actually.'

'Well I'm Anya,' she replied unperturbed, holding out her hand, smiling engagingly. 'Matthew Chevening I presume!'

* * *

When Florence awoke some time later she was no longer sure where in time she was or which of her many summers this could be. Then she caught sight of the slender figure of a girl skirting the edge of the lawn. Florence struggled to rearrange herself and gather her wits. 'Rosemary! I'm over here. Come and talk to me.'

The girl turned and waved cheerfully, then changing direction hastened over to the terrace and sank down at the old lady's feet. 'You've been dreaming, Auntie! I'm not Rosemary. This is 1959 and I'm Dorothy.'

Florence's old eyes filled with apology. 'Oh dear me, Dorothy, of course you are. How foolish of me. I must have been half asleep. But you know you do look so like your poor mother at times.'

Dorothy smiled unperturbed, unable to share any real sense of loss for the mother who had not survived her birth. Besides it had proved no bad thing being raised and more than a little spoilt by

15

every kind of relative except an actual mother. At almost eighteen, scarcely younger than her mother was when she died, she rather enjoyed the comparison to a woman whose remarkable looks were her main legacy.

'Yes, you are like her in many ways,' Aunt Florence continued. 'But fortunately only in appearance I think.'

Dorothy gave a self-effacing little shrug, equally aware that the Chevenings had had precious little time for Rosemary as a person. 'In this family we all tend to look like each other,' she said.

'Yes – that's very true. Now look at your father. Dear Matthew. He's your grandfather all over again - and if you had only known my brother Freddie, your great grandfather...' Florence's eyes became glazed for a moment, then sprang back into focus. 'Where is your grandfather anyway? I thought you took him to the physiotherapist.'

'I did,' Dorothy said. 'But I dropped him at the Stud on the way back. One of the mares is about to foal ...'

'I see. So that little trip was a waste of time and money.'

'Of course it wasn't,' Dorothy protested. 'His leg gets stronger all the time. Besides, it's good for him to take an interest in things. It makes me sad to see him looking so old.'

'Old?' Florence snapped, so that even the whiskers on her chin bristled. 'I'm ninety-four and I'm not old. It's all a question of mind over matter. Dorothy, put my pillow right for me, will you?

16

There's too much nonsense talked about old age. You are not as old as you feel - but as old as you *let* yourself feel ... Ah, that's better dear.'

Dorothy gave a wry grin. 'So that's your well-kept secret, is it?' But the words were wasted. Florence's chin had already disappeared into her collar, and she was asleep again. Moments later she was gently snoring.

Dorothy tiptoed into the house. French windows led from the terrace into the drawing room. Here it was dark and cool after the brightness of the day. She paused, suddenly conscious of her own dim reflection staring at her from above the mantelpiece. In this light - and in the light also of her old aunt's unwitting mistake - Dorothy saw herself as her mother's daughter with a little tremor of recognition. No wonder her father gave her strange looks at times. She had always considered herself to be all Chevening in appearance. But the something that had stirred old Florence was there also – unmistakably. All at once she could have been looking at the photograph that stood on the chest of drawers in his room.

Although Rosemary's hair had been auburn, and Dorothy's was fair, cut short so that it waved softly close to her head, it framed a familiar face, with an expression she was shocked to recognise. There were the same candid grey eyes and thick dark lashes that went against all the rules of her colouring. And there too was that unmistakeable hint of petulance. Dorothy watched as her own lips parted in astonishment at this sudden revelation. The tomboy in the shabby jeans did not match this unfamiliar image.

For a long time she stood motionless in the half-light of the drawing room and measured what she saw by what she had been told. Then she smiled at herself. Maybe she too was destined to be headstrong like her mother. She supposed that already she showed signs – largely due to her attachment for Luke Robson with his fast car and fast friends.

A shadow darkened the window behind her. She turned, embarrassed, to discover Angus – officially an uncle, although in Dorothy's eyes more of an elder brother. He was ten years younger than Matthew which put Dorothy's own age practically half way between the two of them. He certainly did not act like an uncle. At this moment he was staring at her bemused. 'You look as though you've seen a ghost.'

Disconcerted to be interrupted in the middle of her introspection, she answered tartly, 'What do you expect when you creep up behind me like that?'

'I came to tell you that the foal is here - a beautiful little colt. I thought you'd want to come down. What a pity you didn't stay when you dropped Father at the stud.'

'I came up to tell Granny what's happening.'

'You did? Then you haven't got very far.'

Dorothy gave him a cool look, but Angus merely returned it with a lazy grin that creased his sun-tanned face as he ran a filthy hand through a thatch of hair. 'I didn't think you were so vain Dorothy.'

'I'm not.'

'You were smiling at yourself.'

Dorothy scowled. 'And you want to know why.'

'Not if it's a dark secret.'

'Well it is - so there.'

Angus continued to eye her speculatively. 'I suppose you were daydreaming about that dashing boyfriend of yours.'

'Wrong,' she said, wondering how he had hit the nail so cleanly on the head. 'Wrong as usual. So just tell me about the foal.'

'Better find out for yourself. Come on. Hurry up and make your peace with Mother.'

Minutes later they were on their way across the lawn, careful not to disturb Florence as they passed. A gravel path skirted the shrubbery and led through an iron gate set into a high brick wall. The kitchen garden beyond was deserted. Hodges had probably gone home for tea, which was just as well, since the he was an inveterate gossip and probably would have delayed them for the best part of half an hour.

Angus paused on the threshold and surveyed the garden. Sheltered in the lee of the stable buildings, it was a tranquil place, neatly tended and already sown for spring. 'Splendid, isn't it?'

'Yes – it always is.'

'But at what price, Dorothy? It's probably just as well that the Hodges are retiring soon.'

'Is it?'

'You know it is - now that we're all beginning wonder how much longer we can afford luxuries like this.'

'I didn't know. Surely thing's aren't that bad.'

'Pretty bad. Dry rot – costly repairs – that sort of thing. You know perfectly well they are.'

'But we'll get by. We always do.'

She closed the gate behind them and paused for a moment, solemnly looking about her. Hodges had been faithfully tending this plot since long before she was born. It epitomised every familiar thing she had ever known. With its mellow, crumbling brick walls and little iron fences, the glinting glass of the old greenhouses, and wisps of steam rising from the damp earth, it smelled wholesomely of freshly turned soil and good stable manure – and of every April she had known in her life. She drew a deep breath. 'Yes, I suppose when they retire all this will have to change.'

'It will certainly need to be rationalised.'

'You mean ploughed up and left for Dad and me to cobble together.'

'Something like that – so long as the roof hasn't fallen in by then.'

'Oh Angus, don't say that.'

He laughed at her. 'Okay, I won't – because of course things aren't quite that bad yet. Besides you're talking nonsense. Long before it comes down to that you'll be married with a home of your own to worry about. It won't be your problem anyway.'

She paused in her tracks and fixed him with an earnest gaze. 'Hold on, Angus. You're quite wrong there. Foxsteads will always be my problem because I have no intention of living anywhere else.'

'You an old maid? What rubbish. Someone will soon come along and sweep you off your feet and carry you away. It's the way of the world.'

She eyed him in mild contempt. 'It may be the way of the world in general, but I hadn't noticed it to be a trend in this family.'

He took the rebuke good-naturedly, well used to having his own matrimonial disaster under scrutiny. Angus had barely left home before returning with the unthinkable blot of divorce on his copybook. It was sufficient to turn any remark of his on the subject of marriage into a case of kettle and pot. 'Perhaps you'll be luckier - or wiser - than me,' he said with a shrug. 'Besides, you must know they're relying on you to marry into a fortune. And isn't that boyfriend of yours rolling in money?'

'Oh Angus, change the record.'

'I thought it was a tune you liked.'

'Okay then. So where's the big deal?'

'Is there a big deal?'

'Apparently not. No-one encourages us, believe me.'

'Only because he's a rake.'

'Yet you'd have me marry him!'

Angus lolled indolently against the iron railings and eyed her in lazy speculation. 'I hope my brother appreciates the altruism.'

'He deserves it.'

'What? Good God, he has all the soft options. He wants to try my life.'

'Yours?' She laughed scornfully. 'It was

entirely your own fault that you couldn't keep your hands off Millie Carter.'

At this Angus stirred himself and marched towards her along the path. 'You devil! I'll have you for that! A good hiding might teach you some respect!'

'Touché - and no disrespect intended!' she called boldly as she took to her heels.

He was swift in pursuit. Laughing now, they flew along the maze of little paths that chequered the plot, suddenly not caring too much for Hodges' painstaking efforts. Out by a green painted door they went and round the back of the high brick wall. He did not catch her until she was safely in the stable courtyard where their roistering laughter rang sacrilegiously through the respectful silence surrounding the new arrival. Then like two naughty children they struggled to wipe the smiles from their faces, and composing themselves, crept like a pair of guilty conspirators towards the inner sanctum of the foaling box.

CHAPTER TWO

Matthew was well used to being the subject of gossip. It came with the package of living in one of the notable houses of the district, of being part of a long established and respected family, which gave rise to a misguided impression of opulence. And of course it was greatly exacerbated by his being a widower and consequently considered to be the most eligible man in the district. As far as Matthew was concerned it all lacked any kind of substance, since the family was actually in financial straits, which in turn called his eligibility into question. Nevertheless this was how the locals viewed him. To be seen in the company of any woman was sufficient to arouse immediate interest. To be seen in company someone like Anya Paris was enough to inflame gossip to fever pitch.

Matt knew perfectly well what was coming the moment he escorted Anya over the threshold of the White Hart. All eyes turned in unison at first sight of her, attracted by her slender grace and Pre-Raphaelite air of having stepped straight from a gilt frame - as unlike any female form to be found in this neck of the woods as was possible. Then all eyes widened incredulously as they saw that it was Matthew Chevening guiding her to a secluded table in the corner of the bar. The silence that accompanied them was conspicuous.

'They'll get over it,' he told her wryly, settling her in her place. 'Villages thrive on the unexpected.'

Anya Paris was clearly unperturbed. 'Then that's a change. In London you'd have to walk naked into the middle of the road to be noticed.'

'I can imagine.'

'But of course it also has the advantage of being fairly anonymous. This little trip has been something of a revelation.'

'You've been to the Borders. On business?'

'I've been returning some restored works of art to a stately pile near Melrose. That's what I do, you know. I don't want to give any wrong impressions, because professionally speaking I'd scarcely call myself a portrait painter. It's just something I do because I'm good at it. By profession I'm a conservationist and I work for a company that does just that.'

'I know all that,' he said smiling at her earnest declaration. 'I also know that you are something of an artist.'

She shrugged this aside. 'I prefer to think of myself as a scientist. Restoring old pictures is a wholly scientific craft. If I have a talent for capturing a likeness, then it is a bonus.'

Matt nodded in pensive agreement as he rose to fetch drinks. Lunch had been declined, much to his dismay since he himself was rather hungry. Instead he ordered sandwiches, soda water for Anya and a beer for himself, then returned to the table before any of the locals could make overtures. He did not wonder at their interest. Alone in the corner Anya cut an arresting image, a slender wisp of a girl with an elfin face, whose amber hair shone in a bright halo against the window. For a fanciful moment he was reminded of a stained glass depiction in the Lady Chapel of the church across the way. But the moment was fleeting. There was actually nothing in the least angelic about this young woman whose curious blue-green eyes had already proved mischievously disconcerting.

'And so,' he said, placing the glass before her, 'you are a scientist whose work takes her to Scotland. It must have been a precious cargo you were conveying.'

'It was. That's why I was delivering it in person. It was part of an extraordinary collection that included a wonderful and very unusual icon. It was in our hands for the purpose of provenance.'

'And did it turn out to be all the owners had hoped?'

'Oh yes. And much, much more. It turned out to be as rare as it is beautiful. The most glorious example I've ever seen.' Her own face shone as she talked. Clearly her profession was her obsession. He feared that the portrait he had come to discuss could only stand in the shadow of such brilliance.

'So you have completed the errand.'

'Yes , and to be truthful I'm more than relieved to have delivered it safely. Do you know of the Boswells – at Skelby Park?'

'Only by repute. They open their garden to the public – although not the house I think.'

'Then they should. It seems all wrong that such a wonderful collection should not be seen by the whole world.'

'It was that special?'

'Titian, Canaletto, a sublime Stubbs – the best I've seen in private hands and the only one I've ever handled. It was pretty astonishing really.'

For a moment she concentrated on the sandwich that had been placed before her, as yet untouched. Then after a couple of hasty nibbles her thoughts once more scattered, and she was back telling him about the icon which every museum in London had wanted to examine, believing it to have sprung from the earliest roots of Christendom, and of the nonchalant disregard with which its owners had treated it. 'But not any longer, Mr Chevening. I think it has earned its respect.'

'I'm glad. And please call me Matt.'

Twisting the glass in her fingers, she played with the elliptical pool of light shifting on the polished surface of the table, momentarily lost in thought. Then she looked up with a rueful glance. 'I'm afraid sometimes I talk too much, Mr Chevening.'

'Matt,' he corrected for a second time.

She responded with a smile. 'My apologies anyway Matt. Of course you don't want to hear about other people's property, even if they have had a stroke of such good fortune. Good fortune always comes to the already-rich, doesn't it?'

'Sadly yes. We could do with a little of our own just now as it happens. Things have been very hard for us this winter.'

'Yes, Giles told me.'

'Then you probably know that my father has had a poor time. No doubt Giles explained about his riding accident. Actually he's lucky to be walking at all. He had a crashing fall last autumn, and for some time we wondered whether he'd ever walk again. But he's doing well and making the best of everything.'

'Yes, I did hear. It must be hard for him to come to terms with such a misfortune.'

'Yes, it's tough. That's why we are looking for something special to mark his seventieth birthday later this year. Giles came up with the idea of the portrait. Possibly through meeting you.'

She raised her eyebrows. 'Really? I didn't think he'd seen any of my work.'

'He didn't say. But we were glad enough to take his advice – since only Giles has the remotest knowledge about art. We have some fine family portraits, but beyond that I daresay we are a bunch of rustics.'

'That isn't at all what I was told.'

'I see. What did you hear?'

'That there are masses of you - and you have an aunt who is as old as Methuselah and a house that dates back to the dark ages.'

She toyed for a moment with her sandwich, then laid down her knife. It had been hardly touched. No wonder she was so thin. It did her no favours, he thought. Besides it was a waste, especially when he himself was still famished. 'So how did you meet my brother?'

'We met working on a television script together. He must have told you.'

'Not that I remember.'

'It was with the new ITV people. We were both hired to research a programme about the National

Gallery. I gather research pays the bills for Giles while he waits for his ship – his bestseller – to come in.'

Matt gave a rueful laugh. 'Oh dear! Poor Giles – ever the optimist – ever the loser.'

'Oh no,' she protested. 'Not a loser surely. He's a splendid person and he really believes in himself.'

'And do you believe in him?'

'I believe that extraordinary things can happen to anyone.'

Matt emptied his glass and gazed contemplatively into it. Maybe that was true, but also it could not be denied that sometimes the extraordinary brought little enough joy. It was certainly true of Giles's life so far, and it was certainly true of those at Foxsteads. Things that he would not have believed a year ago had lately come to blight his family, making it hard to feel that kind of optimism.

Anya was gazing pensively into her upturned palms as though reading secret thoughts. He watched her quietly, welcoming the chance to study her more closely as for a moment or two she was lost in contemplation. In repose there was something quaintly appealing about the solemn little face beneath the halo of red curls; the skin almost transparently white, the downcast eyes fringed with thick pale lashes. He noticed just the faintest smattering of freckles across her nose, which somehow restored her to her place in the twentieth century. 'You're fortunate to have choices in what you do,' he told her.

She gave a little shrug. 'Not that it changes anything. Restoring – conserving - that is my real love. My obsession. Always has been. Once I had high-flown ambitions of working abroad. Italy. I really wanted to do that.'

'Yet you claim it's science, not art.'

'Science is art. And art is science.'

'It is?'

'Truly it is. The blending of pigments, the understanding of the chemistry created by time and light - it's a wonderful subject! At times I feel privileged to understand even a little of it.'

Once again she was lost to him, absorbed in her thoughts. Then she looked up at him with a smile and pressed her palms together as though to close the book. 'How pretentious I am! I didn't come to deliver a lecture but to talk about your portrait. Please forgive me.'

'I feel thoroughly edified'

'Oh dear. Then that's terrible.'

She began to rummage in her handbag, a huge, shabby container of an awful lot of everything, eventually producing a small folder. 'These are some photographs of work I've done. Not much to go on really – but the best I can do at the moment.'

He took them from her and slowly leafed through them. Even from these Matt recognised the quality of her work. There were portraits of people, of animals; a wonderful picture of a man in hunting pink mounted on a handsome horse. 'This,' he told her, 'is how I visualise my father's portrait.'

She laughed. 'You have selected the only one

29

that I was reluctant to include – simply because it was done entirely from photographs. The family wanted it done as a surprise - for a birthday I think it was – I forget exactly. I don't usually work from photographs alone.'

'So now perhaps you'll believe in my lack of knowledge. Because you see, for me it works.'

'Yes – it did work.'

'And I truly think it would work for us. It's the perfect concept for my father's portrait.'

All at once her eyes clouded and her face grew solemn. 'Not for me, Matt. You see I need a reason to be away from London for a while – and a proper commission to come to.'

He wanted to ask why, but her expression forbade it. Instead he said, 'I assure you that is how we would want it to be.'

'I'm glad - because in any case I believe a portrait should never simply copy a photograph. It has to be much more than that – to have life put into it – something that takes it beyond just an image. That's what I dream of perfecting.' Once more her face filled with apology. 'Oh dear, I'm lecturing again – and being very pretentious, aren't I?

'There is nothing pretentious about having a dream,' he said. 'I rather envy your indulgence.'

'Is it an indulgence? I mean to say, don't you have dreams?'

He gave a good-natured shrug. 'Age and responsibility tend to change one's focus. The dreams I once had no longer matter that much. And the things I want now are too practical to be called dreams.'

Anya appeared to consider this for some moments before she said, 'I think that's terribly sad.' And slowly she replaced the photographs in their folder and quietly closed it.

* * *

Later that afternoon Angus settled himself on the porch steps to await the return of his brother. He was still smiling to himself as he thought of that wild chase through the vegetable garden. The teasing words that had provoked it passed lightly through his mind like a mild stimulant. He shuffled the pages of the newspaper spread before him, and remembering Dorothy's reproach on the subject of his own shortcomings, stretched his long legs with a yawn and congratulated himself on his good sense in recognising what was good for him. Behind him his few gloomy years of responsibility lay discarded. Before him an undemanding future in the shelter of the place he knew and loved best seemed assured. And the tranquil scene beyond the porch, bathed in thick yellow sunshine where the shadows lengthened across the perfection of the afternoon, seemed to stamp its seal of approval upon his sense of satisfaction. Angus sighed complacently. No longer did he seek a challenge from life - at least not beyond an occasional challenge thrown at him by his wayward niece, which after a lifetime of teasing and bantering, he had come to expect.

He was dozing when his brother finally arrived.

Matt snatched the paper from his hands, folded it and delivered a brisk blow to the head. 'Thanks for running things in my absence!'

'All done,' Angus replied airily. 'Everything accomplished. Even delivered a new foal.'

'Well *well!* Fancy that.'

'A colt – a little beauty – and no problems.' Angus looked smug.

Matt beamed at him. 'Excellent news.'

'So what about you? What's your news then? How was the artist woman?'

Dorothy appeared at the top of the steps. 'Don't you dare to tell him anything before me!' she yelled. 'Angus, you're a pig.'

'Steady on!'

'Well, I'm dying of curiosity too.'

Matt smiled. What a baby she was! He watched indulgently as she flew down the steps. Then as breathlessly she arrived he looked again. Or was she? The stab of recognition that earlier she had seen in herself now pierced his consciousness. Perhaps his daughter was no longer quite the child he thought. He returned the hug she delivered and drew her down onto the step beside Angus. 'Patience young woman and I'll tell you all about it.'

'Was she nice?'

'Yes, she was charming - even taking into account Giles's tendency to exaggerate. Different, I have to say – but interesting. At least I felt there could be a real basis for working out a scheme.'

'A scheme?'

'Yes, something we hadn't thought of before –

the possibility of working from photographs.'

'And so?'

'Well, if it were done that way we could keep the whole project to ourselves - which let's face it, could be fun.'

'Gosh! That would be something, wouldn't it?'

'I thought so. The snag is that she insists she'd need to be here anyway to make a real success of it.'

'I don't get.'

'No, I didn't really. I rather think it had something to do with wanting to be out of London for a bit. Not a problem, I suppose, if we can find some pretext for having her here.'

'I don't see why we'd need to,' Angus reasoned. 'The lodge is lying empty and needs a tenant at the moment. Why not an artist? We've got the finest scenery in England, haven't we?'

Matt looked from one eager face to another. 'Well yes, why not?'

'If she agrees.'

'And if we can afford it. Does she come at a high price?'

Matt hesitated. He fingered the scraps of paper in his pocket on which he had scribbled the flimsy terms of an agreement - ambiguous to say the least. He said slowly, 'That rather depends on how we look at our priorities – whether we can afford such a luxury in the light of our present difficulties – not to mention the repairs to the roof we're about to have to finance...'

'Or whether we need something mad and wonderful to lift our flagging spirits,' Dorothy said.

He smiled at her. Dorothy, ever positive, whatever the situation, had hit the nail on the head as usual. His Pollyanna baby, he had once called her. And yet she was no longer a baby. In fact at this moment he hardly recognised her.

His smile became contemplative. Yes, somehow it had escaped his notice how grown up and lovely she had become. Yet the wide grey eyes that eagerly returned his scrutiny from beneath a fringe of thick dark lashes concealed no feminine wiles whatsoever. She was lovely without even knowing it. Her flaxen hair fell lightly into place whether or not she troubled to comb it. He was looking into a face destined soon to turn heads. For a moment his thoughts vacillated between pride in what he saw, and reluctance to accept that all too soon others would see it for themselves and she would be taken her from him. In a moment of panic he searched for the little girl in her, but found only a young woman who reminded him sharply of his youth. How strange that he had not noticed the metamorphosis.

Later that afternoon as he strode across the garden towards the Stud he was still smiling to himself, thinking of Dorothy's eagerness, and Angus's guile, and acknowledging how much he welcomed the prospect of a diversion however it was achieved. Yes, even as he trod this familiar path, anxious to find his father and the new foal, his mind strayed quixotically. He had found himself curiously captivated by Anya Paris and was still haunted by echoes of the afternoon.

After lunch the final shards of ice between them had melted in the spring sunshine. It had become wonderfully warm, with the gardens grown colourful in a mere couple of hours. A carpet of daisies appeared to open up before their feet as they crossed the wide expanse of the green towards the church. Anya said she wished to see inside. He was surprised. The slender figure in green, stepping lightly through the lych-gate, her red hair burnished bright, somehow looked more pagan than Christian. Two elderly men sitting sunning themselves on a bench clearly agreed They stared as they recognised Matthew, turning their heads in unison, then nudged each other sagely. Matt did not wonder. Rural Northumberland did not often see her like. Moreover, she had probably made their day.

Inside it was dark and cold. 'I love old buildings,' she said. 'Especially churches. Mediaeval art is fascinating. Even at its most primitive it has a beauty that is full of truth and simplicity.'

'Yes, yes I agree it has.' He imagined she was still thinking of the icon. 'This is a wonderful old building. It has Norman origins, so I understand. I have known this little church all my life' He looked about him, suddenly seeing the familiar little building with new awareness. It had indeed always been part of his life. It was where he had been baptised, confirmed, married and where he had buried his young wife. It contained graves and memorials of his family. And today he was acutely aware of it place in his whole psyche. 'Being here with my family is one of my very earliest memories,' he told her.

She nodded slowly and said, 'My very earliest memory is of being in a church too. But it was not this kind of tranquil experience.' She paused by the font and ran her hand over the worn carving of its cover. 'It was in France. I was with my mother and we were hiding from the Germans.'

'Occupied France.'

'1940. France in free fall. Of course I don't remember much about it. I was scarcely more than a baby at the time, and my mother had lost my father and we were trying to get to England. We sheltered in this little church and waited for help to arrive. It was a wonderful, peaceful place, and there was an old man – I don't think he was a priest – who prayed with us. Anyway help arrived. I don't know how we came to England, only that it was in an open boat, and that we did. I never found out how. You see my mother died before I was old enough to ask the proper questions.'

'How very sad.'

'Not really. It just explains why I like churches. This one is lovely.'

She turned and began to wander down the flagged aisle towards the altar. 'My earliest memory is of being a fugitive. I suppose in a way I still am.'

'Is that what you meant when you said you needed to be away from London for a while?'

She became thoughtful. Then she shook her head. 'Perhaps, although I don't think so. My reasons are very much of the present.'

His expression silently questioned her, but she turned away, and for a few moments stood quietly gazing about her – at the simple altar with its carved rail – and gleaming eagle supporting the ancient Bible – at the crumbling flagstones before it, with the worn brasses lying in a bright pool of stained glass.

'Yes, it's lovely,' she said. 'Really beautiful. English churches are so simple and straightforward. In France it's much harder to believe in all that symbolism. Don't you think so?'

'I'm afraid I'm not familiar with French churches.'

'No, I suppose not. My work has taken me to many.'

'And I'm guessing that you yourself are French.'

She replied with a Gallic gesture. 'Who knows what I am? The war rather smudged the facts. Anyhow my mother took up with an Englishman called Brown after my father disappeared, so I claimed the only name that seemed to make for kind of an identity.'

He opened he mouth to question her. But all at once she laughed. The absent look left her eyes and she returned to him. 'I told you I talk too much! I'm so sorry.'

Once more he started to speak, but nothing came. Somehow he could not quite meet her gaze, as though dazed and disconcerted by the swiftness of her smiles and the way her ever changing moods were reflected in her eyes; extraordinary eyes that were brooding, fathomless one moment, bright and shining the next. He could not even discern their colour. Rather like the sea they were shifting shades of blue and green. Instead he mutely followed her down the aisle.

As they reached the porch, she paused once more to study the carving about the door, worn almost smooth by the countless hands that had caressed it as she caressed it now. 'I shall remember this little church for its simple beauty and its northernness. Do you think it has a collection box?'

When they had found one and emptied their pockets, together they wandered outside, blinking in the bright sunlight. The clock in the tower chimed the hour, sending a shower of birds chattering into the air. The two elderly men could be seen retreating across the green in search of tea. It was then that his voice returned to him – and he invited her to come to Foxsteads.

Now as he approached the stable yard the rapture of that moment slowly seeped away. Reality returned. He remembered that his father's day had been about treatment for his troublesome leg and discussions concerning the pele tower roof and not least the arrival of a new foal. Suddenly his extraordinary meeting with Anya Paris receded into the unreality of a half forgotten fantasy.

Passing beneath the archway of the Stud, with the clock on its tower catching the last rays of sunlight and the old fox of the weathervane turning a disinterested back, Matt tried to reassemble his concentration. Not least was the thought that now he had to concoct a tale for his father about the man he had been to see about a horse.

CHAPTER THREE

'Lunch was good?' William asked, as he and Matthew returned from the stud.

'Fine,' Matt replied, warily wondering whether this was merely polite conversation, curiosity, or an indication that gossip had already spread beyond the White Hart. 'Although I'm sorry I missed the foal's arrival. What a little beauty.'

'Yes - splendid. One little ray of hope amidst all this gloom, wouldn't you say?'

Matt met his father's worried look. The fellow seemed weighed down by the bleakness of everything. He had yet to come to terms with the bitter truth that life had irrevocably changed. As they covered the few hundred yards back to the house, it was painful to see how heavily he relied on his sticks and how arduous his progress was. Matt was saddened to see his father so suddenly aged, yet determined as ever not to give in. Six months ago he had worn his age lightly, and of course he was still a remarkable looking man, with fine grey eyes and only the slightest thinning of the hair which once had been thick and fair like Matt's. Even the slow progress across the garden did not entirely conceal the energy of the man who only months ago had been a bold and accomplished horseman. But the brave endeavour to keep going in defiance of the truth was fast becoming a painful effort.

'So there was no better news from the survey,' Matt ventured.

'I'm afraid not. It was exactly what we already

knew I suppose.'

'And chose not to believe.'

'*Tried* not to believe,' William said with a sigh. 'It's pretty hard to take when someone employed to clean a few gutters tells you that half the roof is about to collapse.'

'Especially coming from Robson.'

'That makes no difference really.'

'Probably not – if we really think we can trust him.'

'Not liking him has nothing to do with not trusting him, Matt.'

'Okay, I take the point. So we had hoped he might be wrong.'

'But it appears he was not.'

The path they followed, skirting the lawn, now rounded a great mound of rhododendron, bringing the house into view. Set against the trees was a wooden bench onto which William lowered himself with a hydraulic sigh. 'Looks invincible, doesn't it?' he said, looking towards the house, where the old pele tower cut a bold and defiant silhouette against the sky - a vista unchanged in generations. It was indeed hard to accept that such a threat hung over its future. The tower was quite simply part of that landscape. It had claimed a place in the histories of border raids since the fourteenth century, and was reputed to have sheltered the ill-fated Earl of Derwentwater during the intrigues of the Rising, a legend that had given it an immortality of its own. 'But facts have to be faced. It seems that time is running out for the old place.'

Matt sat down beside him. 'Dry rot.'

'Apparently so.'

'Treatable then.'

'Yes, of course – but only at a price. They found serious damage in all the main timbers of the tower. Large parts of the roof will have to be replaced. It could cost thousands. Thousands that we haven't got at the moment.'

'How much are we talking about?'

William shrugged. 'Robson will have to be brought back to estimate.'

'Robson's company isn't our only choice, Dad.'

'No, but he has a good reputation as a builder – and he is our neighbour, whether we like it or not.'

And his son's trying to lead my daughter astray, Matt thought to himself, but said instead, 'Don't you mean whether we like *him* or not?'

William gave him a rueful look. 'I'm afraid we can't afford to dislike him in the circumstances. We're simply going to have to bite the bullet and try to raise some capital somehow.'

They were silent in thought. All about them their assets were there to be seen - land in good heart as far as the eye could see, valuable livestock, and at its the centre the house and its many treasures. Yet a deep innate reluctance prevented them from considering these possibilities in any kind of rational light.

'We can't contemplate selling land or stock, Father. It's our income and our livelihood. It isn't just the past. It's the future.'

'I know, and of course we can't. But we shouldn't be thinking of investing in more stock either.'

Matt swallowed. Something to do with seeing a man about a horse, was it? He took the rebuke without comment. Already his father was beginning to struggle to his feet, his frustrated sigh echoing a painful grimace. 'I suppose we *are* living in the past,' he said. 'Before we know it the world will be full of Robsons, covering the countryside with little boxes, and people like us will be nothing but an anachronism, a memorial to a bygone age, a small chunk of history living in a charming ruin!'

'What nonsense!' Matt protested, helping his father to organise his sticks. 'You know perfectly we'll never allow that to happen.' Nevertheless a contemplative silence accompanied them as they continued their slow progress to the house. As they reached the steps Matt paused to sweep up the day's paper from where it lay abandoned by Angus, while his father, with an audible sigh of relief, stepped ahead of him into the welcoming refuge of the house - the ancient pile whose immortality he still could not call to question.

* * *

That evening Foxsteads wore an air of almost painful familiarity. William was assailed by the heady scents of logs and lavender polish and something distinctly appetising being concocted in the kitchen. The dogs, barred from the stables on account of the foal's arrival, flung themselves in a tangle of sliding rugs at his feet. Sounds mingled -

voices from the library, the clatter of cutlery from the dining room, strains of Chris Barber issuing from his granddaughter's bedroom. William quietened the dogs and slowly made his way upstairs to his room, steeped in melancholy, knowing only that the welcome worn by this beloved house was probably where familiarity would begin and end in the not-too-distant future.

'I suppose we have to accept that something has to go,' he told Katherine bleakly.

She was seated at the dressing table, winding her silver hair into its customary chignon, and returned his look through the glass with raised eyebrows. 'Something? What kind of something?'

'Land. Property. The family silver.'

She regarded him impassively. 'You know perfectly well you don't mean that.'

'Well, you think of something then.' He came and stood behind her, a hand on each shoulder, and regarded her reflection with a sad little sigh. 'The simple fact is, Kate, that we can't easily put a hand to the kind of money all this is going to take.'

'We don't know that yet.'

'I think we do.'

'We've always got over things before.' The final pin secured the chignon and she turned to face him. 'And we will again.'

Smiling, he dropped a kiss onto her brow. What a comfort she was - with her air of calm optimism, her reassuring smile, the ability to make him believe in the impossible. How sad, he thought, that in his heart he always wondered if he had failed her. A square peg in a round hole she was, stoically making the best of everything, even though the persona of the country wife sat uneasily on her slender shoulders. 'I'd like to know what,' he said.

She returned to the mirror to fasten her pearl earrings. Then she said, 'For a start look at me now, William. As always in my pearl studs, while all manner of treasure lurks in the jewellery box. Most of it's only on a kind of loan anyway – in trust for my lifetime – inherited from heaven-knows-where. And Elizabeth is our only daughter and she hates jewellery. You know that. She'll never hanker after it. If something has to go, why not start here?'

For just a moment he stared at her in outrage. Then he gave a hollow little laugh. 'Darling Kate - just as if I'd sell your jewellery – least of all to pay for a roof! Too right you are. We'll simply have to think of something.'

She watched him as the smile faded and the old haunted look returned to his face. She could feel the pressure of his infirmity as he supported himself, albeit lightly, on her shoulders, and could sense his air of helplessness.

'William, we haven't even received an estimate yet,' she reasoned. 'We don't know what it's going to cost. We could easily be meeting trouble halfway.'

'Kate, I have never been a pessimist. I can't be accused of that. But in this I can see no real reason for optimism. Robson's face said it all. Do I need to spell it out?'

A little tremor crossed her face as she shook her

head. Of course there was no need. William's own face said it all. And in many ways she understood him better than she understood herself. She emitted a philosophical sigh. There were indeed times when she wondered whether she knew herself at all. William, dear William, was an open book, while it was she who constantly endeavoured to conceal her feelings beneath a flimsy veil of pretence. How such an unevenly balanced marriage had worked was a mystery to Katherine. Yet somehow, against all the odds, it had. 'Robson is a loathsome man,' she said. 'No doubt the thought of dry rot gives him enormous pleasure.'

William smiled wryly. 'Yes, I rather think it does.'

'Can't we get a second estimate then?'

'I don't think so. Robson isn't out to fleece us you know.'

'He didn't make his money by being charitable either.'

'No, but here it's different. He has a vested interested in us, doesn't he?'

'Does he?'

'Of course – together with local society as a whole. What's more his son appears to have a vested interest in our lovely granddaughter.'

Katherine replaced her comb on the dressing table with a forceful stroke. 'William, I refuse to allow that thought to enter the equation,' she declared. 'That - like everything else probably - will simply have to take its natural course – and the sooner the better.' Stunned to silence, he watched as she rose to her feet, bestowing on him the enigmatic look that he knew so well and understood so little – a wise woman too often underrated.

* * *

One thing was sure. Being in love with Luke Robson had changed Dorothy's life. Just the summer before she had been nursing disappointment, having failed the exam that would have taken her to university. Now she was spending a reluctant three days a week in college, studying for her retake, together with a secretarial course 'in case' on her father's insistence (oh, he of little faith!). But it was this that had turned out to be the proverbial ill-wind.

Whilst the college course was unspeakably dull, with boring reiteration of her English Language course, and the incomprehensible vagaries of shorthand and typing for which she could see no useful purpose, the social life was a revelation. Never before had Dorothy experienced such fun and freedom. And she was quick to adapt, and quick to learn, emerging from the experience as a shining imago, stepping into the sunshine, surrounded by a brand new circle of friends in which she was the indisputable centre of attention - not least because of her enviable position as girlfriend of the legendary Luke Robson.

Everyone wanted to be in Luke's set. He had it all - the looks of James Dean, more money than the rest of them put together, which he spent freely, and a shiny black Aston Martin. He was the personification of glamour. And for the time being at least, he was hers.

It was mostly because of Luke that Dorothy had had to reinvent herself. Swiftly she had cast off her schoolgirl image, updated her wardrobe in a burst of enterprise, and shed the trappings of her rather narrow childhood. Growing up had been difficult in a household where she was so many things to so many people, and she had assumed something of a chameleon character. Supposedly this helped when it came to shaping herself to Luke's ideal girl. Metaphorically at least her beloved pony had been put out to grass. Her Picturegoer magazines and most of her old records had been given to her cousin Philip. Traditional jazz was now her music. The sounds emanating from her prized Dansette were no longer dreamy ballads, the Dickie Valentines and the Mario Lanzas of before, but Chris Barber and Humphrey Lyttleton, and swinging Sinatra. And suddenly heaven itself was joyously squeezing herself with Luke into a sound booth at Granger's record shop in Hexham.

That morning she was punctuating a shopping trip with a visit to Granger's. She enjoyed being sent out for things, having just made herself available by passing her driving test, and was grateful for the few extra hours of freedom. She and Luke were crushed into a booth, trying to share a pair of headphones between them. His arm was tightly wound about her waist and his hand was already making its way inside her blouse. She was weak with ecstasy.

'Listen to this track, Dorothy. Basin Street Blues done quite differently from Kid Ory's.'

'I can't concentrate. Give me the headphones.'

Obligingly Luke removed his hand and relinquished the set. Dorothy recovered herself. 'It's better than Ory's. More up-to-date.'

'Of course it is. Shall we have it?'

'You can have it. I'm out of funds.' He gave her a doubtful look and she frowned at him. 'We're all out of funds actually. Your father has thrown the cat amongst the pigeons. You must know that.'

'Not exactly his fault, Dorothy. It's probably fortunate that the problem came to light before it got out of hand.'

'It is out of hand already. We're all trying to work out how to afford it.'

He eyed her scornfully. 'You must have plenty of assets. Look at who you are and where you live. You're all so – you know – substantial.'

Dorothy laughed. On the face of it, she supposed it must appear that way. Indeed assets there were. She knew that perfectly well. It was persuading her father and grandfather to relinquish some of them that was the tricky bit. Dorothy had already wondered why they had not considered offering some of their valuables for sale. She had worked once or twice during the college recesses for her father's friend, Henry Crisp, who ran fine art auctions in Newcastle. It had been an edifying experience. She had been astonished by the vast sums raised by art and antiques, and was well aware that her family had masses of everything. But the very suggestion had at once been shot down in flames. Inadvertently Luke had put his finger on the pulse of it. It was all down to who they were and where they lived. That and an inability to move with the times.

'When it comes to assets, I'm afraid my family can't see the wood for the trees,' she told him. 'They simply don't see the things they own as currency.'

'You mean spending in itself is a problem.'

'What? Have you ever looked at us? Everything we own we've had forever. I mean, look at the shabby old cars we drive. We seem to like things better when they're falling to bits. And if my grandfather tells me one more time that he still wears the shoes he was married in I shall scream!'

Luke laughed at her. 'Not a problem I can identify with. My father makes money simply so that he can make more money. And he does it so that he can spend it.'

'Then you're lucky.'

Luke shrugged. 'In a way, yes, I suppose. But we've come a long way the hard way. It's simply your good fortune that you had your country house given to you on a plate.'

For some reason Dorothy bristled. The implication that her family did not work for its living was somehow deeply offensive. Farming, the breeding of livestock, supporting a way of life from the land was not the easy option. It could be cruelly hard at times. The Robsons, for all their wealth and bluster, still had a lot to learn.

She removed the headphones and handed them back. 'Okay, buy the record. It's good.'

'I'll buy it for you if you like.'

'Why should you do that?' His hand slid back into her blouse and found her breast. Her stomach seemed to turn inside out and her legs become jelly. 'Why should you want to?'

'Because – because you're irresistible.' He said, kissing her gently. 'And because I want you.'

Dorothy gave a little shudder, alarmed by her own aching response. Of course she wanted him too. With every instinct. Yet somehow she could not quite shake free of her grandmother's old world upbringing, despite the fact that most of friends made extravagant claims for themselves. Lurking in the back of her mind there was always a little spectre, reminding her that the reality of succumbing to Luke Robson might have the power to rob her dream of its magic, and cast her back into the role of just the girl-next-door – or worse, the discarded girl-next-door. Fiercely she pushed him away, aware that his kisses were becoming intense and that probably they were attracting the attention of everyone else in the shop. 'Luke Robson, you're a rake.'

'I know. So do you want the record or not?'

'Of course I want it.'

'Then it's yours.'

He bought the record and she carried it home in triumph, with half the items on her grandmother's list forgotten, and her resolve seriously shaken.

* * *

Katherine was delighted to have a whole day to

herself. Robson was due to come that afternoon to discuss the pele tower roof with William, but she was not expecting the meeting to involve her. The rest of the family had already dispersed and gone about its business. Including Dorothy. How useful it was, Katherine thought, to have her granddaughter available to run errands, today sent to collect the shopping from Hexham. Dorothy had cheerfully driven away in the old Morris Minor, and left Katherine with the rare luxury of time to enjoy what was another perfect spring morning. She had already ensconced Florence in the wicker chair on the terrace, and was setting about making the most of her time in the garden.

Florence waited until Katherine had assembled her tools, changed into her gardening shoes and put on her canvas gloves before she decided that she wanted her footstool brought to her. Katherine inwardly sighed. 'I'll just bring the stool from the drawing room, Auntie.'

'But it's the wrong height for this chair. I can't think why you didn't bring down the wicker stool yesterday. You know I like to have it. The other one gives me a crick in my knees.'

'I'd have brought it if I'd known where to find it - but it wasn't with the chair, and you know how dingy the attic is.' Katherine's expression was one of martyred patience, while her fingers in their gardening gloves tightened around the trowel. 'I'll send one of the men to find it for you as soon as they get back.'

Florence drooped and shifted in her chair, flinching with exaggerated discomfort. 'Very well dear. I expect I can manage without it until then. Oh, how dreadful it is to have to be so dependent - to be old and stiff and such a nuisance to everyone.'

Katherine put down the trowel, peeled off her gloves and suppressing another sigh moved towards the house. 'Very well then. I'll have another look...'

'Bless you Kate! What a trouble I am!' Even a casual observer would have noticed how quickly Florence recovered herself, so it could scarcely have escaped Katherine's practised eye. However nothing but patient acceptance showed as she patted the old lady's hand and said, 'No trouble, dear. I'll not be a moment,' before disappearing to the attic.

Florence leant back in her chair and gazed across the lawn with a sigh of satisfaction. A contented feeling stole over her. The garden was looking beautiful. Such a sudden transformation - such warmth and greenness! She fancied she could almost hear the vital thrusting and unfolding of all that greenness, as every single rustle and movement served to deepen the colour of the garden before her eyes. She listened intently. But for the singing of the birds, she was sure she could have heard spring more clearly than she could actually see it. But tired though Florence's old eyes were, she could still make out familiar things - a bee hovering over the cascade of aubrietia on the terrace wall - a blackbird on the lawn tugging with all his strength at a stubborn worm to take home to his mate - the old tabby cat lurking in the shrubbery watching. Suddenly Florence was seized by a paroxysm of alarm. She saw that the cat was stealthily approaching the unwary blackbird, still manfully struggling with his dinner. Fond though Florence was of the old cat, she now pulled herself bolt upright in her chair and clapped her hands sharply. There was an echoing crash from somewhere in the house. Whether it was this or her own prompt action that did the trick, Florence did not know. But a moment later the lawn was deserted, except for the worm perhaps, hurrying back to earth. Florence grinned benignly. She had made someone's day at least!

A few moments later Katherine reappeared at the garden door. 'Did you find it?' Florence began. Then she straightened herself and stared. Katherine's face was as white as a sheet; she was covered from head to foot in pale grey dust, and looked as though she had seen a ghost. 'Something wrong?' Florence demanded in alarm. 'You haven't fallen down the stairs, have you?'

'Not quite,' Katherine replied, sinking unsteadily onto the doorstep, her lips trembling. 'But for a hair's breadth I almost came down rather quicker than that. The floor of the attic has just fallen through!'

CHAPTER FOUR

Arthur Robson was a self-made, self-satisfied man - which in his own considered opinion he had every right to be. He had made his way up the slippery ladder of success by old-fashioned hard graft and the ability to grab the main chance when he saw it. His building company had grown out of the bomb devastation of the war, where he saw the vast estates of housing he had built as the phoenix rising from the ashes, fanned by a proverbial ill-wind.

He had bought Fallowfell Hall just over two years before – a solid, Victorian mansion that also traced its origins to the entrepreneurial success of industry. Shipbuilding money it was, he understood, although he had bought the house from the estate of a retired Colonel who had allowed the place to fall into disrepair. Hard times apparently had also necessitated the dispersal of its land many years before, which was the only disappointment to blight Robson's pleasure in his splendid acquisition.

Once or twice he had considered approaching William Chevening, his immediate neighbour, with a tempting offer to purchase a tract of the adjacent pastureland. Chevening had intimated that times were tough and it was very clear that his house was in need of considerable restoration. Indeed the idea was still mulling in Robson's mind when the emergency call came from Foxsteads that morning.

'My God,' he said to Rita as he replaced the telephone receiver. 'Their bloody roof's gone and fallen in. So now perhaps he'll believe me.'

Rita Robson put her hand to her face and gasped. 'At Foxsteads. Heavens above! Do you mean the whole roof?'

'I don't really know what I mean. Chevening was in a right panic. The man's a complete fool of course. He was very well warned. I told him weeks ago that this would happen. I spelt it out in words of one syllable.'

'Is anyone hurt?'

'Apparently not. But I'll have to go straight over, I suppose.'

Robson sank back into his chair and returned to his coffee, plainly in no hurry to do so. Time was, he thought - and not so long ago - when he would have dropped everything and responded to a man like Chevening in short order. But times had changed. Recently the ground between them had levelled out. These days he knew he was no longer just on the up. He had arrived. And he wished nobody to forget it.

Rita, for whom the transition from Gateshead to Fallowfell Hall still remained very ragged at the seams, eyed him anxiously. 'Yes, Arthur, I do think you ought to go over right away.'

'Aye woman. And I shall when I'm good and ready.' She still had a lot to learn, he thought. She looked the part of course. Even in middle age she was a pretty little woman with an empty head of blonde curls and a look of permanent surprise. But she had yet to come to terms with the reality of her new position. 'As a matter of fact I feel quite sorry for Chevening,' he told her. 'This could be a disaster for him. He's already hinted that money's tight at the moment.'

'Surely not.'

'I dare say that means ready money - but even so it's a bit surprising coming from substantial people, isn't it?'

'It is – very surprising,' Rita agreed, 'Although I suppose their house is quite shabby, isn't it? It's all a bit – well – faded.'

'People like that don't go in for smart furnishings,' Robson said dismissively. 'With them it's all land and cattle and horses and the like. But even so I didn't expect Chevening to admit to being strapped.'

His contemplative gaze swept his surroundings. Shabby and faded had no place here. He was the first to acknowledge that setting this house in order had cost a small fortune, but it was worth it. Moreover he'd had the good sense to personally undertake only the renovations that fitted his own field of expertise, and had put the interior décor in the hands of the best firm he knew. A wise move. He had come across the London firm of J.P. Castaletz in the course of business, and on the strength of this had invested his trust and a great deal of money in making sure that Fallowfell Hall was restored to its original splendour. He considered the result to be a mutual achievement.

Rising from his chair he strode over to the handsome Chippendale mirror above the chimneypiece – the mirror described by J.P. as 'in the style of' - and adjusted his tie. The image reflected his sense of purpose. A burly man with a florid complexion and brindled hair, he wore a sense of arrogance like a badge of office, a visible declaration that he was astute, confident and always right. 'I have a bargain to strike with Mr William Chevening,' he said. 'Accounts can be settled in different kinds of currency you know.'

Rita nodded and looked about her with a bird like gaze that was curiously devoid of any actual comprehension. 'You mean cheques and the like?'

'I mean land,' he replied.

'Land? But do we need land?' He ignored her and made for the door. Then he turned on the threshold and said, 'Trust me. When I've assessed their problems they'll be given an offer too tempting to refuse. So just wait and see.'

* * *

At Foxsteads, less than two hours later, William took his place at the lunch table. Still dusty and distraught from the morning's discovery, he was stunned by the news that not only had his wife nearly killed herself, but that his house was about to crumble about his ears and plunge him into unavoidable and unsustainable debt. His interview with Robson still rang in his ears. 'The impertinence of the fellow! Can you believe it?' he said to the family.

'But it is a generous offer, William,' Katherine said. 'Surely accepting it would solve our problems more neatly than we could have dared hope.'

'It is, I know, very generous,' William agreed. 'But I cannot accept selling off land at any price. And coming from Robson of all people...' He paused, ashamed of his attitude, and added, 'No, it's not just that. There's a life-long principle at stake too.'

He sighed despondently. Of course it was a pity that he and Robson were not better friends and had not made a more promising start in their acquaintance. It would have made everything so much easier in a situation like this. Moreover it was possible that the fault was more his than Robson's anyway. But it had been hard to accept the arrival at Fallowfell Hall of someone like this, who thought to buy himself into the community at any price, throwing money at any cause that would further his own. For as long as William could remember Fallowfell Hall had quietly mouldered away in the custody of the old retired Colonel whose family had owned it since time out of mind. But now it had taken on a new character. Robson had already spent what William considered to be an obscene amount embellishing the place. And then there was the matter of the four great oaks on the boundary, which had been felled. Water under the bridge now of course, but a bad start in their relationship. Much thought had lain behind the decision to ask Robson's advice in the matter of the roof repairs at Foxsteads. At least it had seemed to be a step in the right direction, since neighbours they were and likely to remain.

'And do you really trust his judgement?' Matt

asked.

'After this morning's disaster we have no choice. The man knows his job.'

'And he knows how to grab the main chance when he sees it.'

'That too. I rather think money provides all the answers to a man like that. I dare say he even believes he can buy himself a place in heaven if he so chooses.'

'But isn't a hundred acres really very little?' Katherine said.

'We can't afford to part with one acre of our lowland pasture,' Matt replied. 'We have too little of it.'

'It's the best and most profitable land we have,' Angus agreed. 'Besides he'd probably only fill it with some faceless housing estate.'

'Nonsense,' William said.

'Is it? Are you sure of that?'

'Of course. He'd never get planning permission to build on Friar's Meadow – even if it were practical, which it isn't.'

'But if he did, the price would be a fraction of its worth.'

Florence who was trying to follow the argument and dribbling soup down her front, said, 'Who's going to build a housing estate?'

'Nobody's going to build anything, Auntie. We only said 'if'.'

'Then why don't you build one yourself, William? There's money in that, you know.'

'Because even if I wanted to it wouldn't be allowed.'

'Auntie, you're spilling soup,' Katherine said with a weary glance.

Florence fumbled for her napkin, grumbling. 'Then why waste time talking about it?'

William's gaze swept round the table, and against all odds, felt a smile tugging at his lips. Florence was winding herself up for a lively altercation on the subject, whether warranted or not – a prospect as ever relished, even though nowadays she could not always keep up with the train of thought.

'Why haven't I met this dreadful man?' she demanded.

'You have, Auntie. We're talking about Mr Robson.'

She grinned so fiercely that her teeth slipped awry. 'Well, well - if he's wanting to build his houses on our estate you'd better up the price.'

'Except that no-one's building anything.'

'Nor selling anything. End of subject.'

William's gaze travelled the length of the table and rested on Katherine - dear Kate, who alone hated these pointless arguments which came thinly disguised as discussions. In fairness it didn't show. Her tranquil expression betrayed nothing of the truth that what was grist to the mill for most of the family was to her a painful irritation. 'One thing is certain,' he said, trying to meet her eyes and failing, 'However we meet the cost of our repairs, the repairs cannot wait. We have to accept that almost all the roof timbers of the pele tower need to be replaced - and that it's going to cost a very great deal of money.'

'But for heaven's sake,' Matt said, 'let's consider all the possibilities before we decide to chop our estate into pieces.'

'Agreed. But we have to think quickly if this splendid old house is to have a future.'

He looked about him. This very room, set beneath the ancient timbers of the pele tower, was acknowledged to be the glory of the house. With the heavy panelling of its original oak, and intricate plasterwork of its lofty ceiling unchanged since the seventeenth century, it was remarkable for its beauty and preservation. A great open fireplace dominated the room. A Jacobean mantel spanned the wall from floor to ceiling in heavily carved black oak, the date 1657 entwined amongst the convolutions of fruit and leaves. And opposite were stone mullions, added at a time when windows were heavily taxed and an expensive luxury, the ancient glass still spilling milky light onto the flagstones and worn rugs. It was a room rich in history and heavy with atmosphere. Silently he surveyed the portraits ranged about the walls, and strangely, when all was considered and all controversial remarks taken in their proper context, these faces told him much the same as the flesh and blood faces ranged about the great oak table itself - that there had to be another way - though what that way could be William still could not tell.

* * *

When lunch was over Katherine went out into the garden, slipping away on her own. She carried her trowel and trug basket with her, but with no real intention of working amongst the weeds. She wished only for a little time to herself, away from the argument and counter-argument and feeling of being constantly in demand. Recognition of this gave her the mildest pangs of guilt. She was hiding from them all, she knew - especially from Florence – which did her very little credit. Katherine reached the lower stretch of garden beyond and out of sight of the house and rounded the tall beech hedge that divided it from the adjoining shrubbery. A niche had been created in the hedge, paved with stone slabs, and a semi-circular seat built there to provide shelter where one could sit and contemplate. Katherine often used it when she felt the need to be alone.

She sank onto the seat with a little sigh and closed her eyes for a moment or two. Her thoughts reflected the drama of the morning and the worrying questions that Robson's findings had raised. Yet to Katherine it seemed absurd that even such a contingency could cause this scale of financial anxiety in the family. Slowly she opened her eyes and looked about her.

The lawn sloped gently away and melted into a rural landscape, framed by the distant Pennines. It had been farmed by generations of this family. Much of what she saw belonged to them. Surely, she reasoned, when they had all this, it could not be so difficult to afford a crisis of this kind. Surely with all this land - acres and acres of it - they could spare one small pasture to keep faith with their past. Then she contemplated all the other possessions they had, probably worth hundreds of thousands of pounds, and wondered how it was they could not raise the money to repair the roof without a major family crisis. Somehow it made no sense.

But then, Katherine thought ruefully, there were things about this family that would never make sense. More than forty years in their midst had not provided so much as a ray of enlightenment.

So deeply absorbing were these thoughts that she did not notice Dorothy's approach across the lawn until a slender shadow fell across the stone slabs. She looked up, startled, suppressing a little shudder of irritation at being discovered in her idle solitude. Ashamed, she gathered herself together and began to make a hasty pretence of assembling her tools.

Dorothy was not deceived. 'Am I invading you in your hiding place?'

'No of course not. Come and join me.' Katherine patted the seat beside her.

'I thought I'd find you here. Are you sure you're all right?'

'Of course. Why?'

'Well after this morning's dramas?'

Katherine smiled. 'I wasn't dwelling on it. Not really. Just thinking over all the problems it has uncovered and wondering how we're going to find such a monumental sum of money to solve them.'

Dorothy eyed her grandmother sagely. 'We can't sell land, Gran. We really can't. Dad and Grandpa are absolutely agreed on that.'

'Oh, I know they're quite adamant.'

'And perfectly right. Honestly they are.'

Katherine slowly replaced her trowel, fork and gardening gloves in the trug and set it back on the ground. 'Probably they are. And I dare say some other way can be found.'

'I suppose we can borrow or mortgage or something.'

'Maybe. I'm afraid these things do happen to large old houses. Sadly it's been the demise of far too many. That and death duties.'

'That will never happen to Foxsteads. We simply wouldn't let it. Besides, there are just as many people who've done heroic things to save their property. Look at Lord Taylor. Don't you remember that amazing auction sale he had at Holsworth? It raised hundreds of thousands of pounds. We could easily do something like that.'

Katherine smiled and shook her head. 'Holsworth Park is a stately home, Dorothy. He was selling works of art and antiquities. But I agree, it was heroic.'

'But I've seen how auctions work. Foxsteads is just as historic in a different way. Of course it isn't large or important like Holsworth, but it is unique and we own masses of wonderful things. Besides everything is relative. His repairs were probably a great deal costlier than ours.'

'Yes, I do see that   and there could even be sense in what you say.'

'There is sense in it. Think of all that china and silver we have – half of it never leaves the pantry. And the attics are stuffed with unused bits of furniture and pictures – dozens of pictures. No wonder the floor fell through.'

Katherine laughed. 'You're perfectly right of course. Maybe we should give it some thought.'

* * *

Later that afternoon Matt and Angus set to work clearing what remained in the attic, carefully avoiding further disturbing the unsafe timbers. They passed it all down the stairs to Dorothy and their sister, Elizabeth, who although now married with a home of her own, was quick to assume charge of the operation. Together they stacked it in the unused nurseries on the second floor immediately below. There were dusty boxes containing papers, trunks of old clothes, quantities of furniture and a great many pictures.

'Why have we so much of everything?' Dorothy demanded.

'It's the accumulation of several households over the years,' Elizabeth said. 'It happens.'

'So why keep it all? It bears out what I was saying before. We should sort it and sell it.'

'Most of it's just junk.'

'But not all. Look at all these pictures. Why have they been thrown away in the attic? I mean look at them - oil paintings - portraits. Some of them look pretty reasonable to me.'

Matt, grey with dust, came to help with the stacking. 'Probably are,' he said. 'I just think they were replaced by better things at different times. Some probably came from our Grandmother's house up in Perth. Actually I can remember one or two of them. This portrait hung in the hall when I was a boy.'

Dorothy eyed it disdainfully. 'I hope she's not an ancestor of mine.'

'I'm afraid I think she is. Not much of an oil painting, is she?'

'She's not. And what about this?' Dorothy held up a large canvas, a dark and grimy still-life with a crumbling frame, its corners bound with rusted metal brackets. 'This looks really old.'

'I believe it is. I remember that too. Believe it or not I was unaccountably afraid of that picture when I was little. It hung on the landing outside my room, and I was sure I could see a face peering out of it.'

She stood back and looked at the painting, her head on one side. 'I can't imagine why – although maybe perhaps I can - *if* you have a vivid enough imagination.'

'Or happen to be a child.'

'It was one of a pair as I remember. The other hung in the north corridor. Both pretty dreadful, but interesting I suppose. Definitely only fit for the attic.'

Angus was more interested in a pair of Lakeland studies. 'Grasmere. I once fished right here on this very bank. Got stuck into a massive pike of all things and lost pounds worth of tackle. These are good. Really good.'

'I told Gran today that we should have a sale – that we have more valuables than we realise.'

'And what did she say?'

'Actually she said she'd speak to Grandfather. I

think she quite approved of the idea.'

'I imagine he'll take some convincing. But yes, I think you could be right.'

Together they assembled the stacks of old prints, dark paintings and old photographs, relics of family history, silent testament to events long forgotten. There were strange faces looking back at them from the past, and strange places that might have been recognised had history and nature not somehow changed them. It was all curiously revealing. Dorothy found a painting with a torn canvas. 'Pity about this. It's not a bad picture. Can a tear like this be repaired?'

'By experts, yes.' Matt said. He paused in thought. Then after a moment he sprang to his feet. 'Good Lord, that's it!' He brandished a couple of pictures aloft, his eyes bright. 'I've got it!' The others stared uncomprehendingly.

'You've found a Van Gogh?'

'A Picasso.'

'The Mona Lisa.'

He laughed. 'Better than that. Don't you see? We've found the perfect pretext for bringing Anya Paris to Foxsteads. No need to mention the portrait. We can keep that to ourselves.' He paused and encountered nothing but incomprehension. 'Come on all of you. Wake up. Don't you see the point? We'll ask her to restore the lot. We'll make that the basis for an auction. How about it?'

And so it was that by teatime a sketchy scheme of sorts had been shaped into a viable plan - which even a battle-wearied William reluctantly agreed to pursue.

* * *

As Henry Crisp checked the auction rooms before closing up for the day, he paused to wonder about the telephone conversation he had earlier that day with William Chevening. It had come out of the blue, taking him quite off guard, and in the midst of an unusually busy day in the auction house. There had been little opportunity thus far to dwell on the implication. But now the staff had gone home, he had met his targets, and all was set for an important sale. He looked about him in satisfaction. Most of what he saw comprised the furniture and effects of a man, known to him by sight and repute as a collector of Lalique, and this collection, amongst other things, was going under the hammer the following day. It promised to be an interesting sale. Henry went on his rounds, checking the doors and alarm systems. There was also some important Georgian silver locked away in the safe for the night. This also he checked carefully. Henry, who was the senior partner of Wise and Crisp, could look back on a long career that was succinctly summed up by what he saw about him. The wonderful melange of the beautiful, the valuable and the just plain curious that passed through these rooms represented as many tastes, interests and obsessions as there were items in a catalogue, and Henry loved the sight and smell of it.

He returned to his office and sat down at a desk

still littered with a great deal of paperwork. Carefully he stacked it together and filed it away. Its job was finally done. What it contained had been concisely assembled and bound into the thirty glossy pages of the next day's catalogue. Only now, as slowly he turned the pages, did he at last permit his thoughts to stray.

William Chevening was one of his oldest friends; a man he had known since his young days when their two wives had first struck up a friendship together. Certainly he was someone Henry knew sufficiently well to enable him to read between the lines of the most innocuous conversation. He had had good practice of late. In William's own words, life at Foxsteads had recently become 'just one damned thing after another' – a sentiment with which Henry could scarcely argue – since yet another drama on the Foxsteads front could only be thought more sad than it was surprising.

On the telephone William had confided that the house needed major repairs. This in itself was scarcely surprising, when one took into account that the ancient pile had survived centuries against all the odds. It was the family's inability to deal with the crisis that puzzled him most.

'We are strapped for cash,' William had told him bluntly. 'Need to raise some capital somehow. Is there anything you can do to help?' He had then talked without enthusiasm about some old paintings the family had retrieved from the attics. 'A load of neglected jumble, I told them. Not worth the money it'd cost to put them right. But I agreed to find out.' With even less enthusiasm he spoke of Katherine's desire to thin out the furniture and pass judgement on some of the porcelain that lurked deep in the cupboards. Henry closed his eyes and considered it all. He knew Foxsteads intimately. As an aficionado of antiques he had often weighed up the value and rarity of much that he had seen there, marvelling at William and Katherine's apparent disregard for it all. Now as an auctioneer he could not suppress a small frisson of excitement at the prospect of handling some of it. But then Henry opened his eyes again and shook his head remorsefully. He was also uncomfortably aware that such thoughts were unworthy of him. As an old and trusted friend of the family he could not fail to recognise the reluctance and dismay in William's faltering tone.

Later as he drove homewards, with all thoughts of tomorrow's sale at last filed into the back of his mind, he contemplated long and hard upon the situation - and tired though he was he resolved to go over to Foxsteads that same evening.

Amanda was horrified. 'How *could* you, Henry, after the day you've just put in, and the day you're facing tomorrow? It's madness. Surely William can wait a bit.'

'Probably he can. But he sounded pretty down. I really feel I have to go.'

'Shall I come with you then and chat to Kate?'

He put an arm about her. 'Of course if you'd like to. But I think it might be as well for me to go alone.'

William greeted his old friend warmly. 'It's so

good of you to come over. And I must most sincerely apologise.'

'Apologise? What on earth for?'

'For dragging you all the way over here – when you're so busy.'

'It's nothing.'

'Besides I'm deeply embarrassed to have to ask this. It goes against the grain, Henry, and offends every fibre of my being to have to admit - even to you - the state of my insolvency.'

Henry was at once sympathetic. 'Good God, William, there's no need to apologise for that. I'm just sorry that everything seems to have hit you at once. As for embarrassment - you have to understand that this is very familiar territory for me.'

'I realise that.'

'Most of my time is spent in situations of this kind – handling things that people no longer want or need - or are able to keep - for reasons very like your own. It's quite simply what I do - in my very respectable professional life.'

William gave a brittle little laugh. 'Of course I appreciate all that. But I'm still not sure how far I can take on this sale thing. As you can well imagine, it clashes with everything I feel about my home and family.'

'Then perhaps you haven't thought it through.'

'I haven't dared,' William said wearily. 'Probably because the only real point is that I'm going to have to raise a very large sum of money, which could mean stripping my home of half its heirlooms - something I just can't bring myself to contemplate.'

Henry removed the steel rimmed spectacles from this nose and quietly polished them while fixing William with a myopic gaze. 'You don't have to do that. Make the things you don't consider to be heirlooms your starting point and take it from there. I'm always astonished to discover how often it's the so-called cast-offs that produce the most extraordinary results.'

'I'm afraid I'd find it hard to imagine value in the things I'm prepared to part with, Henry - things like the heap of second rate pictures from the attic that my family seems to think has a future.'

'Yet they could be right. You can't tell. The grime of ages can cover all sorts of unlikely truths.' Henry replaced the glasses on his thin nose and ran a hand over his thin grey head.

William responded with a wry smile. 'Or quite the reverse of course!'

'All right then, let's put it to the test. Why don't we have a look around?'

Henry was already very familiar with Foxsteads, but still never ceased to wonder at its diversity. Old and rambling, it spread haphazardly about a lofty hall, wearing its mysterious air of antiquity like heavy cloak, beneath which one could imagine a myriad of secrets. The hall itself was dark and atmospheric. A massive oak staircase rose from its centre onto a galleried landing. Beyond this a labyrinth of corridors led in three directions. In the hall Henry cast a glance at the pair of sporting pictures that hung there. He had always admired them and recognised their quality.

William strode past without looking. Presumably these were of the heirloom ilk. Henry was reassured by this thought at least.

At the far end of the hall a low gothic doorway led into the dining room - that wonderful monument to the Jacobean origins of the house. It was a room frozen in time, even while its atmosphere remained vibrant and very much of the moment. Nothing, Henry decided, should be changed in that splendid room – not outwardly at least - for William had already declared his intention to delve into its deep cupboards where a quantity of fine porcelain, collected down the generations, was stored. Most of this seldom saw the light of day, although Henry was familiar with much of it. He remembered seeing many rare and beautiful pieces.

Moving on, a door at the foot of the stairs led into the library – a mellow room owing its distinguished label to a wall clad in dusty, largely neglected books, and dominated by an immense desk, its tooled leather a depository for newspapers, unanswered letters and photographs. The library was indisputably the beating heart of this house. It was the place where the family gathered and the dogs sprawled before a massive hearth and shed their hairs on the faded chintzes; a room strewn with the detritus of everyday life.

Henry knew it intimately and had long admired many of the fine old books that gathered dust there. Apparently nobody appreciated them greatly. Some were of value, Henry knew, and he had long harboured the desire to handle them. The opportunity was half-heartedly offered to him. 'We could include some of these,' William said, with a dismissive gesture. 'Not that they're up to much most of them, I dare say. But we have far too many.'

'Then I would like to go through them at my leisure. You'll have to tell me what can be spared.'

'Katherine is fond of some of the great classics of course – but on the whole we're not what you'd call book people.'

They moved on to the far end of the hall where the drawing room awaited in almost sterile contrast. This was a room seldom used and stood in silence, bereft of the echoes of family life, as though waiting only to be brought to life by times like Christmas, high-days and holidays. It was a pity, Henry thought, for it was beautifully proportioned with tall windows and a fine carved chimneypiece, and contained some important pieces of fine English mahogany.

'I'm told that the chiffonier can go!' William said with a wry smile as they looked about them. 'Kate has always hated it.'

'I wonder why,' Henry replied. 'Because it will be very much liked by a large number of collectors unless I'm much mistaken.'

'It came from my grandmother's Scottish home – as did the linen press on the landing – which Kate has also declared must go. Honestly, Henry, I can't help feeling that I am being drawn into some kind of conspiracy.'

'Really?'

'Well I seem to gather the impression that

they're all in league of some sort over the whole thing. Come upstairs and I'll show you what else they've uncovered.'

There was a great deal to consider. Certainly the acquisition of the grandmother's possessions - and probably countless other households over generations - had cluttered the upper rooms of the house. Each bedroom appeared to contain two of everything. No wonder Katherine was conspiring to create a little space. With mounting enthusiasm Henry began to make notes as they progressed from room to room. At the end of the east corridor was a locked door. Beyond were the unused nurseries beneath the pele tower, where the contents of the attic lay in store.

'This door will be sealed when the work begins,' William explained as he opened it. 'The workmen will use the old outside stair, and hopefully we will be left on this side in relative peace.'

Henry was shocked by the damage caused by the fallen timbers. 'Kate is lucky to be alive.'

William's face grew sombre as he nodded. 'Yes, I realise that. It was a near thing - a very lucky escape. I suppose it should make one aware of the finer degrees in all things – even problems.'

In silence they sifted through the debris – the paintings, the prints and artefacts – the little microcosm of the past that had lain forgotten in the attics since time out of mind and now emerged as a beacon in the dark.

'Conspiracy or not, William, I do agree with your family,' Henry said, as afterwards they returned downstairs to the library. 'I do believe you could raise considerable capital from the little I've seen.' They were silent for a moment, as Henry completed his notes. Then he added, 'I need hardly tell you that there is a great deal of collectable porcelain. We both know there are some splendid pieces there, especially the German dinner service. It's quite unique. And some of the old engraved Newcastle glass could be quite sought after.'

'And the paintings? You won't easily convince me there.'

Henry smiled 'I can only say that in my opinion it would be worthwhile having them looked at by an expert.'

'That's why I asked you, dear fellow,' William said.

'I'm afraid I'm not an expert in nineteenth century art. But undoubtedly there are works of quality amongst your so-called cast-offs - possibly of value, and certainly worth looking into. I would suggest that the services of a good restorer would be well worth a modest investment.'

William gave Henry a long affectionate look. 'Thank you. That's all I needed to hear.' Dear Henry. He was a rock and a refuge. This quiet man of books, kindly, cultured and erudite, whose reassuring friendship over the years could not easily be explained, nor measured in terms of worth, was surely to be judged simply by the restorative effect of his company.

But somehow the conspiracy theory persisted. The following day, even before Henry's advice had had time to form an echo, the family had discovered a suitable restorer – someone of repute – a friend of Giles – and were suggesting that arrangements be made for her to occupy the lodge while she worked. It all appeared a little too succinct and coincidental.

Henry merely received the news with a wry smile. William's call had come at the end of an exhausting but highly successful day, while he was still in his office tying up the ends of the sale. Still smiling to himself he replaced the telephone. Finally he closed the file on the day's events, as eagerly he prepared to open another – on the even more interesting event to follow.

CHAPTER FIVE

'When is our artist expected to arrive?' Angus enquired as he deposited a sheaf of brown envelopes in front of his brother on the work-worn desk in the Stud office.

Matt did not look up, but continued to work his way down a column of figures. 'Not until late afternoon. She's driving up from London.'

'I thought she had a fast car.'

Matt pushed the papers aside and gave an irritable sigh. 'It's a bloody long way.'

Angus perched himself on the corner of the desk and began to sort through the mail. It was mostly bills of course, and he supposed that they would have to get used to it, since bills would be arriving thick and fast before much longer. The following day Robson was to begin work on the pele tower, and then the fun and games would really start. 'I suppose Dad still has no idea that he's about to be painted.'

'Of course not. He's hardly come round yet to the idea of a few pictures being restored.' Matt took the letters, pushed them to the end of the desk and gave Angus a disparaging look. He wanted to finish his work at the Stud before lunch and to be at home afterwards, free to greet the visitor. Angus was probably perfectly aware of this, and was making a nuisance of himself on purpose. Matt eyed him balefully, 'I was hoping that you might hold the fort for me here this afternoon. We're expecting a call from the Broderick Bloodstock Agency.'

Angus shrugged. 'No problem. As you like.'

'Well, for one thing I feel it's only polite for me to be around when she arrives. And for another, I did think I ought to check the attics just once more.'

'Whatever for? I thought we did it to destruction yesterday.' Which was true enough. A team of Robson's workmen had thoroughly cleared the rooms the day before and the family had sifted through every minute item that had been recovered. Finally most of it had ended up in the rubbish cart anyway. 'There can't be anything left now.'

'No, probably not – but it all got a bit chaotic yesterday didn't it? Everyone trying to read things into the least bit of rubbish – and then Philip turning up to try to resurrect World War Two!'

'Yes, funny kid, Philip.'

Philip was their sister Elizabeth's teenage son, whose young life appeared to be punctuated by obsessions of one kind or another – the current one seemingly the war, which the class at his school had been discussing. As Elizabeth observed, at least it was progress of a kind, since nothing even remotely academic had ever touched her son's imagination before.

'Yes, his face was a study when we unearthed the gas masks, wasn't it? I dare say I can find plenty more artefacts for him about the place – when I have time to look.'

'Anyway Elizabeth wasn't much better herself – trying to turn every broken toy and mouldy book into a collector's item. I suppose it's a Chevening failing. Hoarders the lot of us.'

Matt responded with a smile, then returned to his accounts. 'Maybe you're right. Anyhow, give me a bit of peace so that I can get this finished – and then I'll leave the chair to you.'

'Thanks a bundle,' Angus said with a rueful look. But it did not contain much venom. His usual role in this establishment varied very little between the mundane and the menial and he was more than happy to occupy his brother's very comfortable position in the office for the afternoon. Stuffing his hands into his pockets he wandered, whistling, into the hazy sunshine of the languid summer day beyond.

At last the desk was cleared and Matt too emerged, blinking into the sunlight. He had not realised how warm the day had become. It was almost June, and today he saw the summer expanding before him. Hazy sunshine had risen out of a misty dawn, throwing the bold contours of Northumberland into soft focus. Far to the east a grey line blurred the horizon suggesting that a North Sea fret had claimed the coastal strip, but inland the mercury was high.

Up on the roof the air was refreshing and comparatively cool. Matt emerged breathlessly onto the turret and leant against the cool stone of the parapet. Had there been no better reason for building a house around a tower the view from here would have claimed it. Little pockets of mist curled in from the east coast, giving the far horizon an indistinct, almost mystical quality. Outlines were softened, colours subdued, and the stillness in the air seemed to accentuate the least tiny sound and magnify it. From the village, a distant grey sprawl in the valley, came one ringing note as the church clock chimed the quarter. Below him the metallic clink of trowel on soil conveyed that his mother had returned to her summer-long battle with the weeds. He heard the gentle cooing of doves from the stable roof.

Sights and sounds to inspire an artist? Matt hoped so. Maybe the pictures waiting to be restored would not raise the roof – this or any other – but there had to be sense and reason in trying to cast a little light into his father's diminishing optimism, and he was fairly sure that the arrival of Anya Paris would cause a welcome diversion whatever the outcome. He glanced at his watch, then pensively scanned the landscape once more, tracing the winding course of the road into the distance. There was not a car in sight.

At last he turned to descend from the turret, caressing the old stones with his hand as he went. No sign of deterioration up here, he thought. These old walls and parapets were wonderfully preserved and would stand for ever. Nevertheless, he made his way cautiously back to the winding stone stair, knowing where the stone buttresses could be relied on and where the failing timbers could not. Once more in the attic he made his way back to the door, keeping close to the sides of the room.

All at once a resounding crash shook the rafters. Matt's heart thumped with such force that he was thrown back against the wall. For a moment he froze there listening, trying to adjust his eyes to the darkness. Before him he saw a great cloud of dust rising from the gaping hole which had all but swallowed his mother. As the air began to clear he realised that this had become even larger than before. Then from far below came cries of help. Matt rattled down the stairs and stared in disbelief. Young Philip was lying on the landing, his knee grasped under his chin, groaning.

'For God's sake man – whatever's happened?' Matt dropped down beside the writhing figure of his nephew in consternation. Philip was suddenly all arms and legs, flailing like an anguished crane fly.

'The floor just went – crumbled. Oh hell, Uncle Matt, I think I've broken my leg.'

'Let's have a look. What on earth were you doing up there? We all know it isn't safe.'

'I was just looking… I thought…'

'You didn't think. That's just the trouble. If you had you wouldn't have gone near the place.'

'I was only having another quick look round.'

'What for?'

'For things – you know - and then I fell over something.'

'Something? But there's nothing left up there.'

'Well there is. It was a door or a picture or something. It sent me flying. *Ouch!*'

'Come on now, try to straighten it out.' Carefully Matt manoeuvred Philip's protesting leg into more or less its normal position and performed a few rudimentary tests on it. Many a time he had done much the same at the scene of an accident in the hunting field.

Philip ceased protesting and muttered, 'Am I going to be alright?'

'Probably. And I'll tell you something else. If this was the war proper, instead of your idea of a history lesson, they'd sharp have you back at the front line.'

Philip looked sheepish. 'Shall I see if I can walk?'

'Okay, stand up and I'll help you downstairs.' Slowly they made it to the bottom. Matt helped him to the hall chair. The injured ankle was already starting to swell. 'You'd better take it easy for a bit, then perhaps see whether your mother thinks the doctor should take a look at it. I'll get someone to run you home.'

There was no-one about. Matt looked again at his watch, gave a deep, frustrated sigh, and went to fetch the car.

The timing could not have been more exact. It was pure precision. For after all the planning and contriving, it turned out that there was no-one about when at last the red MG turned into the tree lined drive of Foxsteads, and no-one to greet the visitor.

* * *

The little car ground to a crunching halt on the gravel sweep before the house. Anya Paris stepped out of it, and shaking the red curls from her eyes, stood looking about her. The old house that rose imposingly before her, its grey stones warmed by the soft sunshine, was her only welcome. Her face registered pleasure and surprise. It was not the house she had expected to find after a journey through the brisk, smoke-blackened metropolis of Tyneside and wild open spaces of Northumberland, where stern grey buildings stood braced against a bitter climate. This house was different. Its mellow warmth suggested that it had grown accustomed to the elements ravaging it since the Dark Ages; that it welcomed the lusty encroachment of nature. Its many-paned windows seemed to smile benignly through the untamed convolutions of the old creeper that wound itself thickly over the porch. Vigorous tendrils spread in all directions, and the roof sagged cheerfully beneath thick stone slabs down which a number of white doves were slipping and sliding with apparent enjoyment. 'It's beautiful,' Anya said aloud. And although there was not a soul in sight, the house alone seemed to welcome her. She looked towards the porch, approached by its flight of shallow steps, and seeing the door wide open, stepped confidently towards it across the gravel.

'Young lady - come over here if you please!' An imperious command from an unseen source stopped her in her tracks. She looked about her puzzled. The place still seemed to be completely deserted. 'Over here!' the voice repeated impatiently. Obediently Anya stepped back a pace or two, looking all about her, until she could see, beyond the corner of the house, a stretch of lawn and the edge of a stone terrace on which stood a wicker chair. At first sight there appeared to be nothing but a pile of rugs on the chair, but then an arm appeared from the midst of it, waving and beckoning her. Anya glanced once more towards the deserted hall, before stepping lightly across the lawn in response to the command.

On the terrace she found herself face to face with a lady who had to be at least a hundred years old. Wrapped to the chin in a tartan rug, there was not much of her to be seen – just a tiny face, creased like a withered leaf. Clearly the heat of the day had not been taken into consideration.

'You must be the young lady from London,' Florence said, offering a tiny hand that was unexpectedly firm and cool. 'Miss ?'

'Paris. Anya Paris,' Anya announced loudly and distinctly. 'And you of course must be Aunt Florence.'

Florence looked slightly taken aback. 'Yes - yes - so you've heard of me, eh?'

'Yes, I have – and I do apologise if that sounded very rude.'

'No matter,' Florence said abruptly. 'And no need to shout. My hearing is excellent. Young people always imagine that old people are deaf, blind and simple - and I assure you that I'm none of these. At least, I don't perhaps see as well as I used to - but I see plenty. Aye, I see more than you'd think! And you're a pretty little thing, aren't you?'

For a moment Anya was stunned to silence. She paused, chastened and rather taken aback to find the old eyes unexpectedly bright and disconcerting in their scrutiny.

'Not that I'm over fond of red hair,' Florence

went on. 'Rosemary had red hair, you know, and an evil temper to go with it. Though of course you won't have heard of Rosemary. Have you a temper, Miss..?'

'Paris. Anya Paris. Yes, I think perhaps I have at times. Driving can make me pretty angry, that's for sure.'

'Good. I'm not against a bit of spirit in a woman. I've still got plenty myself - and I'm ninety-four. Now would you believe that?'

Anya answered with the expected platitudes, inwardly a little disappointed that her companion was not the centenarian she'd thought.

Florence straightened herself in her chair and grinned widely until her teeth, which looked far too large for the tiny wizened face, slipped awry. 'Of course at my great age one tends to be forgetful,' she confided, 'and I'm afraid I'm a bit confused about you. Which of them is it that you're sweet on?'

Anya responded with a little laugh. 'My goodness! I'm only here to restore some paintings!'

'Oh yes. Foolish of me. But if you'll forgive my saying so - rather a fool's errand for you, Miss... Miss Prague, if you believe they're worth your trouble. But perhaps you don't know that.'

'I know nothing about them.'

'Then prepare yourself for a big disappointment. They're all fooling themselves if they think those mildewed old pictures will pay for as much as the gutters of the roof. I remember when they were thrown into the attics - and the proper place for them too. They're nothing but a load of Victorian jumble. No-one wants that kind of thing anymore.'

'Yet the nineteenth century produced some of our finest painters,' Anya said. 'And strangely of late even the lesser-known of them are being rediscovered and becoming vogue.'

Florence bristled. 'Are you trying to tell me that I don't know rubbish when I see it?' she demanded. 'Are you trying to tell me about something I know intimately and you've never set eyes on in your life?'

Anya was fortuitously spared the struggle of digging herself out of trouble when the garden door opened and Matt stepped onto the terrace. He paused, his face flushed scarlet from rushing around, grime from the attic still clinging to his hair and clothes. He faced her apologetically. 'After waiting in all the afternoon I had to be missing when you got here! I'm so sorry. It really is too bad.' Almost as bad, he thought, as the excruciating humiliation of their first meeting.

'I was here, wasn't I?' Florence said.

'Yes, Auntie, of course you were. Thank goodness for that. And have you introduced yourselves?'

'Indeed we have,' Florence said, grinning at Anya in a confidential manner. 'And I've decided that she'll do.'

'Do?' Matt repeated, looking bewildered. 'Do for what?'

Florence now grinned from ear to ear and gave Anya a lopsided and conspiratorial look. 'For whatever it is you want her for!' she replied.

It was quickly agreed that Anya Paris brought a breath of very fresh air into the well-worn realms of Foxsteads.

'I like her very much,' Katherine told William after their first meeting, unable to conceal her surprise. 'And I didn't expect to at all. Giles' friends are usually so alarming.'

William raised an eyebrow. 'You're still remembering that woman he brought here from some back street in Bloomsbury.'

'Not really – although she was perfectly dreadful of course. Giles's friends always *are* disreputable. This one couldn't be more different. I feel she brings a little bit of London – real London – to us.'

'Yes, I suppose she does.'

'Well she certainly seems to know her way around. I shall enjoy getting up to date on all that's going on.'

William responded with a rueful smile, 'Don't you really mean all the things you're missing out on?'

'No, no, not at all.'

'Oh come on, Kate. I know it's hard on you.' He smiled gently at her, aware as ever how at times she hankered for the London of her youth. 'Admit it.'

She laughed, protesting fiercely. 'Not in the way that you think William. I'm perfectly aware that I wouldn't fit into London these days. It's all memories – you know - the old adage which says that the older you get the more you like to talk about how it was!'

'I know that.'

'But that's just the wonderful thing about being human – when everything looks good in retrospect. Besides it *was* good - but that doesn't mean I'd change a thing.'

'I'm glad to hear it! That's a relief.'

'Well it also happens to be true. But it'll be nice just the same to have all the latest gossip.'

Angus too was clearly impressed. 'No wonder that sly brother of mine didn't have much to say about her,' he said to Elizabeth. 'She's pretty amazing, isn't she?'

'Yes. She seems nice.'

'I didn't mean nice.'

Elizabeth gave him a baleful look. 'Why is that some men can't see a pretty girl without metaphorically picturing her between the sheets?'

'Who said anything about sheets?'

'In the hay then.'

'Believe me, if you had as hard time as I do getting your oats you'd understand!'

'I hadn't noticed it to be a problem of yours,' she replied coldly.

Florence was intending to dine out for the next month on the fact that she alone had greeted the visitor. 'Independent woman. That's what I like. Can't be doing with these feeble flighty types.' Matt observed these reactions with amusement tinged with more than a little relief – although why he should feel personally responsible for the family's reaction to Anya was not clear - only that he did.

The tiny lodge where she was to be accommodated had been tidied in readiness for her. It nestled in a great mound of rhododendron at the entrance to the drive, alongside tall iron gates that stood permanently open between imposing stone piers. Mrs Hodges had cleaned it as best she could, while the family had assembled a few extra pieces of furniture and creature comforts. Anya was clearly delighted.

'It's the perfect rural idyll,' she said, eagerly looking about her. 'I hadn't expected anything so splendid.'

Matt, who passed it several times a day without a glance raised his eyebrows. 'Hardly splendid,' he protested. 'But yes, I suppose it's pretty.' The lodge, half hidden by its own overgrown garden, seemed to peer back myopically from tiny gothic windows - straight out of a bygone age.

Inside it did not amount to much - just a couple of rooms with an attic above that was quaintly reached by a winding stair concealed behind a low door. 'My studio,' she said at once. 'It's perfect.'

'I hope you won't feel too cut off and lonely.'

'Solitude is exactly what I like,' she told him earnestly. 'Especially at the moment. I badly need time to myself to draw breath, and privacy for my work. For me it is essential – and being on my own is what I do best.'

He felt questions entering his mind, but she moved quickly on, looking about her, examining things. 'Who put the flowers on the dresser?' she asked. 'Was it you?'

'I'm afraid it wasn't. I daresay my mother or sister was responsible.'

'That was very nice of them - such a lovely welcome.'

'Despite everything?'

'Oh yes. Your wonderful old aunt saw to that!' Anya paused beside the table, picked up the little vase and thrust her nose into it. 'Early roses always smell the best.' She replaced the flowers and turned to him solemnly. 'Everyone has been very kind. Your mother invited me to dine with you – but as I've explained – well anyway, I'm not sure that I should…'

'I'm perfectly sure you should,' he protested. 'No time like the present for looking at the pile of work we've got lined up for you.'

She laughed. 'In that case I accept.'

Back at the house Katherine was busy placating Mrs Hodges. 'It really is extraordinary,' she said, 'how this family homes in on us the minute it smells a party. I'm afraid we're going to be ten for dinner tonight. Can you cope?'

'Have to,' Mrs Hodges replied, wiping her hands on her apron and facing Katherine with a martyred look. 'I guess more veg should do the trick. The joint's big enough for twenty.'

Katherine looked relieved. Elizabeth and Edward had wanted to be in on dinner as soon as they heard that Anya was to be included. Then Philip telephoned, sounding sorry for himself, and asked to come too - largely in the hope that Matt would take pity and agree to dig deeper into some cupboards. 'No need.' Matt told him. 'You've got the real thing in Miss Paris. She tells me she was smuggled out of occupied France in 1940.'

'Crikey! Are you serious? Will she talk about it do you think?'

'You can but ask her.'

Katherine began to rummage in the kitchen cupboards, wondering whether to use the Meissen, possibly, she thought, for the last time. 'The Birketts can't keep away of course. Even Philip's coming. Amazing. I'm sure Anya Paris would be astonished to know what a stir she's causing.' She began to count out the pieces of china. 'It's entirely my own fault of course. At tea time they all turned up and one thing led to another.'

Mrs Hodges grunted, and emptied a bag full of potatoes into the sink. 'Looks like we'll have to put on a bit of show then.' And she gave a wry smile, for she knew perfectly well, as Katherine herself knew, that when it came to the crunch, no-one could put on a show to match the Chevenings.

As Matt took his usual place in the dining room and looked about him, he was aware of Anya's gaze absorbing the scene with keen interest. He imagined how it must appear to someone seeing it for the first time, feeling his own senses assailed by its great age and enormity. The room itself was massive, as was everything in it, from the great oaken doors and furniture to the heavy Victorian silver on the table. Even the knives and forks were huge and heavy. It might all have appeared overpowering had the faces about the table not somehow had the strength and presence to match.

The ten of them were comfortably seated about the table. William and Katherine faced each other along its great length, with the family ranged on either side. Dorothy was in her usual place beside her grandfather, looking very pretty, Matt thought. Across the table he faced Aunt Florence. Usually she retired to bed before dinner with a light supper on a tray. But tonight she was fighting fatigue and risking a night of indigestion for fear of missing anything. At her own request their guest was seated next to her and clearly she was being hugely entertained.

'Have you been to Northumberland before?' Florence was demanding. 'It's the finest county in England, you know – but that is a well-kept secret.'

'I'm afraid your secret's out then,' Anya replied, 'because I've heard a great deal about it, and I've wanted to come for some time.'

'Oh so you've been told have you? About our marvellous countryside – or about our terrible climate?' Florence laughed, tucking her napkin into her collar. 'Can't risk spilling me soup!'

'It's your Roman history that's so famous, Miss Chevening. I'm longing to see the Wall for myself.'

'The Wall eh? Well now, does that mean you are a historian as well as an expert on Victorian art?'

'Oh dear, please forgive me that! I'm not an expert in either really. Restoring is a skill rather than an art - and my knowledge of history is very sparse. But Hadrian's Wall is something everyone should see, don't you think?'

Florence snorted rudely. 'When you've walked it once from Steel Rigg to Housesteads you'll have seen more than enough!'

Edward caught her eye. 'Certainly you'll have seen the best of it.' He put down his knife and fork and leant towards her, a recognisable sign, Matt knew, that he was about to expound on the subject, or throw some controversial spanner into the works. 'The Wall, I'm afraid, is little more than a heap of rubble in most places. Half the houses in Northumberland owe their stones to the Romans' industry. Now if our ancestors had nurtured the interest shown today in such a heritage...'

Matt sighed. Edward Birkett, pompous and pinstriped, whose attraction for Elizabeth had always been a mystery to the family, was also a man of opinions. At one time he had had aspirations as a politician. Probably, Matt thought, he would have been good at it. He interrupted. 'Surely not, Edward. That doesn't detract in the least from its appeal. You can't but agree with that.'

'I agree that it's remarkable for the fact that any of it's still there.'

'Then we'll make sure Anya sees what there is.'

'I mean to see as much of everything as I can,' Anya said

Matt rose to carve second helpings of beef. This was one of several duties, traditionally William's, that had fallen to him since his father's accident , and he was aware of critical eyes upon him as he performed the ritual task. As his knife deftly reduced the baron of beef to a few bones, it also crossed his mind that the word economy might be bandied about this table and the family question how the impending repair bills could be met, but it would never reduce the Chevenings' idea of a roast of beef – nor truly reflect the delicacy of their financial situation.

'Do tell us more about your work, Anya,' he heard his mother asking. 'Do you work in a museum or a gallery?'

'No, not at the moment,' she replied, 'although I've only just finished a contract with a private gallery. Just now I'm on my own - self-employed. I'm trying to treat this as a working holiday in a way - which actually I haven't managed for some time. Then I hope to find something in the autumn to take me abroad.'

'You must come across some extraordinary treasures in your work.'

'Oh yes, I do. I was involved in work at Lord Hazelwood's home a short while ago. It was just before they opened Longhirst Park to the public. You probably read about it. It was given a lot of publicity – and was so exciting.'

'Yes, I did read about it. The Longhirst collection is famous of course and highly respected. Quite a responsibility.'

'It was. But then restoring always is. That's why it has to be so slow and scientific and handled with such care.'

'And painstaking.'

'Yes, very – and the older the work the more exacting'. Anya's eyes had begun to shine as she spoke.

'I'm afraid our pictures are nothing special,' Katherine said. 'Probably just in need of a bit of cleaning.'

'That doesn't necessarily diminish them, Mrs Chevening. Just to see wonderful original colours emerging from years of yellowing varnish can be like discovering treasure.'

Florence noisily put down her spoon. 'I'm afraid you'll find no treasure in that mildewed rubbish you've been brought here to clean,' she remarked scornfully, wiping soup from her chin with her napkin. 'And this family knows a thing or two about treasure.'

'Yes, I can see that.'

'You can't see what I'm talking about,' Florence said. 'Isn't that so, Matt?'

Matt glanced from his Aunt to Anya with an indulgent little shrug. 'My aunt is bursting to let you into our family secrets.'

'Oh no, spare us that,' Elizabeth groaned.

'Hidden treasure,' Florence said ignoring her. 'Isn't that right?'

'So the legend goes.' Matt smiled tolerantly at the old lady who was drawing a deep breath.

'Yes, yes,' Florence said. 'It's an old legend. The Jacobites you know. Rebels riding into Fallowfell - and our ancestor - an ardent king's supporter - hearing them coming and hiding his silver.'

'I'm sure Anya doesn't want to hear all that nonsense,' Katherine said.

'Oh please, I do. I'd love to hear.'

'There you are, she does,' Florence said triumphantly. 'Anyhow the Jacobites were about to invade…'

'No, no,' Matt interrupted. 'You've got it the wrong way round. Foxsteads was a stronghold of the Jacobites - and it was a family called Flynne who lived here in those days. They were amongst many families around here who supported the Jacobite claim to the throne. Foxsteads was known to be a safe house during the Jacobite Rising.'

'I'm afraid I don't know very much about the history of that period,' Anya admitted.

'It was one of the last really romantic conflicts,' he told her. 'And of course like all the old houses around here we have our own romantic legend. I'm afraid visitors usually have to endure it!'

Florence looked sulky. She preferred the tale the way she told it, no matter which persuasion it was. 'Alright then, tell it your way.'

'Come on, Philip, what about you doing the honours?'

Philip had not yet opened his mouth. He looked up, alarmed, pushed a lank strand of hair from his line of vision, and shook his head. 'Crumbs no. Let Angus. He does it best.'

'It was at the time of the '15 Rising,' Angus obliged. 'James Stewart, the Old Pretender, was pressing his claim to the throne – with the help of Flynne and the ill-fated Earl of Derwentwater. You've probably heard of him.'

'I haven't I'm afraid.'

'Well, the King's men were bearing down, so Flynne rushed to hide all evidence of his allegiance by concealing his valuables – including his wife and daughter - in a niche in the tower – which he secured with bricks and mortar.'

'Goodness!' she exclaimed. 'How gothic.'

'It was. The outcome was that Flynne was brutally murdered – and it was close to a century before the silver and the bones of the unfortunate women were discovered –probably the last time the pele tower was renovated.'

'Had no-one had missed them?'

'Who knows?'

'What a discovery!'

'It was. Spectacular. Wonderful Jacobean silverware – some of it ecclesiastical – all of it immensely valuable.'

'So who claimed it?'

'There were a few tenuous claims. In the event it was divided between the Abbey church in Hexham and a museum in Newcastle. Just one rare and beautiful chalice is now kept under lock and key in the local church.'

'The lovely church I visited when I first came to Fallowfell?'

'Yes, St. Bede's – which of course is very old.'

'And what of the poor ill-fated women? Do they still haunt the house? Surely they do.'

'Certainly not,' Katherine said brusquely.

'Now mother, you can't be sure of that.'

'Take no notice of him,' Katherine admonished, wondering what kind of a welcome this was – and wondering why this family still clung to the absurd ritual that all new-comers to Foxsteads seemed bound to endure. 'Believe me, Anya,' she said.

'No-one, as far as I've ever discovered, has been haunted by those or any other ghosts at Foxsteads.'

Florence became morose. 'No-one can rule out anything for sure. I prefer to keep an open mind.'

Angus shook his head and winked at Anya.

She fell silent for a bit, and sat looking about her, relishing the history and atmosphere, and quietly observing the gallery of portraits ranged about the panelling. Matt followed her gaze. His ancestors impassively returned her scrutiny, protagonists probably responsible for passing the old Foxsteads legend down the years and generations. 'And what,' he asked her, 'do they say to you – as an artist?' She shook her head noncommittally.

He wondered whether she was contemplating how her own portrait of his father would rate amongst them. Or whether she searched beyond the heavy gilt frames and the military scarlet and hunting pink that bore testament to their diverse achievements, to find real people with tales to tell? He smiled to himself. She could not fail to be moved. They were not just large in size - although Mortimer Chevening's portrait was almost the height of the room. They were, in the same sense that everything in that room seemed large to Matt that night, powerful, intrusive and arrogant. He knew that with an unusual perception he was seeing Foxsteads and his family as Anya herself saw them – maybe guilty of being clannish, closely bound together by these ancient walls, even something of an anachronism. But beyond doubt larger than life.

CHAPTER SIX

Matt stood at the top of the pele tower steps and watched as a cavalcade of vehicles wound its way along the drive and into the yard behind the house; trucks, vans, diggers, as unwelcome as they were necessary. He was not often given to fanciful thoughts, but as he watched, warming his back against the weathered oak of the great doors, he could almost sense the reluctance of the old house to be torn apart, to have its secrets laid bare. Its ancient substance seemed to convey a little tremor through his body. He felt unreasonable resentment towards Robson and the purposeful team preparing to tear into its fabric. Maybe they would succeed in outwardly preserving the tower - but if indeed it had a heart then he knew that afterwards it would never be quite the same again.

When the unloading was complete, he saw his father stepping forward to speak to Robson. Matt hesitated at the top of the steps, then turned on his heel and let himself into the tower.

He made his way up the winding stone stair beyond. All inner doors to the house had been locked and sealed so that now this was the only entrance. The need to have one final look around was thinly disguised in the name of necessity to salvage whatever had caused young Philip to almost break his neck the day before. For a fleeting moment he smiled, considering how thoroughly the incident had robbed Anya's reception of dignity. Then he grew solemn. As he emerged into the attic, now stripped of its packing cases, furniture and boxes of jumble, looking strangely empty and sanitised, he saw this last errand for the milestone it was. It was not just an opportunity to search for whatever had been inadvertently left behind - but a final chance to gaze on the old pele tower as he knew it, before the roof which for centuries had darkened it, surrendered its ancient timbers. And even though Robson had promised that the new should match the old as far as modern techniques made possible, he knew that much of the dank mysterious atmosphere of its great age would inevitably be lost, a small intangible piece of history simply dispersed into thin air. He was looking his last on what remained of his childhood memories, soon to be lost forever.

As though to impress it on his mind, he breathed deeply of its strange but familiar smell. It was an odour, which he still did not associate with the menace of dry rot, but with childhood games of hide and seek, and the annual retrieval of Christmas decorations, and the reading of forbidden schoolboy literature by torchlight. A great wave of nostalgia engulfed Matt as he prepared to search for the forgotten debris, which Philip believed to be a picture. Unlikely, Matt thought, but he had to be sure.

As he paused motionless with his silent thoughts he was all at once aware that he was not alone. For a moment he froze, his blood turning cold. Then as his eyes became accustomed to the dimness he made out the figure of a woman standing on the far side of the room. Once again he chided himself for entertaining fanciful thoughts and called out, 'Who's there?'

The figure stepped towards him. 'It's Anya.'

'Good God. And for heaven's sake don't move any closer. This floor isn't safe.'

She stopped in her tracks. 'I didn't mean to intrude.'

'Then what on earth are you doing here?'

She met his defensive look with an apologetic little smile. 'Am I trespassing? If so, I'm very sorry, but suddenly felt I wanted to see the tower just once before it's taken apart. Please forgive me.'

'Of course,' he said abruptly, wondering why she hadn't bothered to ask. 'I'd be pleased to show you round - just as long as you're careful where you step. I'm afraid this floor is thoroughly rotten.'

'I was forgetting. Goodness, how sad.'

'It is. The whole bloody business is sad - sad, expensive, and an urgent necessity, I'm afraid. Nothing we can do about it. He retrieved a torch from the recess where it was kept and led her across to the safe side of the room. The powerful beam revealed nothing of Philip's alleged obstruction. The room was completely bare. 'I suppose I was saying goodbye to a few childhood memories,'

She eyed him sagely. 'And that's probably the saddest part of all.'

'Yes, curiously it is.' He pressed his palm against one of the broad oak beams. It looked and felt so solid, so permanent, that it was hard to believe it no longer had the strength to shoulder its great burden. 'English oak,' he said, unable even in the face of the facts, to keep the pride from his tone. 'The kind of wonderful timber that couldn't be produced today, no matter what Robson tries to fool us into thinking.'

'Such things are irreplaceable,' she agreed. 'I've always believed that old buildings – even old objects and pictures – absorb little bits of the past and keep something of them for ever. There is no substitute for that. Do you know what I mean?'

'I know that this place holds priceless memories for me.'

'And they'll have left a mark on it. That's for sure. It's what I've always believed anyway. I'm not sure that I give much credence to ghosts as such – but there has to be something that remains of lives and happenings. Once it's gone, it can't be put back.'

He eyed her thoughtfully. Her theory somehow put into words the feelings he had about this whole operation, the breaking into the timeless pattern of things, the exposing and final destruction of moments of history.

'Sadly it can't,' he agreed. 'There's plenty to remember of course – but you're right - the evidence will be gone.'

As they wandered about the room he recounted little anecdotes from that vanishing past and showed her small details - the low beam with its pattern of initials carved by himself and his countless unknown predecessors - a place where the plaster had crumbled and he and his brothers had concealed the precious documents of one of their many boyhood secret societies – the recess behind the fireplace where they had all hidden. 'It's believed to be a priest-hole,' he told her. 'We used to imagine that we'd find more bones and undiscovered silver from the old legend in here – but of course we didn't!'

'Maybe they'll be discovered now.'

'I'm afraid not - if they exist at all. The stonework won't be disturbed. So there we are – no ghosts – no evidence. Only hearsay!'

'Do you believe in the legend then?'

His mood had begun to lighten. He smiled at her. 'It's more fun to believe it than doubt it. Don't you agree?'

She nodded. 'Oh yes, of course I do.'

They had reached the far side of the room where a short flight of stone steps led up to the turret. He stood back to allow her to pass, then followed her into the crisp air. She emerged with a sharp intake of breath. The view, which on a clear day like this practically stretched from coast to coast, was truly breathtaking when seen for the first time. And at least nothing could destroy that, Matt thought, as he watched her. 'Splendid, isn't it?'

'Stunning! How marvellous to have a view like this that belongs to you.'

'It is,' he agreed. 'It is something we have without owning it. There's a lot to be said for that. And of course it's a wonderful refuge at times. I for one am known to come up here to escape when things get steamy downstairs.'

'Do they get that steamy then?'

He gave her a shrewd look. 'Don't tell me you

can't imagine it - from what you've seen already.'

'Okay – so I can.'

In a companionable silence they leant together on the parapet and gazed out over the landscape's wild undulations – at the patchwork of meadows in the valley, tidily edged with crisp stone walls, which gradually gave way to distant heather-strewn moors. In the distance a great rocky outcrop cut a jagged outline against the sky. He directed her gaze along the horizon. 'The crag you can see above that young plantation of spruce is the Foxsteads Crag – marking our northern boundary. The river marks the southern edge on the other side. The best of our pasture is there. But this is the view I prefer.'

'It's beautiful.'

'Yes. It's wild and wonderful.'

She gave him a circumspect look. 'You love it, don't you?'

'Of course. It's my home.'

For a moment she turned away. Then she said, 'That doesn't necessarily signify. Just believe me, I envy you for the way it makes you feel.' The wind had whipped her hair into a shining halo, hiding her face from view. He sensed rather than saw her pensive expression, as she added, 'I envy you for belonging.'

He opened his mouth to speak, but she met his gaze and shook her head with a little smile. 'Nothing to add to that – except that I think I should leave you to enjoy your wild and wonderful refuge by yourself. You know, personal goodbyes and all that! But thank you for showing it to me.'

She did not wait for his protest, but disappeared down the stone stairs. He was left with a deep sense of melancholy, first lightened by her company, then deepened by her departure. It was an extraordinary paradox that left him questioning.

After that he did not remain long, but glanced about him in one long last reflective sweep, then followed her down the rickety stairs. Finally he closed the door quietly behind him, closing with it a cherished chapter of his life.

* * *

Anya appeared to slip easily into life at Foxsteads. The family took to her at once. Even young Philip became become infatuated, aware possibly for the first time in his sixteen years of the stirrings of manhood. Only Dorothy had misgivings, which surprised her. Anya was unfailingly charming, and fairly unobtrusive on the whole. Perhaps it was simply some instinct concerning her father that promoted the antipathy. Dorothy was not sure. She only knew that her father was strangely stirred by Anya's arrival.

She observed him with a kind of detachment new to her, obliged to recognise that he was still a good-looking man, perhaps even more so now in middle age. The deep tan of an outdoor life accentuated his Chevening looks - the thick fair hair, weather-bleached as were his brows, and the intensely blue eyes that ran in this family. Even the deep lines about his mouth and eyes, carved by wind and weather, did not detract from this.

Strange, Dorothy thought, that she had not appreciated all this before. But of course fathers were not usually considered in that light. Besides, she was fairly sure that Matt was quite oblivious of his own appeal - even blissfully unaware that Diana Bell had been mad for him for years. Poor Di. If she had visualised any kind of future with him, even Dorothy could have put her wise and prevented the gossips from suggesting that she had been ill-used. But that was water under the bridge – and this was different. Dorothy was aware of a different kind of chemical reaction between her father and the newcomer, and she did not like it.

'The trouble is,' she told Luke, 'I'm afraid he's falling for her.'

'And that's a problem?'

The two of them were embarking on an evening of jazz - usually an infallible source of high spirits. Dorothy sank down on the floor amidst the litter of records waiting to be sorted, looking like a thundercloud. 'Of course it is. It's a disaster.'

Balefully she looked away, knowing that she was being unreasonable, a little perverse even, since she was entirely dismissive of her father's far more reasonable concerns over her own burgeoning romance. Had he known that these music sessions were actually held in Luke's bedroom he would have expressed them in the strongest possible terms. But he did not know. And it was of course part of the attraction.

Besides this was a bedroom with a difference, once and for all blowing away the myth of cold, draughty places, fit only for sleep. All about her were the clean lines of very contemporary furniture, providing a magnetic venue for Luke's many parties. Perhaps his far-sighted parents had planned it that way, for it was more like a small apartment, with armchairs, a desk and the most fantastic radiogram. A low-slung cabinet accommodated books, records and, behind closed doors, bottles and glasses, from which Luke was at this moment busy extracting refreshments for their evening.

'I take it you don't think much of her then,' he said with a wry grin.

'Do you blame me?'

He shrugged. 'I can't judge. She seems nice enough to me – pleasant, friendly and – well, she is pretty attractive, isn't she?'

Dorothy's disenchantment increased tenfold. 'If you like red hair and freckles. Honestly, she's got everyone eating out of her hand. She only has to turn on her charm and everyone falls at her feet. I wouldn't trust her an inch.'

'Do I detect a touch of the green eye?'

'No you bloody well don't. I detest green eyes.' Dorothy scowled as she began to assemble the records into order of a kind. 'I don't know what I think. Call it instinct if you like. I just know it doesn't feel right.'

'Your Dad's a full-grown man Dorothy.'

'Luke. For God's sake. He's my *father*.'

He sank down beside her and ran his fingers up the back of her neck. 'He's big enough to look after himself. And so are you, Dorothy. Can't we forget Anya Paris for a minute and get on with the music?'

She allowed her head to collapse onto his shoulder with a little sigh. 'Okay. I'm sorry. Let's then. Who's coming over tonight?'

Already his hand had encircled her slender waist and was finding its way into her blouse. 'Just some of the crowd,' he said with a non-committal shrug. 'The usual.'

Adroitly she detached herself. A likely tale. Probably they had not even been invited. Not that it mattered half as much as it should have done. Dorothy's emotions were so mixed up that they did not make any logical sense.

She shuffled through the records in a desultory way and attempted to measure her attitude to her father against his towards her. Of course he did not trust her with Luke. He had every good reason, since she was almost certainly going to be led astray in the long term, if not in the short. However she had always believed her own attitude towards him to be different and philosophical, since women like Diana came and went in his life from time to time, usually without serious threat to the status quo. Which was fine. She had never wanted a step-mother and it had never seemed likely. Theirs was an entirely satisfactory one-to-one relationship in which no spare places existed. There had never been any real reason for this to change. But then on the other hand, Dorothy thought, staring into the cover of 'Music for Moonlight' with its evocative imagery, she had never before seen a light in his eyes like that engendered by the mere presence of Anya Paris.

Aware that Luke was watching her, Dorothy buried the record in the pile and began briskly to busy herself again. 'Are we dancing or just listening?' she asked, brandishing a Chris Barber in one hand and a very new and shiny Frank Sinatra in the other.

'We're still thinking evil thoughts about Anya Paris, aren't we?'

'Not really,' Dorothy said, looking contrite. 'I have no real reason to – beyond my unfounded feelings of instinct.'

'How did she happen? I mean, where did you find her?' Luke withdrew a packet of cigarettes from his shirt pocket and offered her one.

'No thanks. I don't. Anya? She restores pictures.'

'I know that. But what was the contact?'

'Giles knows her – you know, my writer uncle from London, who knows just about everyone. The one I'm going to stay with later this summer.' Luke lit a cigarette and exhaled in a fragrant plume of French tobacco, reminding Dorothy of her one and only visit across the Channel. 'You have a brother in London, haven't you? You should come with me.'

'Marco? Yes, Marco lives in London – but we're not particularly close. Nothing in common. He's the odd-man-out in our family – the arty one.'

'There you are then. They must be two of a kind. Giles is totally the odd man out in our family

111

too. The circle he moves in is littered with writers and artists like Anya Paris. Anyway he seems to think highly of her. You'd like Giles. I'm sure you'd get on.'

'I'm not sure you'd be that keen on Marco though.'

'Why's that?'

'He can be pretty off hand. I'm afraid he's rather detached himself from us all - and probably wouldn't want to know. I dare say he doesn't even acknowledge his Tyneside roots anymore.'

'Marco doesn't sound a very Tyneside name.'

'It isn't of course. Marco Bellini is a pretension. As you know he's a television director and totally pretentious. I suppose in all fairness he's entitled to it. Bellini is my mother's maiden name.'

'It sounds Italian.'

'Way back it probably was. Apparently my grandfather sold ice cream on South Shields sea front – a legend in our family! – at least I always thought so.'

Dorothy relaxed back against him laughing. 'So there you are. We should all get together. Giles the aspiring writer and playwright and your brother Marco, the television director. It's tailor made.' Suddenly she returned to bolt upright and became solemn. 'It is, Luke. Really it is. I'd love to introduce them to each other. Poor old Giles has struggled so long and hard for some recognition. Years and years he's tried to make a go of it – and all he needs is a bit of nepotism – I'm sure of it - because getting *heard* is the hardest part of all. Even I know that.'

Luke shook his head and gave her an indulgent smile. 'No, Dorothy,' he said. 'Getting Marco to listen would be the hardest part. Believe me.'

He took the Frank Sinatra from her and went over to the radiogram. 'We'll have this,' he said. 'This one's the latest.' Clearly the subject of Marco and whatever spectre it had raised was closed.

Dorothy watched in silence as he busied himself, reflecting on the new revelations about his family and ancestry, which in her mind at least explained quite a few things. For a start, his legendary charm could only have come from his Latin roots. She might even have guessed, looking at him now in this fresh light. The crisp dark hair and fathomless eyes - with the kind of long lashes that any self-respecting girl would pay a king's ransom for – undoubtedly spoke a Mediterranean language. She smiled to herself as she watched him, conscious that good looks and hot blood were a dangerous combination. Especially when taken with alcohol.

Luke had returned to the floor beside her with two glasses of wine, one of which he placed without question into her hand. Dorothy took a minute sip and still toying with her theory, said, 'I'd rather have a Coke if you've got one.'

'Well I'm afraid I haven't,' he replied. And placing his glass on the floor, he slipped his arms around her body, which was temporarily immobilised by the brimming glass, and began deftly to unfasten the buttons of her blouse. 'I really don't know why I bother with such a goody-

goody. You don't smoke - and you don't drink – and you don't…'

'No I bloody well don't,' Dorothy said, ridding herself of the glass and his advances in short order. 'You're a rake – and you smell like a French taxi.'

'Don't you like my Gaulloises?'

'Yes, I suppose I do. Where do you get them?'

'My father's interior designer brings them.'

'The famous Mr Castaletz.'

'So you know him.'

'Of him. I should do. His name's all over the packaging in your hall. What's in it all?'

'Paintings I believe. More paintings rather. He has a gallery in London – and my father seems to have more or less given him carte blanche here.'

'Extraordinary,' Dorothy said. 'Well, ironic really. Here are we Chevenings struggling to raise money from paintings we don't need, simply to settle our debts to your father, while he buys up half London by the crate-load. You'd have thought we might manage some kind of a barter system between us, wouldn't you?'

Now it was Luke's turn to become serious. He nodded slowly. 'You would. But then isn't that the whole point of what's been said already?'

'I don't know what's been said.'

'Surely you do. You must have heard about the offer my father made to your grandfather - about debts being settled in kind. They all could be, Dorothy - or almost. Probably not with paintings of course - but with land.'

Despite herself Dorothy bristled. 'Of course I heard about that.'

'And so?'

She scrambled to her feet and turned away, afraid that her face would betray her. A moment of fierce anger threatened to engulf her altogether, as though by whatever quality it was that made her Chevening through and through she now rebelled to the very soul. 'And you know what my grandfather replied,' she said tartly. 'That's precisely why we're having the sale.'

'But it doesn't make sense to me.'

She crossed the room and stood silently gazing from the window. 'If you don't understand, then I probably can't explain.' For here was the answer - beyond, where the sky was slowly darkening and a mist was beginning to obscure the distant hills. Most of the windows of this house shared the same view – her view - a sweeping landscape fronted by the gardens of Fallowfell Hall, but embracing an undulating patchwork of pasture and woodland that faded into the distant grey hills of the Pennines. Almost all of what she saw belonged to her family. It was breathtaking. Small wonder that Robson, with his ambitions for buying himself into Fallowfell at any price, wanted to make inroads there. She perfectly understood why he was prepared to make his offer so generous and attractive. But it did not alter anything. Focussing her gaze on the enclosure immediately in question, a lush expanse of water meadow dotted with the black and white of Friesian heifers from her father's prized stock, she said coolly, 'My grandfather would consider selling any of our land as a breach of trust – betraying a kind of landowner's Hippocratic oath if you like.'

'But that's crazy.'

'Is it?'

'Landowners don't make oaths – Hippocratic or otherwise. My father has the money. Your family has the land. It seems a very simple equation to me.' He had joined her at the window. She could feel his warm breath on her neck. Slowly he drew her round to face him, ignoring her unconvincing attempts at resistance. 'Can't you see what's in it for everyone - our two families – you – me. We have everything to gain.'

'I don't think so. As I see it there's everything to lose.'

'Then you're wrong. Think about it. For instance, aren't you and I the perfect catalyst?'

She eyed him in astonishment. 'And what's that supposed to mean?' she asked, knowing the answer perfectly well. But as she tried to resist the irresistible, hot blood coursing through her brain, all but drowning out the evocative strains of '*Too Close for comfort*' issuing from the record player.

'At this moment it means I want you madly.'

She gave him a sardonic smile. 'Me or my grandfather's acres?'

'You are a cynic.'

'I am a realist.'

'Then you must see what we could achieve together.'

She scoffed at him. 'How dynastic – archaic.'

'Is it?'

'Of course it is. What if I agreed?'

'Oh, how I wish you would!'

Her gaze sank to the floor. 'You know I can't, Luke,' she protested, even as his gentle touch evoked a sensual tremor which challenged the very concept of *knowing just when to say when.* 'I just can't.' In a moment of panic she demanded to know when their friends were expected to arrive. Probably they had forgotten, was his reply. She had expected as much. And as he pressed her hard against the sill, she could feel his urgency, recognising it to be more of the present than of some future dynastic plan.

'*Too close, too close for comfort now,*' the song crooned. And gazing with uncertainty into the fading light beyond the window, she saw that the mist had at last obliterated the hills. Now it was creeping silently across the pastures in thin grey fingers, as though to conceal the material considerations tainting the sweetness of the moment. Minutes later her skirt was tumbling to her feet and he was gently taking off her blouse. Was '*too late now*' part of the song, she wondered? She could not recall.

Then all at once the music ceased, and into the questioning silence came the sound of cars, followed by the crunch of tyres on the gravel, and noisy, laughing voices. It seemed that someone had remembered after all that there was a party about to happen at Fallowfell Hall.

CHAPTER SEVEN

'If it's family history you're after my memory speaks volumes,' Florence told Anya, discovering her one day in the library with her nose buried in a book. 'You see, I remember a quite different age – a real chapter of history.'

'Then I'd like to listen.'

'Some of it is hard to imagine. No, you wouldn't believe it, but once upon a time this house was teeming with servants – an opulent place. There were always parties and visitors and we were never short of anything - not in my father's day.'

'The handsome man of the moustaches and braids in the portrait on the dining room wall?'

'Ah, yes, and he was so handsome. You never saw a finer looking man.'

'There is a strong family resemblance amongst you all, isn't there? I can see it in the portraits and in real life. Not just the fair hair and blue eyes, but a real likeness between you.'

'You notice it because you are an artist, I expect,' Florence said looking pleased. 'I suppose you'd say we were a good looking lot really.' Anya smiled at her with a twinkle that was not lost on the old lady. 'Oh yes, I was handsome once you know. I was acknowledged to be a fine looking woman in my day. I had the young gentlemen of Northumberland at my feet.'

'I'm sure. I've seen pictures of you too.'

'So I expect you wonder how I ended up an old maid.'

'Not really, Miss Chevening. I also know that lots of ladies of your generation did not have the opportunity of marrying, or lost loved ones in the war.'

'I lost my Robert – you're right about that. But that wasn't all, Miss Prague - whatever it is you call yourself.'

'Anya.'

'No, Anya, if one tragedy wasn't enough, worse was to follow.'

'Worse?'

'Much worse. I was compromised.'

'Compromised?'

'Yes, everyone knew that Rossiter and I were the perfect match. His family lived next door at Fallowfell Hall - the house where the Robsons are now. The Rossiters built it. Shipbuilding money you know. Anyway the bounder got one of the village girls into trouble and that was that.'

'He had to marry her instead.'

'Goodness, no. She was dispatched in short order. But if you imagine that I was going to entertain Mary Bigstaff's cast-offs, Miss P. - then you don't know a Chevening when you see one.' Florence's eyes flashed, then slowly began to glaze. Moments later she was asleep.

Katherine too welcomed Anya's company. It was so long since she had had a breath of London in her life that she had begun to wonder whether it was still really there, and still the wonderful, vibrant place she remembered.

Anya assured her that it was. 'I'm sure you would recognise it all,' she told her. 'They say

London doesn't change much.'

'I dare say it's much busier than I recall,' Katherine said. 'When I was a girl growing up in Hampstead it was like living in a village - a cultured, rarefied place, where you met people you knew in the High Street.'

'An urban Fallowfell perhaps.'

'Oh no, less like Fallowfell than anywhere in the world,' Katherine said vehemently. Then ashamed of the flatness in her tone and the transparency of her thoughts she gave a brittle little laugh. 'Oh, I can't hide it, Anya. I'm a terribly square peg in a round hole, you know!'

'Of course I agree that Northumberland must have been different.'

'Northumberland - the Chevening Family - it all was. It was wonderful of course. As an only child, brought up so carefully, I couldn't believe such a family existed! I think I fell in love with the whole lot of them. My parents were both teachers - my father was a university lecturer actually - and steeped in literature and love of music and theatre. There was scarcely a London production we didn't see. I can't tell you how I missed it when the dust had settled here. Do you like the theatre, Anya?'

'I enjoy ballet a lot - although I haven't enjoyed that for a long time now. It's strange how when the opportunity is there on the doorstep one doesn't always take advantage of it.'

'How true. I used to return every year while my parents were alive and devour it all. But these days I scarcely think about it at all. Life has changed. Responsibilities have closed in about me, I suppose.'

Katherine was beginning to speak her private feelings, as she thought of those who now depended upon her so heavily - William, still recovering from his accident; Dorothy, scarcely independent herself; and Florence, who throughout her life had been so dominant, demanding, so, well, always there. She sighed and gave an apologetic little smile. 'Dear me, Anya, I am becoming an old complainer. And I have nothing to complain about really.' Nevertheless, Katherine thought, it was good to have a companion who listened and who understood, and she looked towards a summer in such company with a renewed sense of pleasure.

* * *

Before long Anya had completed the first example of her work. A hefty landscape, newly cleaned, was carried down from the studio loft and placed in a prominent place on the dresser in anticipation of a visit from Matt that evening. She had grown accustomed to these visits. He had lately taken to walking the dogs past the lodge after dinner and calling in to pass the time of day – or night, as it usually was. She had not discouraged him, but he was conscious of wariness in her manner. The appearance of the completed picture, clearly set for his appraisal, was the first real sign of welcome he had received.

'Astonishing!' he exclaimed, pausing on the threshold and seeing the picture before him. 'What a transformation.'

'Yes it is. See what a simple clean and brush up can do.'

'Simple? I doubt.'

'Yes, truly. This one turned out to be pretty straightforward, just needing the old varnish removed, some careful cleaning and new applied. I fancy the rest won't be as easy.'

Matt drew closer and examined it. 'How's it done? Or is it all tricks of the trade?'

'Not really. It's simply painstaking work - a case of choosing the right solvent then applying it bit by bit. But it takes a great deal of patience. And the older and rarer the original the more critical the choice of materials. Of course sometimes a painting can be damaged or need re-stretching or retouching. That's when my skill is really put to the test. But not in this case.'

'It must be very rewarding to see a transformation like this.'

She smiled. 'It is. Colours suddenly spring out of the dust of ages - and in a way it's almost like bringing back a little bit of the past.'

He nodded and stepped back in appraisal. 'I can see that. This picture looked like Fallowfell Moor on a wet day when I last saw it.'

'Actually it's Carter Bar. It's lovely - painted about a hundred years ago I think. There's a signature there - T.H. Bloomfield - but I've never heard of him. Probably a local artist.'

'It is,' he agreed, 'Lovely.'

For a moment they stood admiring it. Then she offered coffee and disappeared to make it. While he waited he wandered about the room, now containing the reassuring clutter of occupancy. Books littered the table, mostly works of reference, and a number of well-thumbed magazines. On the mantelpiece a couple of dark photographs had appeared, one of a small girl who was the epitome of the wartime generation. A little child lost in time. He knew he would not presume to ask about it. 'Make yourself at home,' she called from the little kitchen, 'if you can find anywhere to sit. It's a bit of a mess, I'm afraid. Housework's not my strong suit.'

He acknowledged this with a wry smile and sat down on the window-seat with the dogs at his feet. 'You've got it all looking homely. Believe me it's good to see the place lived in again.'

'I'm loving it. Sugar?'

'Not for me thanks.'

She returned with two steaming mugs and sat down beside him. 'This for example. Isn't it a splendid view? I could spend hours just sitting here watching.'

'It is. And yet I've probably never actually noticed it before.' He nodded in silent agreement as he surveyed it. The jungle of shrubs beyond the window, mostly rhododendron noisy with birds, obliterating all but the tallest trees, gave the room a secretive and secluded atmosphere. 'In fact the last time I sat here was as a child,' he told her, 'when one of our gardeners lived here and kept it all neatly manicured. I'm afraid it's become terribly out-of-hand these days.'

'I like it this way. It's a wonderful inspiration.'

'So dare I ask how the project's going? Have you started on the portrait?'

'Only a few preliminaries and first attempts.'

'May I see?'

She gave a very deep sigh and responded with a rueful look. 'I'm afraid not. It's house rule number one. No previews. No half-finished exhibitions.' And she ran a paint-stained hand through very unruly hair. 'I'm afraid I guard my privacy jealously. There's this line you see – and no-one is allowed to cross it. It's my personal territory. You do understand.'

That she was warning him to keep his distance? That she could sense the way the wind was blowing? Matt understood what she was telling him – but not the reasons why. 'Of course.' He replied with a speculative shrug. 'That's your prerogative.'

'It's just that I'm very secretive about my work,' she continued. 'I can't perform any other way. My studio has to be my sanctuary where no-one can enter. And then when the work is done.' She met his gaze and smiled brightly. 'Then of course I want the whole world to see it!'

He laughed. 'And meanwhile you plough a lonely furrow.'

'I'm never lonely. I love every minute of my work. In fact I tend to lose all sense of time when I'm absorbed in something.' He imagined that this evening he had disrupted one of those times. She had plainly been working until the moment of his arrival, for she was dressed in paint stained jeans and an artist's smock, which had once been a man's shirt. There was a strand of green paint in her hair and an aroma of linseed oil and turpentine surrounding her.

'Like tonight,' he said, lifting her paint-stained hand and looking down at it - a small hand capable of great work. 'Was it perhaps the portrait that was absorbing you?'

She shook her head and at once drew her hand away. 'No, I was working on one of those Lakeland scenes. Do you remember the pair? They're quite good, I think, but badly damaged. I've removed some of the varnish and now I'm not sure what to do about the losses.'

'Losses? You mean something's missing?'

'Paint losses. Part of the picture. I can't decide whether it would be expedient to retouch.'

'What decides the expediency?'

She shrugged. 'Instinct I think. Discerning whether it's value would be improved with restoration - or depleted.'

'Surely it would improve it.'

'Not necessarily. It's all bit of mine field of decisions.'

He smiled uncomprehendingly. Then his eyes slid to the streak of paint in her hair. 'I think you decided to retouch.' She did not answer. Her look seemed to suggest that the subject, like the studio door, was closed.

The old Labrador laid a soft muzzle on his knee and he sat fondling the velvet ears, quietly watching as dusk crept over the woodland beyond the window. The noisy chatter of the birds was beginning to fade, and the more subdued sounds of the night to drift on the still air. The cracking of a twig betrayed that nocturnal life was already astir. They heard the distant barking of a fox. Then they sat for a while with the window wide open and absorbed it in silence.

Paradoxically Matt felt at peace with himself, even as he fought against a frisson of excitement. Anya seemed to touch a nerve that sharpened the senses and brought him face to face with the man he had once been – before tragedy and responsibility and the passing of time had tarnished it. Now it was as though he had begun to peel away all the layers of debris – and could begin to breathe freely again. But while that same young man wanted also to touch the hand that had been so quickly withdrawn moments ago, and trust the instincts that suddenly assailed him, he was wise enough to know better. As with the closed door of the studio loft, for the time being he had to respect the privacy she demanded, and allow her to remain an intriguing mystery.

* * *

It appeared that everyone wanted a little bit of Anya. 'Even Phillip,' Elizabeth confessed to Dorothy. 'I know he hangs around the lodge, pretending he's finding out thing about the war, but I'm sure it isn't that at all.'

'I'm quite sure it isn't!'

'And it worries me. It just doesn't seem healthy in a boy of his age.'

Dorothy laughed. 'I would say it's very healthy – in fact a lot healthier than being obsessed with the guns and things.' The two of them were sharing a pot of tea at Elizabeth's scrubbed kitchen table. Dorothy enjoyed dropping into Larch Hill from time to time, where there was always tea on the go and the prospect of a good gossip. Many were the times when she had listened to Elizabeth's tales of woe regarding Philip – who seemed to present one problem after another. Privately Dorothy thought that her cousin would have fared better with a few siblings to widen his parents' focus.

Shortly afterwards Philip blustered in at the door, absorbed the homely scene with what appeared to be a sigh of satisfaction and flung himself down beside them. 'Sorry I'm late.'

'We were beginning to worry.'

'I got waylaid, that's all.'

'At school?'

'No. I stopped for some tea at Foxsteads.'

'That was nice', Elizabeth said. 'How did that come about?'

Dorothy gave a snort of laughter. 'He was hanging round the lodge again I suppose. One of the eager beavers!' She and Elizabeth exchanged glances.

'Nothing of the sort.' Philip eyed her resentfully. Dorothy was usually one of the few people who treated him with respect, and could be counted on to take his side.

But she continued to grin at him. 'Isn't it true? You might as well. Everyone else does.'

Elizabeth shook a bemused head. 'Was Anya at Foxsteads too?'

'Yes, looking things up I think. Then Robson came, full of himself, so I left.'

'Hm. All a bit social isn't it?'

'You could say so,' Philip said, taking a mug from the dresser and helping himself to tea from the pot. Then he took four biscuits from the tin on the table and began to ladle sugar into his tea. After a bit he said, 'Speaking of things social, I thought it was a bit odd when Grandfather introduced Robson to Anya they shook hands as if they'd never met before.'

'Perhaps they hadn't'

'Well I know they had. I've seen Robson at the lodge. More than once. I've seen them talking.'

'Him too!' Dorothy said with a grin.

Philip scowled at her. 'That's not the point.'

'No, I suppose not. How odd.'

'I have my theories of course.'

'Which are?'

'Only theories.' He said, his tone becoming dismissive. He shrugged. 'Anyhow - what of it?' He helped himself to another biscuit, scooped up his school bag and disappeared muttering something about the incomprehensible behaviour of so-called adults.

For some time Elizabeth and Dorothy regarded each other with raised eyebrows. Then Dorothy slid from the table, gathered up the mugs and plates about her and plunged them into the sink. 'Well,' she said, 'what, I wonder, was all that about.'

Elizabeth gave a heavy sigh. 'Who knows? Although I strongly suspect that our problem son is about to start giving us some new problems.'

Dorothy glanced at her aunt, still toying with the thought that Philip's behaviour was pretty normal. 'Is he really such a problem son then?'

'You know very well he is. Toppingham doesn't expel boys for nothing.'

'No, I suppose not. But that's in the past now.'

'But it doesn't cure anything.'

'So you really believe he started the fire there.'

'He started one in the barn at Cribbs Farm, didn't he?'

'Did he?'

'You know full well he did.'

'It was never actually proven.'

Elizabeth shrugged and began to tidy the tea things away. Dorothy stirred amongst the dishes in silent contemplation and wondered about her adolescent cousin who seemed to make such heavy weather of everything.

Elizabeth and Edward had never appeared to handle Philip very well, she decided. Considering how like his father he was, it seemed extraordinary that Edward disapproved of everything about him. And Elizabeth herself simply attributed each problem that arose to his 'going through a stage', as if to excuse his tendency to disruptive behaviour which at times included arson. Adolescence, apparently, was the latest stage. Dorothy gave a little grimace. He should have tried growing up with a father and grandmother who shied away from the mere hint of a teenage issue, as though growing up was an unmentionable disease. Now that had been a problem. At the time, Dorothy recalled, Katherine's sole contribution to presenting her with the facts of life had been to say, 'You do know about these things, don't you dear?' to which Dorothy had answered 'yes' and meant 'no'. Ah well, she reflected, now that she no longer needed to know 'how?' but rather 'how far? and 'when?', she supposed that this too she would just have to work out for herself.

Dorothy picked up the tea towel and began to dry the dishes. It rather seemed, she told her aunt sagely, that Philip was about to enter yet another stage – and if hanging around Anya Paris was part of it, then he could well be playing with fire of a different kind.

CHAPTER EIGHT

The Great Whin Sill was a rocky outcrop rising like the crest of a wave above the powerful landscape of Northumberland. Just to have found the perfect foundation on which to build a wall was itself a stroke of genius. The formidable crags and undulating ridges provided a fortification in themselves and Hadrian had undoubtedly fallen on his feet. From the high point of the Great Whin Sill it was possible to see the lie of the land from the mouth of the Tyne to the Solway Firth, and North to the Cheviots and into Scotland. Today the grasses shimmered like ripples on the water, laid flat by a stiff easterly breeze. A 'droughty wind' Hodges called it, which even Matt was at odds to explain. Certainly it was not the prevailing wind in this part of the world, for the sparse vegetation high on the wall was braced in the opposite direction, with stunted furze and hawthorn shaped in subservience to the bitter weather to which it lay cruelly exposed.

Anya looked about her. The jagged contours drew her attention into a hazy distance. There was no evidence of life beyond a scattering of hardy sheep, the odd grey farmhouse sheltering in the lee of a crag, and the broken lines of dry-stone walling dividing one tract of wilderness from the next. Breathless from the steep ascent, and awed by the overwhelming view that lay before her, she found herself unable to utter a word. It was Matt who broke the silence. 'Amazing, isn't it? This is the northernmost boundary of the Roman Empire.

They got no further than this. And do you wonder?'

She turned to him, her eyes alight. 'No – truly I don't. It's magnificent. Nothing I've read has done it justice in the least. I heard that there was little of it left – and now this.'

'Well, it's true in a way. You're looking at the best of it. Parts have disappeared altogether under concrete – which of course would never happen now. Thank goodness we value such things these days. In fact this is a favourite public footpath.'

'I'd heard that - but certainly there aren't many people about today.' There had been one or two tourists visiting the fort of Housesteads when they passed, exploring a camp that had once housed a thousand infantrymen. But that was all.

'Would you like to walk? Some parts are a bit rough going in places – but worth it – if only for the view.' He looked doubtfully at the cotton skirt and flimsy shoes that Anya had chosen to wear, and the bulky canvas bag slung across her shoulders, but she nodded eagerly.

'Of course. Isn't that why we're here?'

The footpath path ran along the broad top of the wall and switch-backed its way between turret and milecastle, rising high over the windswept crags. They paused once or twice to survey the scenery, and for a while stood looking down into the still, dark waters of Crag Lough far beneath them. 'It's such a natural boundary, isn't it,' she said. 'I can't imagine that many marauders managed to breach all this.'

He laughed. 'They kept trying though. Long after the Romans were history this was still a permanent battleground. You must have heard the legends of border reivers and raiders. It went on for centuries. I was brought up on it of course.'

'Of course. But then probably your ancestors were part of it.'

'Yes, very probably they were.' He smiled at her. 'We'll walk as far as Steel Rigg if you like, because from there you have *the* definitive view – the one you see in all the guide books.'

'I'm hoping to sketch it if there's time.' She indicated the canvas bag, which she explained contained her drawing materials. That at least had answered one question.

They paused in awed silence as they reached Steel Rigg. Ahead and beyond the view was vast. Fundamentally it was exactly the same vista that had attracted the Roman legionnaires nearly two thousand years before. Nothing had changed - scarcely a tree. The same rugged contours swept upwards to Winshields Crag, the highest point on the wall, towering above the sheer and terrifying escarpments that had first excited the imagination of those pioneers. Anya absorbed it spellbound. Then she began to scramble down from the wall, casting about for the perfect spot from which to make her sketch. 'You see, my vision has to be different from the usual,' she explained as he caught up with her at the bottom of the hill. 'I want to look up at those crags and see them against the sky.'

They found a grassy knoll some hundred or so yards north of the great edifice. Matt spread his coat on the ground for her to sit on and perched himself on a flat rock. 'I shall just observe, and I shan't utter a word.'

He did not know how long he sat watching her. It might have been minutes or hours for all he knew, for seeing her at work, watching the familiar landscape taking shape on the page, held him fascinated. Her small hands worked feverishly at the task, while the wind ruffled her hair into a fiery halo which she kept pushing from her eyes. He was not even sure that it was the sketch itself that intrigued him, but rather the sight of the small figure in the context of that vast landscape that held him in thrall.

At last she turned to him. 'Knowing when to stop is one of the hardest parts. Did you know that?'

'No, I didn't.'

'Well, it's true. So do you think it's complete?'

He slid from the rock and sank down beside her, taking the drawing from her and studying it. 'I think it's beautiful.'

'It's the subject that's beautiful.'

Her hair brushed his cheek. It smelled of very fresh air. 'Yes,' he said unevenly. 'That is exactly what I meant.'

She returned to her drawing and added a few more strokes. Then at last she put it aside. 'Beauty is different things to different people,' she said. 'In the same way that for me this is so much more than just a landscape. It's wild and wonderful, isn't it? There's simply so much space.'

'Yes, so much that I don't believe even you, Anya, could feel claustrophobic here.' He was teasing, but she did not smile in response.

'It's not walls that oppress me, Matt,' she said solemnly. 'This or any other. It's people – or to be more exact, people when they move in on me. I need to be free.'

He put his hands on her shoulders, drawing her towards him and kissed her gently on the lips. He felt a moment's response before she drew back sharply and turned away.

'So you don't believe me.'

'Freedom can be very lonely, Anya.'

'Freedom is uncomplicated,' she replied. 'And privacy is the right of anyone who chooses it.'

He could still taste the sweetness of the kiss, and light-hearted though he had meant it to be, it was immediately addictive, leaving him craving more. But her eyes forbade it, and he knew better than to ignore the warnings. Instead he said, 'I would have thought that erecting fences around oneself would be claustrophobic enough.'

'Oh no,' she said. And eying him thoughtfully, added, 'Not if you're the one who has the key.' Then with a whimsical smile, she hastily began to gather together her drawing materials. Moments later she was scrambling to her feet and beginning to scale the steep path leading back to the wall.

He followed. 'Here, let me carry that.'

She relinquished the bag, allowed herself to hauled onto the wall and briskly set off along the path back the way they had come. They scarcely spoke until they had reached the car, parked below the ruins of the Roman fort. Then she took the bag, and opening it, withdrew the drawing. She handed it to him. 'Would you like to have it?'

'Thank you, I would.'

'A memento of a wonderful afternoon.'

'It will be a fitting souvenir – to remind me of something worth remembering.' And smiling, he added to himself, 'For what it was - or for what it might have been.'

* * *

At the desk in the library Katherine was busy writing lists – a habitual occupation that kept her tidily employed. There would be lists for Mrs Hodges and lists for Dorothy to take shopping, garden lists, laundry lists, and any number of 'must do' lists of her own. Today's was one of those. The atmosphere in the library was heavy with after-Sunday-lunch lethargy, and the unaccustomed quiet, broken only by Florence's vibrating snores, was given to thought. Katherine wrote busily, then said aloud, 'Yes, Anya.'

William appeared over the top of the Sunday Times, his reading glasses perched on the end of his nose. 'Did I hear you say Anya?'

'I did. I was thinking aloud actually.'

'About Anya?'

'Only because the Crisps are dining with us on Friday – and I thought it would be nice to ask her to join us. She must get very lonely down at the lodge.'

136

'A good thought then. I'm sure she does.'

'Oh, I don't think so,' Dorothy remarked. 'She gets plenty of visitors.'

'Does she?'

'Well Dad calls in most nights, so I understand. Hadn't you heard?'

'No – but of course I'm glad if he does.'

Dorothy glanced at her grandmother's preoccupied back and screwed up her nose at Angus who was lolling on the sofa beside her. 'Good. I'm sure we're all ecstatic.'

Angus grinned at her. 'He's not the only one either.'

'Meaning what?'

'Robson – some guy from Whittingham - Philip - to name but a few. And you want to keep an eye on that boyfriend of yours, Dorothy.'

'Luke?'

'Him too. He's been seen there. The lodge is turning into a real honey-pot.'

'I don't believe you,' Dorothy said, all but shoving him out of his chair. 'You're just a jealous pig. I refuse to be rattled by you.'

Katherine turned in astonishment. 'I hadn't meant to start a controversy. Is having Anya for dinner going to cause some kind of a problem that's lost on me?'

'No of course not,' William said, scowling at the others. 'She will be very welcome.'

Katherine returned to her list. It was very little wonder, she reflected, that Anya Paris was causing a stir, and it even amused her to think of the likes of young Philip hanging round her door. Then the smile faded. She had suspected that Matt's evening forays on the pretext of walking the dogs had other motives. And of course it was none of her business, and many years too late to be concerning herself over how her son chose to spend his time, but she sensed that an attachment to someone like Anya – a butterfly creature, as elusive as she was enchanting - would only end in disappointment. She gave a little sigh. How lovely it would be to think otherwise. Already she had grown fond of Anya. But Katherine was a realist and had seen Matt hurt once too often. She returned to her list deep in thought.

The same list went shopping with Dorothy the following day – as did the unwelcome thoughts provoked by Angus. She chided herself, knowing full well that she should know better than to allow him to unnerve her. Angus liked nothing better than to have Dorothy as a victim rising to his bait. Nevertheless for some reason she could not dismiss the fact that Anya's presence seemed to pose a threat to the comfortable normality of the status quo, and she did not like it.

Even the village buzzed with gossip. Dorothy's shopping trip turned into one of parrying impertinent enquiries - people intrigued to know Who? Why? and What for? - all questions that could not be answered with any honesty and would therefore be misconstrued from the outset. Ah well, Dorothy thought, if nothing else it gave them something to chew on.

Relieved to have at last completed her errand she turned in at the gates of Foxsteads and drove round to the back of the house where the family cars were kept. Here a cluster of mellow outbuildings surrounded a paved yard. Most of this had become something of a builders' yard in the past few weeks, with an assortment of trucks parked alongside a cement mixer and great piles of building materials. Dorothy wondered whether it would ever be referred to again as the coach-house yard. It seemed to have lost its splendidly faded identity. She parked the car in what remained of the space and gathered up the shopping baskets from the back seat.

As she closed the door a large black estate car drew in alongside, from which a tall man, dark and neatly moustached, emerged. 'I'm looking for a Mr Robson – Arthur Robson. Do you know where he is?'

'I'm afraid you've got the wrong house,' Dorothy told him. 'He lives at Fallowfell Hall, about a mile north along the road from here – huge gate posts with eagles on top. You can't miss it.'

'I understood he was doing building work here – that this was where he could be found during the day.'

'Oh, I see.' Dorothy looked from the man to the car, and saw a large, official-looking brief case lying on the passenger seat, suggesting a business call. 'I'm sorry. I wasn't thinking. Yes, he is here quite a lot. Anyway, I'll slip over to the site if you like and see if I can spot him for you – Mr?'

'Smith.'

She put the basket back in the car and set off towards the house, taking a stone flagged path which skirted the pele tower. From within came the sounds of hammering and falling masonry. She winced. It was dreadful to think of the tower being taken apart and overrun by workmen who probably felt little sense of its great age and no real concern for what they were doing. She hurried by.

The path turned and followed a high wall for a few yards, before passing through it by way of an arched gate, leading into the garden in front of the house. From here she could see the pele tower door with its flight of stone steps. At the top of these Luke was sitting with Anya. Dorothy stopped in her tracks. Anya was perched prettily on the top step, her skirt spread out about her, a sketchbook open on her lap. Luke reclined languidly against the door, smoking one of his French cigarettes. The sound of their laughter wafted towards her on an aromatic cloud of Gauloises smoke.

Dorothy stepped back into the recess of the gateway, suddenly not wishing to be seen. On the face of it there was nothing untoward in this exchange in full view of the garden, but with Angus's remarks still echoing in her mind, somehow she did not wish to acknowledge it. With an unreasonable sense of betrayal, she returned to the yard and the stranger who still waited by the car.

'I'm afraid I can't find him at the moment. Maybe you should go into the building yourself and ask the foreman if he can help.'

The man nodded. 'Okay. I'll do that. Thanks for trying anyway.' And he departed, leaving Dorothy to reclaim her shopping, recover her equilibrium, and head for the house.

* * *

By Friday itself Katherine's dinner party had diminished to a slender complement of six. 'Which will be nice for a change,' she said to William. 'Especially as it started out promising to mushroom into the usual invasion. Dorothy seemed to think that I should ask the Robson family to come.'

'Which thankfully you didn't.'

She smiled at him. 'Not after you were so vitriolic about it!'

'And quite rightly so. Let's get the business side of things dealt with first, before we start socialising. Fair enough for Dorothy – but personally I still have my reservations.'

'Well I have serious reservations about Dorothy too,' Katherine said. 'I'm sure that friendship shouldn't be encouraged either.'

'Probably not – although I'm afraid our disapproval won't change her opinion of him.'

Katherine's face registered dismay. 'Yes, she has become very contrary of late. Really, William, it worries me the way she dashes around after that young man.'

'Then I shouldn't worry too much. Wasn't it ever thus? Can't you yourself remember dashing around after young men and upsetting your family?'

'I cannot!' Katherine said, looking affronted. 'I hope that I allowed you to do the dashing.'

'Ah well, be that as it may, those days are well and truly over,' he said, eying her ruefully, and shifting his weight on his stick with a small familiar grimace of pain. 'See what an old wreck you finished up with!'

Her face fell in remorse, and she slid an arm about him, pressing her cheek against his broad shoulder. 'For shame, William. Nothing of the sort. We'll soon have you good as new again.' And she shook her head, ashamed to be fretting over the trivialities of a mere dinner party, and questioning her granddaughter's very natural attachment for their good-looking young neighbour. The real problem was the here and now. In moments of doubtful optimism, she tried to convince herself that William was recovering from his accident, or that at least he accepted the status quo with equanimity, but the frustrated shudder that now passed through him brought a sharp return to reality. 'Bless you, William,' she said remorsefully. 'You don't have to be dashing with me anymore. I was caught and conquered long ago!' And with an embarrassed little laugh, she gave him a peck on the cheek and returned to her fast diminishing list.

By Friday the party remained a rarefied six. Dorothy herself had finally decided to take off with Luke to meet the gang at the Red Lion in Whittingham - clearly making her point, Katherine thought - while Angus had extricated himself on a similarly flimsy pretext. This turned out to be a solitary assignation with a fishing line down at the river – but only after he had hacked his way into Katherine's special French bread and helped himself to half the cheese-board. The six guests remaining were an intimate group.

The Crisps and Anya immediately found so much in common that it made fascinating conversation – so different from the usual that was bandied about this table. Over the years she had played the part of the rural hostess, enduring endless discussions about livestock and husbandry - or even worse, perennial hunting anecdotes of five-foot-walls and ten-mile-points - conscious that she could only hold her own in such company when it came to the entirely domesticated business of entertaining. For some reason this had never done much for her self-esteem. It was always different with Amanda of course, but usually the two of them were overpowered by louder voices than theirs.

This evening Anya was the perfect catalyst – somehow managing to span the space between two worlds. Amanda and Henry clearly took to her at once. 'You are one of a rare breed in this part of the world,' Henry told her. 'We are always on the lookout for skilled restorers. Few of the clients who come to me seem to understand the importance of presenting works of art – even minor ones – in the best possible condition.'

'Which is mostly because they are afraid of depleting the value rather than improving it, isn't it? And I can understand that of course.'

'And that is why there are experts.'

'I'm afraid I don't claim to be one of them,' Anya confessed.

'Yet I heard that you did some of the restoration at Colburn Park,' Amanda said. 'A wonderful place by all accounts.'

'Yes – truly magical. There was a fire there some years ago, and practically the entire house had been closed up ever since. What wasn't actually smoke-damaged was neglected and in a terrible state. So the work we did was astonishing. It was positively a voyage of discovery.'

Amanda glowed with enthusiasm. Tonight she was in her element, enjoying a subject close to her heart, so different from usual. She and Katherine exchanged glances. The two of them had much in common, different though their lives and backgrounds were. Amanda had been brought up in pre-war India, the daughter of a diplomat, and both she and Henry enjoyed the English countryside without truly understanding the nuances of English country life. She smiled warmly at Anya. 'How immensely exciting for you that must have been. Was the idea to sell the paintings?'

'Just some of them, but only to raise sufficient funds to repair and restore the house itself. Eventually they're planning to open it up to the public again.'

'Of course, I remember reading that now.' Amanda tucked a strand of long fair hair behind her ear and frowned thoughtfully. 'Who was it then who was selling so much art recently?'

'I expect you mean Lord Hazelwood,' Henry said. 'He's disposing of part of his collection at Longhirst to cover death duties.'

Anya smiled at him. 'Yes, as a matter of fact I did some of the restoration there as well – although I didn't spend much time in the house itself. I worked as an assistant restorer – because of course the Longhirst pictures are utterly unique – and immensely valuable. It took months. I was so lucky to be part of it.'

'Yes, it is an incredibly special collection,' Henry said, warming to the subject. 'He owns some of the best Dutch Masters in private hands. Too bad that most of them will probably end up abroad.'

'I know. It's dreadful.'

'But of course it happens all the time. Blame the wretched tax laws in this country. I see it a great deal.'

'Grist to the mill for you, though, isn't it Henry?' William said, wondering where on a scale of one to ten this put his own collection when it came to raising capital.

Henry read his thoughts. 'Believe me William, selling things for the wrong reasons always makes me sad. But there are times when the wrong reasons can just as easily turn up the right results.'

Katherine read the sympathy in their exchange of looks with a warm sense of pleasure. The evening was turning out famously. She watched as Matt silently observed the scene with an air of contentment; saw that his eyes devoured Anya – who, stimulated by the heady mix of conversation and fine wine, was shining brightly and suddenly looking very beautiful. 'Heavens,' Katherine thought, 'I believe he really is falling in love with her.' And for some reason, which even she was unable to fathom, a small shadow fell across the brightness of the moment and she felt a stab of alarm.

But the moment passed, and the evening was deemed an unqualified success. 'The best ever,' Amanda declared, as afterwards she and Henry paused on the threshold with their hosts, and stood watching as Matt and Anya disappeared along the drive together with the dogs bounding between them. 'Charming girl, isn't she?'

'Yes very.'

'And causing a bit of stir?'

Katherine smiled as she kissed her friend goodbye. 'You could say so. Just a little bit. Tossing cats amongst pigeons could be closer to the truth.' And once again she felt a little stab of apprehension.

Matt and Anya walked along the drive in silence. A questioning suspense stretched between them, both companionable yet reserved - the perfect paradox for the conflicting feelings that were tying Matt in knots. He did not know how to proceed with Anya - whether she would welcome his advances – which thus far she had made plain she would not – or whether this perfect evening would touch her senses too. The scene was theatrically beautiful. A bright moon rose through the beeches, casting shadows in strong black stripes across their path. Scarcely a breeze stirred the foliage, and in the stillness, the mysterious sounds of the night echoed about them.

How she slid into his arms so easily he could not recall - only that she did, and that her lips tasted cool and effervescent and returned the kiss as tenderly as it was given. He felt her soft breasts against his chest, a warm yielding suggesting gentle acquiescence, and heard heartbeats that might have been hers or possibly his own. He could not be sure. Only the urgency of the rhythm was beyond doubt, as they stood closely entwined in the darkness.

Then the moment passed. Sharply she drew away and said briskly, 'You must go now.'

Perplexed by her abruptness, he tried to regain hold of her hand. This too was withdrawn. 'Why must I?' he asked.

'Because it's getting very late.'

'Hardly. Surely it's been far too good an evening for it to end yet.'

'Yes, it's been lovely. And surely far too good an evening for us to spoil.'

'Spoil? Because of a harmless kiss – when you look so beautiful and desirable?'

She shrugged. 'I really have to go.'

Matt stepped back and tried to read her face, remembering how she had reacted on the Roman Wall and suddenly fearful that he had destroyed a perfect moment. 'You mean back behind your invisible line – your mythical fence? Why, Anya? Tell me why? I need to know.'

'You don't need to know and you have no right to ask. If you understood anything about me you'd realise that.'

'That you're afraid to be kissed? But that's incomprehensible. I'm not trying to trick you or seduce you, you know.'

'I know that.'

'Okay, so I just want to talk and know more about you because you intrigue me. Is that a problem?'

'No, of course it isn't – just so long as you respect my need for personal space.'

Matt settled himself on the low garden wall before the lodge and looked up at her in silence, unable to discern her expression in the darkness, but conscious of an air of restraint that was not seen when she talked of her work or her achievements - as she had that very evening, enchanting all in her company. Now the restraint rose like an invisible barrier.

At last she said unevenly, 'Moonlight distorts things, doesn't it?'

'Maybe.'

'I remember standing on the beach when I was very young, and seeing a shining path across the sea made by the moon. And I stood there, imagining myself walking lightly along it, far over the horizon to where there would be a bright shining island – and there would be no-one there but me.'

'And you wanted that?'

'Yes. My young life was a constant tug of love – between me and my mother and the men in her life and the woman who paid us…'

'Who was that?'

'Oh, for a short time my mother kept house for an old lady in Sussex – a huge, dingy house on the sea front in Worthing. I used to pretend she was my godmother, although I never told her. I guess that at that time I wanted to belong to someone – or to have someone belonging to me. Then I came to realise that it was better not to belong – to be free so that nobody could actually reject you or hurt you or push you around. When I saw the moon path on the sea it was my eureka moment. So does that answer anything?'

'Not really. The path and the island were imaginary. What happened in real life?'

'Being the way I am is what happened in real life.'

He gave a hollow little laugh. 'And you think I threaten your freedom?'

'I don't know.'

'Well, I promise I don't.' He stood up and drew her resolutely back into his arms and gently kissed her again. She did not protest, but responded with a little shiver. 'And I'll prove it if you give me a chance,' he said. She did not reply, but quickly turned on her heel and disappeared into the lodge. He did not set eyes on her again for three days.

CHAPTER NINE

Matt reproached himself bitterly for his actions, aware that he should have anticipated her response and known better. Her continued elusiveness preyed on his mind, even robbed him of sleep. Finally some days later he rose early and rode out into a grey dawn – surprising even the spirited stallion he opted to exercise – an expedient choice made in the safe certainty that this would take every vestige of his energy and concentration. Besides, he was very aware that the stable grooms were wary of this one. For Matt it was different. In one glance from a flashing eye, the stallion knew that this man meant business. Returning the look with a sardonic smile, Matt swung himself into the saddle, settled the restless animal, already champing to be off, and headed for open country.

Lorimer was a difficult mount - always a challenge. He was also their most successful stallion, commanding the highest nomination fees that Foxsteads had ever achieved. It was a challenge Matt relished. He was a strong and accomplished horseman, outfaced by nothing, not even this double handful, and had long since resolved that no-one should have to ride an animal he felt unequal to handling.

Of course he would never be able to forget what had happened to Rosemary almost twenty years before - of the ghastly accident which he largely blamed for her subsequent death at the time of Dorothy's birth. Of course in that case the choice of riding too strong a horse had been Rosemary's own, and the doctors had given other reasons for her death, but he had always believed otherwise. He closed his eyes against the raw air beating into his face as the pace quickened and tried to obliterate the memory. But she was always there – in these dangerous tracts of land with their uncompromising stone walls, in this fierce northern climate to which she had never quite adjusted, and in the dark lashed eyes of their only daughter. He could not forget her. And no matter how many times since he had been attracted into serious relationships, no one had ever been able to stir him as Rosemary had. At least that was until now. And she also had red hair.

A cool damp wind beat in his face, air fragrant with the scents of damp moss, heather and rich peaty earth. Pursued by a wake of flying mud Lorimer pounded uphill effortlessly, until Foxsteads and its fertile acres had diminished into mere dots on the landscape.

Matt paused at the summit, where the cloud base plunged him into a grey mist. He could feel the dampness on his face. There was no fool like an old fool, he supposed, as he thought back over the years, then over the past few days, aware - and admitting for the first time - the discomforting truth that Anya had changed everything. Although he had not set eyes on her since that bitter-sweet encounter, she had been seen about the place by practically everyone but himself, and he was all too aware that she was carefully avoiding him. Surely one light-hearted kiss did not amount to a credible reason for such aloofness. The great claims she made for needing solitude and space simply did not add up when weighed against the easy charm with which she captivated all who met her. He shook his head in perplexity. She was an enigma - in all probability more afraid of something in herself than in others. But even recognition of this did not provide an answer. It simply complicated matters and turned the making of amends into a matter of some urgency. Thus resolved, he turned for home. Lorimer was already beginning to dance with impatience. Matt at last allowed him to have his head, and gathering up the reins, squeezed the saddle between his strong thighs, and retuned home at a gallop.

* * *

Back at the Stud his father was at his desk, shuffling amongst a litter of papers strewn about him. 'I am beginning to feel that we must accept Robson's offer for the land,' he remarked, eying the mountain of cheques he had just written. 'I see no other way.'

'Not yet,' Matt said. 'Wait and see how things work out.'

'Wait for what? To see what Henry can raise for a few of our cast-offs and some pretty ordinary paintings?'

'At least you now concede Ordinary rather than Worthless.'

William shrugged impatiently. 'Matt, for heaven's sake let's come down to earth. We may raise a little on those paintings and things – a few thousand at best. We may have a bumper harvest, and it looks as though the Stud is going to have a better year – I have every hope of that. But we're still going to have to mortgage, sell or something. Every day Robson is finding snags which will eventually make his estimate out-of-date – and there's nothing we can do about it.'

'Except keep him dangling a bit longer.'

'And who,' William asked dismissively, 'is keeping whom dangling?'

Who indeed? Matt echoed silently to himself, and turning on his heel, he left his father to his problems and set off in pursuit of his own, striking out towards the lodge.

Lost in thought, he did not notice Dorothy as she converged on him from across the park until she had actually clambered over the iron railings and had joined him on the drive.

He greeted her a little coolly, she thought, as breathlessly she tried to match her stride to his. 'You're an old crosspatch this morning.'

'I've a great deal on my mind.'

'Well, if Anya is part of it you're going the wrong way.'

He stopped abruptly and eyed her suspiciously. 'Meaning what?'

'I mean that she's over in the paddock and you're going the wrong way if it's her you're running after.'

He strode on for a pace or two in silence, then he said, 'I don't much like your choice of words. No-one's running after Anya.'

She responded with a sardonic smile. 'I thought we all were. She's only got to lift her little finger and we all jump. Hadn't you noticed?'

He scowled at her in astonishment. 'No I hadn't.'

'Well it's true. Even me. I can't believe I offered to run errands, but here I am rushing to find some silly charcoals she's left behind. Well, she is busy sketching in the paddock and it did seem counterproductive not to offer. But all the same…'

'Did you say sketching?'

'Yes, she's drawing Mazurka, and it's marvellous. She is pretty clever. I have to admit it.'

'But you don't like her. I wonder why.'

'I just don't trust her,' Dorothy said. 'I don't see why she's here. No don't protest. I know we all know what she's doing here – but why is she doing it? People making their way in the world don't bury themselves in a place like this for nothing.'

'Maybe they do – if they need a break.'

Dorothy shook her head. 'And she'll wreak havoc before she's finished. She got everyone bewitched!'

'What nonsense you do talk!' Matt said, laughing at her. But despite himself he felt a sharp stab of apprehension, as though her words somehow echoed his worst fears.

'You'll see,' Dorothy said. 'And by the way, if you're still looking for her you can take the charcoals, can't you?'

He ruffled her hair until it stood in peaks. 'Oh no, young woman. You can do your own running around. I have business to see to.' And he vaulted the iron fence and strode off across the park in the direction from whence she'd come.

He saw her before she saw him. She was seated on the grass in the far corner of the paddock, a sketch book lying open on her lap, her face hidden from him by the broad brim of a battered straw hat. He paused silently keeping to the far side of the fence, not wishing to disturb so tranquil a scene. She was a picture in herself, he thought as he watched her, her flowered skirt spread out around her and that enormous comical hat drooping over her eyes - a small figure in a great green landscape that drew the eye in an uninterrupted view across the sunlit pastures of Foxsteads and on into the blue distance. His father's favourite hunter contentedly cropped the grass a few yards away, apparently unaware of his own importance, his coat gleaming like a well-polished conker. Then she gave a little sigh and drawing an arm across her face, pushed the hat to the back of her head and saw him there.

He had wondered what kind of reception he could expect, but she smiled and said, 'Ah Matt – are you spying on me?'

He had paused beside the fence, still without crossing it, and could easily have seen over her shoulder, but chose not to. Carefully averting his eyes from the sketch book, he said, 'Heavens no.'

'I've been sketching Mazurka. What a splendid horse he is.' The gelding looked up for a moment then returned to his grazing.

'Yes, he's a grand old chap – probably my father's all-time favourite. The two of them have had some high old times together. I guess he'll be eighteen now.'

'Really? He's still very handsome.'

Matt climbed the fence and sank down beside her. 'I wish you could have seen the pair of them in action.'

'So do I. The problem of matching man to horse is going to be really difficult. I shall have to rely on photographs. I'm afraid there's no choice.'

'Does it really matter?'

'No, I suppose not.' She handed him the sketches. There were several of them in which the old horse had been captured with intuitive skill, a few pencil lines that brought the uncompromising pages to life. He studied them in silence. The matter-of-fact tone of the conversation hung unnaturally between them, their absorption in the drawings and their subject drawing a flimsy veil over the reality.

'I think you have been avoiding me,' he ventured at last.

She shrugged. 'Maybe I have – but not for the reason you're thinking.'

'Then I'd like to know why.'

She met his puzzled look with dismissive shrug. 'I don't think that's necessary. I'm here to paint a picture and I'll talk about that as much as you like.'

He ignored her, and without flinching from the repelling look he received said, 'I've missed seeing you. Where have you been hiding?'

'Matt, you have no right to even ask me that.'

'Okay. Agreed. But I do need to know what's gone wrong.'

She looked away and shook her head. 'I don't think you do.'

'You see I can't believe you were offended by my very natural, if misguided, desire to make love to you.'

'And I'm not. Of course not.'

'Because you've made yourself perfectly clear and I'm not trying to make demands on you.'

'It's of no significance if you are. Demands don't work with me.'

'Then what?'

She struggled to her feet, suddenly angry and defensive. 'If I've been avoiding you it has nothing whatsoever to do with what you might or might not feel about me.' She scrambled to gather together her possessions and began to walk across the paddock, pausing beside the old horse to gently tug his forelock. Two gleaming red heads turned and solemnly surveyed him, the empathy between them seeming only to exaggerate his own isolation. 'No Matt,' she said unevenly. 'You've got it all very wrong. I don't really care one jot what you meant. It's what is happening to me and my emotions that concerns me. That's what it's about.'

* * *

Dorothy was intrigued to find herself alone at the lodge, surrounded by Anya's possessions. In a few short weeks the little house had thrown off the air of anonymity which had made it and the shabby furnishings seem so bleak and impersonal. Now it was littered with the comfortable clutter of its none-too-tidy occupant. A jar of wild flowers stood on the table. There were books and magazines about the place, all changes for the better, Dorothy conceded.

Nevertheless her father was right in thinking that she was ill at ease with the presence of Anya at Foxsteads. She could sense the way the wind was blowing – and she did not like it. Also Angus's remarks were hard to ignore. 'She's a femme fatale, Dorothy, make no mistake,' he told her. 'She needs to be watched.'

'I'm well aware that Dad is smitten, if that's what you mean. But then she has the whole family eating out of her hand, doesn't she?'

'Not just the family, Dorothy. For heaven's sake wake up.'

She knew what he was trying to tell her, but she chose not to understand.

Now, alone in the little house, she looked about her with interest. A faint smell of oil and turpentine pervaded the room – and something else, a strangely reminiscent smell which caused her to pause uneasily. Dorothy sniffed the atmosphere like an inquisitive dog. Then unable to discern its origin, she began to search for the box of charcoals.

There was something uncomfortable about searching amongst Anya's possessions – a sense of spying or probing into personal corners. And yet it

158

was impossible to resist examining things – the books on the shelf, the photographs that had appeared on the mantelpiece, amongst them a framed theatre programme bearing a flamboyant signature which she could not read. It was all curiously revealing. On a small table in the corner she found writing materials spread about; envelopes, an open writing pad, empty but for a few notes scribbled on the blotting sheet. The name Smith sprang from the sheet, simply because it had been underlined. Strange that. There were plenty of Smiths in the world of course, but it was still strange.

The charcoals were nowhere to be found. Dorothy tried the staircase door and was disappointed to find it locked. This also surprised her, for nothing else in the lodge suggested any regard for security. By now she was shamelessly snooping and she knew it.

She returned to the centre of the room and turned herself in a slow thoughtful circle. Gradually realisation began to dawn. The haunting smell pervading the room was suddenly so familiar that she could not imagine how she had not immediately recognised it. It was of course the scent of those French cigarettes.

For a moment Dorothy stood stock still, stricken to immobility, scarcely able to think. It was as though the room still spun about her, while the lingering smell of that French tobacco seemed to bring Luke right into the lodge with her, to conjure up his presence as surely as if he had walked in through the door. But the presence was not hers with whom to communicate. It was Anya's. And she in her role of the casual observer could only stand there motionless while slowly she awakened to the disquieting truth that she minded – minded unreasonably that Luke had passed through the little house recently enough to have left these tell-tale traces. Why should he come calling here? Why? A nasty empty feeling opened up in her stomach into which her heart rapidly dropped.

Thus awakened Dorothy sprang back into life. All the little fragments of doubt she had kept at the back of her mind began to work overtime. Perhaps Angus was right. Perhaps she had been naïve. She closed her eyes tightly, as though to obliterate the thought and banish from her mind what logic was trying to tell her. But it was no use. Frantically Dorothy began to search about her. Unexpectedly she discovered the box of charcoals on the window seat, but she left it untouched. Lying beside it was a half-finished charcoal drawing of her grandfather, his kindly face captured in a few deft lines. But she could not bear to look at that either. Instead she continued her frenzied search. Evidence was not hard to find. A large number of cigarette ends littered the hearth, and in the grate she could see a familiar blue packet, carelessly discarded.

All at once everything went out of focus, then sprang back with awesome clarity. Of course this evidence was circumstantial and inconclusive, but in Dorothy's mind it produced a clear vision of what instinctively she had guessed and naively chosen not to acknowledge. Luke was calling on Anya at the lodge, and there could only be one reason.

She sank onto the sofa and buried her face in her hands as Angus's warnings echoed through her mind. Hot tears began to trickle through her fingers which angrily she whisked away. Then scrambling to her feet she hurried from the lodge, suddenly impatient to return to the warmth and sunshine beyond, and to the world of ten minutes before in its normality.

But that world had changed. It was not as before, but seemed to have ceased turning. Reluctance dogged her footsteps home. Miserably she wandered into the old orchard beyond the kitchen garden, and sat alone for some time trying to make sense of it all. It was painfully beautiful amongst the ancient apple trees. Gnarled and twisted, they had been allowed to grow wild since the planting of the present fruit garden. Sunlight lay latticed on the grass, and the scent of last year's apples, still rotting there, issued a pungent intoxicating aroma that somehow increased her awareness of all that was familiar and beautiful and loved.

She felt betrayed and very lonely, unable to think of anyone to confide in. Angus would probably laugh, and her friends simply shrug and say they'd told her so. Nobody would understand – except perhaps Giles, her unlikely uncle who was the best person in the world to talk to. But it was still a fortnight until her visit to London. Dorothy tried to smile as she thought of it and how much she looked forward to seeing Giles and Imogen, to spreading her wings in their wonderful city. Then she sighed, sadly acknowledging that in the meantime her lonely secret could only be shared by her and the old apple trees.

CHAPTER TEN

From his desk in the window Giles saw the world outside as a series of passing feet; polished city shoes, heavy workmen's boots, high heels rhythmically tapping along the pavement, wheels pursued by a nanny's serviceable brogues. It was a world, yet not a world, from which he felt curiously detached. He was not even aware of Imogen's return until he heard her light footsteps on the basement steps leading from that anonymous street to their little flat below.

Edgewell Street was aptly named, lying as it did on the fringes of fashionable Pimlico. Outwardly it presented the respectable façade of a typical London terrace, with its broad steps and pillared porticos, flanked by neat iron railings. However the front doors and fanlights concealed a conglomeration of flats and bed-sits - some decidedly seedy. Self-evidently a basement flat was as low as it got.

Sitting at his dark window, Giles waited impatiently for Imogen to return. Occasionally he entertained pangs of guilt as he waited, gazing at the passing feet, trying to muster the inspiration to finish his latest play, knowing that Imogen had been on her feet all day. Imogen herself never complained, and somehow his optimism and self-belief protected him from any deep remorse he might have had. Giles simply filed away his failures with a philosophical shrug and presented a convincing image to the world at large of an embryo talent about to hatch from its intellectual egg. Rather like Edgewell Street itself, his life was a fascinating paradox that made the actual and the apparent hard to divide one from the other.

At last he heard Imogen's shabby shoes on the basement steps, and hurried to open the door. 'Here, let me take that.'

'Shopping as usual. And a really nice cheesecake – from Mrs Goldstein.'

They deposited the packages in the scullery and Giles lit the gas under the kettle. 'Excellent – and that delicious bread too.'

'Their best. They are good to us, aren't they?' The generosity of the couple who owned the bakery where she worked indeed provided many luxuries they could never have afforded. 'So anything new today?'

'As a matter of fact, yes. I've been waiting for you to come. News from the North.'

'Really? Good I hope.'

'Very. Dorothy's coming down on Friday.'

'But I thought…' For a moment Imogen's smile wavered, then she said, 'That's splendid. We weren't expecting her until the end of the month. Why has she changed her plans?'

Giles shrugged. 'She's a free agent I suppose. Can't wait for a bit of London perhaps.'

They made tea and carried it through to the living room – a gloomy room made cheerful by multi-coloured rugs and a liberal scattering of bright cushions covering the one sofa and the floor. Books filled the shelves alongside the hearth, and Fine Art posters adorned the walls. Its bohemian shabbiness was somehow homely.

'What about the theatre?' Imogen said. 'We've only got tickets for two.'

'I'm sure I can get another – although I expect I'll have to pay for it.'

'It doesn't matter. Three for the price of one still isn't a bad deal.'

'And we do have to go, Imogen. It's important to me to be there.'

'Of course it is.' Imogen's belief in Giles was second only to his own. And if he expected to meet the elite and influential at this private performance, for which he had worked hard to gain entrée, then she was behind him every step of the way. Imogen had spent twenty years of her life believing in Giles's talent, seeing hope in every envelope that came through the door, and omens in practically next to nothing. 'Perhaps Dorothy will be your lucky charm,' she said.

'Perhaps she will. She sounded a little down I thought. Reading between the lines I felt she wanted to escape for a bit.'

Imogen sipped her tea thoughtfully. 'Probably there's very little excitement for a young girl at Foxsteads.'

Giles laughed. 'How right. They're all off to the Fallowfell garden party this afternoon. Nothing changes, does it? You know, up there they don't really need to change the calendar at all. Life is so predictable.'

'There you are then.' Imogen smiled triumphantly. 'So we'll give her a great time – and in return I'm sure she'll bring you luck. How about that?'

* * *

Earlier that day Dorothy had replaced the telephone feeling very far removed from a lucky charm. The joy of hearing Giles's cheerful voice had quickly evaporated as the reality of her snap decision began to sink in. Why on earth was she planning to go to London now of all times - running away just when she should be staying firmly put and fighting her corner? What sense could there be in leaving the field wide open – and worse, not knowing what was going on? Dorothy sank deeper into dismay, which was almost enough to eclipse the excitement of hearing Giles and feeling so special and wanted. Of course London would be wonderful – but she should have waited.

Matt was quick to pick up on her mood. 'What's wrong, little one?'

'A headache, that's all. I think I'll miss out on the garden party if no-one minds.'

'But they will. Don't do that darling. It's Granny's last year as chairman of the committee and there'll be lots of kind words and probably a bouquet – and she'll want you to be there.' Her excuse did not fool him for a minute. 'Take a couple of aspirins and you'll feel much better.'

Dorothy nodded miserably. She supposed that never in her eighteen years had she missed a village garden party. Even now she could hear Aunt Florence demanding that her ubiquitous straw hat be found, and that the wicker chair be stowed in the boot of the car. Of course it would a shame to miss out on Granny's day – and with a bit of luck the Robsons would not bother to come anyway.

The scene on the village green was reassuringly familiar, the grass freshly mown, the Scouts' marquee straining lopsidedly on its guys, from which strings of bright bunting fluttered. It could well be needed, for the warm sunshine spilling defiantly through darkening clouds promised but a brief appearance and the breeze was fast freshening. Dorothy looked about her. The atmosphere was uniquely all its own, noisy with the cacophony of cheerful voices and music from the youth club band, unchanging and familiar. There were the same stalls, the cakes and bric-a-brac and the lucky dip run as ever by the vicar, so exactly as it had been since she was small that it seemed as though events in Fallowfell passed unchanged from generation to generation. Giles had hit the nail on the head. No earthly need for a calendar. All this was as set in stone as the Carol Concert at Christmas or the Easter Duck Race. Despite herself Dorothy felt a smile tugging at her lips. Even the people didn't really change. Everyone was dressed in garden party best, Elizabeth in her navy dress with the polka dots in which she never looked quite comfortable - while Aunt Florence's black straw had been around for so long that it had become a part of social history. Of course her grandmother looked immaculate. She always did. Dorothy's smile became wistful.

She supposed that only she had changed. And she had changed from just the day before.

She wandered about by herself. In the marquee she examined the entries for the competitions, the flower arrangements, the children's' paintings, the fruit cakes and marmalade. The judges were busily picking the winners. 'What a dreadful task this is,' one of them remarked to Dorothy. 'They should all have a prize, don't you think? It's so hard to decide.'

'With the children it definitely is. I remember how disappointed I was when the masterpiece I'd painted of my beloved pony was beaten by somebody's mangy dog!'

'Well there you are. Perhaps it was your disappointment that brought about some of the changes. You see the young ones are all given a gold star for effort these days.'

'Oh, I assure you there was no nepotism on my part Mrs Chesterton. My little disappointment didn't change a thing.'

'No, of course not Dorothy. I didn't mean that at all. And anyway flower arrangers are all grownups – or supposed to be.' The worthy Mrs Chesterton appeared to be flustered by her own worthiness, so Dorothy moved on. She was interested in the dressed sticks, the beautiful traditional craft perpetuated by local shepherds and farmers, small works of art created in the long winter evenings. Hodges was an exponent of the art and had entered a stick with a handle carved into a trout from a sheep's horn. It was beautiful. Surely it would win a prize for Foxsteads.

A light hand on her arm aroused her from her reflective thoughts. 'Well Dorothy, aren't you going to unravel the finer points of this mysterious country lore for me?'

Her heart seemed to miss a beat, her mind to hover between past and present, as she spun round in dismay. Luke returned her unwelcoming look with his most engaging smile. 'What are we supposed to be looking for? All these look spectacular to me.'

'I wouldn't have expected you to be very interested,' she replied ungraciously. 'In fact I didn't think you'd bother to come.'

'Why not? I always keep *my* appointments.'

'I know what's coming next, so don't bother to say it.'

'You mean I haven't the right to ask what happened to you last night? You said you'd come to the gate to meet me. I waited for ages. I thought we were meant to be walking along the river into Whittingham.'

'Then I'm sorry. I had a terrible headache and went to bed.'

'Couldn't you have let me know?'

She shrugged. 'I thought you'd rather enjoy hanging round the gate. It seems to have become a bit of a habit of yours.'

An uncomfortable silence fell between them. Dorothy picked up a stick and quickly replaced it. Luke shook his head in confusion. 'Whatever's the matter Dorothy? Why are you being like this?'

'I'm interested in proceedings, that's all.'

'You mean a bit of noblesse oblige?'

'No, I don't. I mean I'm interested.'

'Well, I'm sorry if you've got a headache.'

'I haven't. Not now.'

'But you're behaving like a bear with a sore head.' He studied her in perplexity. 'And why should you think I'd want to hang around waiting for you?'

'You could have gone to the lodge, couldn't you? You seem to enjoy hanging around there.'

'What's that supposed to mean?'

For the first time she really looked at Luke. The dark handsome face that had haunted her sleep the night before now provoked a constriction in her throat, which she endeavoured to swallow. She tried to detect guilt in his puzzled expression, but could find none. 'I know you've been calling at the lodge, that's all.'

'What nonsense. Who told you that?'

'Don't talk so loudly. People will hear. They're coming over to judge these now.'

'Who told you that?'

'No-one told me. But I know. Don't take me for a fool.'

'I don't know how to take you. What am I supposed to have done?'

'When you go calling on Anya? I can only guess – and frankly I don't want to know.' She eyed him levelly and said, 'It's none of my business what you do with your time, and thankfully I won't be here to care much longer anyway. I'm off to London to see Giles on Friday – so feel free to do as you please.'

'Thanks. I shall.'

Dorothy felt breathless with dismay at her own words. She sensed the irrevocable unravelling of all that had seemed so light-hearted and wonderful that summer. Now it had become nothing but a tangle of lies and misunderstandings that could never be undone. And far from not caring, she cared so much that it hurt. There was the sting of tears on her eyelids as she turned and walked away, afraid that her face would betray her. He did not follow.

The judging continued, the sun shone bravely, despite distant threats of thunder, and Hodges' stick won second prize. That concluded, people began to pour into the marquee, where cream tea was about to be served by a veritable team of floral, neatly-permed ladies-of-the-parish who had been baking for a week. People surged about the tea table, voices rising to a great crescendo. Dorothy dutifully mingled amongst them.

She was surrounded by familiar faces, those of neighbours, friends and acquaintances. There was Miss Ryan, her first schoolteacher at the village school, Freda Wilkins the post mistress, Charlie from behind the bar of the White Hart, and dear old Dr Barclay who had brought her into the world. Like it or not, they were all part of her life and she of theirs, and a little stab of recognition pierced her unhappiness to remind her that her father had been right and that it was important to be there.

She was immediately submerged by a tide of small talk. 'How lovely to see your wonderful old aunt out and about as usual.'

'Oh, she wouldn't miss the garden party for anything.'

'What an inspiration she is – a marvellous old lady.' Dorothy smiled benignly, aware that her sainted great aunt was at this moment creating the usual mayhem over the arrangement of her wicker chair, insisting that be placed in the optimum position for the prize-giving. 'Yes, she certainly is – inspiring.'

'Your grandmother too. We're all so sorry that she's retiring from the garden party committee. How long has she been in charge?'

'As long as I can remember certainly.'

'I'm told that there is to be a little presentation shortly, and the vicar has a few well-chosen words to say.'

'Not too many, I hope. Granny is very bad at accolades.'

One of the floral tea ladies came past, bearing an enormous brown enamel teapot and jug. 'More tea ladies?'

'Thank you Maud. I was just telling Dorothy here …'

Dorothy spotted daylight and thankfully slid behind the pole of the marquee inhaling a deep breath. Again she felt very close to tears. Suddenly it was all too much. Beyond the bank of potted plants she could still hear her companion holding forth, and shrinking into her hiding place, she looked warily about her. Luke was miles away talking to the Armitages and some of her own friends, which ruled out seeking Jill and Susie for consolation. Even her father and Elizabeth were preoccupied with Aunt Florence, keeping her supplied with scones. They were laughing about something. Indeed, everyone seemed to be laughing or smiling, chatting and enjoying the occasion.

Dorothy was engulfed by the illogical sensation of being sought and surrounded by those she knew best, yet lost in a desert of total isolation. Gingerly she began to edge towards the door of the marquee. Arthur Robson spotted her and stopped her in her tracks. 'Hello Dorothy. Marvellous do isn't it?'

'Very.'

'I hope you're not running away.'

'Of course not. I was just heading for a breath of fresh air, that's all.'

'I shouldn't bother if I were you. It's trying to rain out there. There'll be some storm before the day's over. Hear that thunder?'

Despite herself Dorothy smiled. 'In this din? I can't hear a thing.'

'Besides,' he said with a meaningful look. 'I've just seen Luke over there if you're looking for him.'

'I know. I saw him.'

'I must say it's splendid to see the two of you hitting it off so well together. We're all so pleased about it.' Arthur Robson's florid face creased in pleasure.

She frowned. 'Are you?'

He laid a reassuring hand on her arm and nodded. 'Oh yes, very. It is such a good thing for you two young people – and has to be welcomed by both families.'

Dorothy stiffened. 'Why's that? I'm afraid I don't quite understand what you mean.'

'Of course you don't. I wouldn't expect the young and romantic to understand the practicalities of such a situation.'

'Are there practicalities then?'

His tone became confidential. 'I'm quite sure your grandfather would think so.'

A surge of anger almost provoked an impertinent response. Fiercely she bit her lip and turned away, recoiling from his touch with a little shudder. Such relief it was when at that moment the vicar banged on the table with his spectacles case and requested the attention of the assembly. There was a mild murmur and shuffling as people paused to listen. Hastily Dorothy slipped into their midst.

The vicar was leafing through a sheaf of papers. She watched him absently, trying to swallow her anger. The temerity of that man Robson. The impertinence. And yet, she wondered, would his theory perhaps be less irksome if it were true? And might it even be true? Briskly she re-focussed her attention.

The vicar's glance was sweeping the assembly with a practised eye. Then he drew a very deep breath, which Dorothy knew from long experience could stand him in good stead for quite a while. Thanks were distributed to half the village – the scouts, the band, the good ladies of the tea-table, the gate attendants, the volunteer stall holders, and the good villagers themselves, for spending their money for the good of God and the church. Oh my word, Dorothy thought, perhaps in the circumstance of such appreciation He might also keep the rain at bay for a bit longer. The reply was hefty clap of thunder.

Finally he turned to Katherine who waited patiently to hand out the prizes. 'As you all know, Mrs Chevening has decided to step down as our chairman,' he said. 'And we are at a loss to know how we can replace her. An impossible task. She is quite simply irreplaceable.' Katherine gave a self-effacing little laugh and shook her head. 'What nonsense, Vicar. It's high time for someone younger to come forward.' The vicar, unperturbed, beamed at her. 'We owe you a huge debt of gratitude Mrs C. You will be a very hard act to follow, leaving a truly immense gap at the table. Moreover, I can safely predict that before long we will be begging you to return!' There was a ripple of mirth and a unison of 'hear-hear', followed by another rumble of thunder.

Then there came another pause, as a disturbance of some kind caused a murmur to pass through the marquee. The vicar glanced up from his notes. One by one heads were turning towards the entrance. All Dorothy could see was a halo of bright amber hair against the light – no more – but her heart dropped into her stomach. Holy Jesus, so she had turned up as well – and with the most incredible timing. Dorothy looked on in bitter dismay, aware that had she – or Elizabeth – or almost anyone else - arrived just then, it would have attracted no attention whatsoever. And yet there was Anya Paris, indecently late, turning up at the wrong moment, with people smiling and nudging each other. Once more she felt knotted and angry.

She saw her father pressing his way to the back and drawing Anya into the centre of things - Philip hot on his heels, stupid boy. What a little creep! So where, she wondered, was Luke in all this?

As though in reply he appeared at her side, just as the vicar was taking up his dissertation again. 'I have to talk to you.'

'Not now. Anyway why aren't you buzzing round her like the rest of them?'

'She has plenty of admirers already – and at this moment I don't happen to be one of them.'

'You mean there are others who go calling at the lodge?'

'Dorothy, for God's sake stop this charade and listen. You've got it all wrong you know.'

'Okay, then tell me who it was who littered the place with fancy fag ends.'

A strange expression flickered across his face. Then he said calmly, 'Anya's fancy foreign friend, I imagine.'

'Fancy foreign friend?'

'Dear Dorothy, if you haven't heard of him, then you're not the detective you think you are.'

A round of applause greeted some unheard remark from the vicar. Dorothy whispered angrily, 'Nonsense. I don't believe your fairy tales.'

'Ask the people from Whittingham then. They'll tell you about the foreigner staying at the

Red Lion. And the fellow who came up from London last week and started asking questions.'

'What fellow?'

'A man called Smith. You met him.'

There was another burst of applause. Dorothy was conscious of smiling faces crowding about her, but suddenly they appeared to mock rather than beam approval. She closed her eyes as she turned away, and pushed her way blindly towards the exit. Luke did not attempt to follow. As she reached her goal and turned to look back there was no longer any sign of him, only an empty trail of self-destruction closing in behind her – an irrevocable path which in mere moments had destroyed all that had seemed so wonderful that summer. Dorothy became rooted to the spot. Then in a shock of realisation she saw that she was in danger of missing her grandmother's presentation. Dear God, how could she let such a thing happen? Remorsefully she remained on the threshold, just long enough to see her grandmother receiving a little porcelain vase and an immense bouquet. Then she dashed from the marquee.

Once more on the threshold, she paused, suddenly realising that she faced either a very long walk home or a very long wait for her family to depart. Moreover the sky had blackened and it was beginning to pour. For a while she hesitated, miserable and torn with indecision. Then a shabby car drew up beside her. 'I'm heading back now, Miss D. Do you need a lift?'

Flooded with relief she nodded and clambered in to the passenger seat. Hodges of all people would not ask questions. She was saved. They exchanged platitudes all the way home - how well he had done, how splendidly the vicar had spoken, and what a delightful presentation it had been. 'A pity to leave, but of course I have to get back for the animals,' he said as they drew up at the door, glancing at her with a question on his face.

Dorothy responded with a watery smile. 'I have a very important telephone call that can't wait,' she replied. 'So thanks for the timely rescue.' And she fled into the house through the rain.

True to her word she dashed to the telephone in the library, and in a trembling voice demanded Giles's London number. For a few doubting moments it seemed that there would be no reply. 'Trying to connect you,' the operator said for a second time.

'Then please keep trying.' Impatiently Dorothy drummed her fingers on the desk.

Silence. Then, 'Still trying to connect you,' from the expressionless voice on the end of the line.

'Please, please be there,' Dorothy begged. 'Please, dear God.'

At last there came the click of success. 'Oh Imogen, it's me,' she whispered urgently. 'Can you hear me?'

'Just. The line's not too good.'

'I can't shout. Mrs Hodges, you understand.'

'Okay. I can hear now. Anything wrong?'

'Well, not in global terms exactly – so don't panic. Just for me at this moment. Listen, can I come down sooner?'

'Of course you can.' Imogen's voice was warm and welcoming. Tears filled Dorothy's eyes and began to trickle down her cheeks.

'Tuesday then? Is that too soon?'

'No darling. It can't be too soon.'

Dorothy could say no more. She put down the receiver and began to weep silently into her handkerchief. Waves of despair and relief seemed to converge in a confluence of uncertainty. She felt numb and confused. Then fiercely she wiped her eyes and shook herself. This was no use at all. Besides just perhaps things would look a bit less bleak and unpromising when viewed from the far distance of London.

Imogen was left holding a silent telephone. 'I think,' she said to Giles as she quietly replaced it, 'that our charm - our little talisman - is suddenly feeling fresh out of luck.'

-

CHAPTER ELEVEN

The rain had eased, but the threat of thunder still hung heavily in the air as Angus set out to fish the evening rise. It was always good to escape alone and enjoy the peace of the riverside – and never more so than this evening, with strange currents sweeping through the household, due, he supposed, to the drama of the afternoon. His mother of course was understandably both relieved and delighted. But Dorothy seemed inexplicably down in the dumps and no fit company for anyone - which was all rather unsettling for a detached observer like himself.

Angus was an ardent angler. It had always provided an antidote for most ills, and consequently he spent long hours not just fishing, but tying flies, making casts and brooding over the old book in which he had kept a record of every catch since his boyhood. His preoccupation with the sport, which always seemed a little out of character with the volatile Angus, was even something of a family joke. However tonight he had had some success. Three nice brown trout lay beside him in the grass and Angus, determined to make a couple of brace of it, was now battling against the failing light.

He had been aware of a fish rising for some minutes. He knew within a foot or two where it was, but the wily creature could not be tempted by the fly. Angus, ever patient, with the evening quickly drawing in about him, cast again and yet again. At last, trying for what he decided must be the last time, he felt the familiar shock of contact passing along the line. He struck. He had his fish. But the slippery devil was going to make a play of it.

Angus was so deep in concentration that he did not notice the stranger walking towards him along the riverbank until he was quite close. And he was even closer before he noticed Angus. The man paused in uncertainty before pressing slowly and furtively forward. Angus's instinct at that moment was one of annoyance rather than surprise. 'I hope you know this is private property,' he said abruptly.

'I'm sorry. I did not know.'

'Shush!' Angus said. 'Don't move! I'm going to have this one if it's the last thing I do.'

The man stopped in his tracks and stood watching, apparently fascinated. Patiently Angus played his trout, winding in the reel, releasing it, employing all the subtly and wisdom he could muster. He wondered only vaguely about his uninvited audience. The man appeared harmless enough, a tourist he imagined, judging by the casual clothes, the open- necked shirt and light trousers. He was a tall, slim built fellow of about his own age, and dark in a Latin way, with wavy hair that reached his collar. He did not appear in any way threatening or offensive. And at least he had the manners to keep his distance and remain silent.

'Pass me that net, will you? That one there. Thanks. I've got him I think. Y'bugger, what a fighter!' The fish, a good one-and-a-half-pounder was safely in the net.

'Bravo!' the stranger said softly.

Angus gave him a triumphant grin and began the delicate operation of extracting the hook, a task made difficult by the failing light. 'I must have been after this one for more than an hour. What a fish! The best I've had out of here this season.'

As he bent to his task, he was not conscious that the stranger had moved silently on. He found a rock, put the fish out of its misery and looked up. Then he stared about him bemused. Only a shadow disappearing into the trees beyond provided any evidence of the strange encounter.

'Hey!' Angus called. 'Hang on a minute!' But it was too late. The fellow had gone as silently and as furtively as he had come, and now it was no use starting to wonder about him, or question his mysterious presence in the darkness of the riverbank. Angus began to wonder whether he had imagined the whole thing. Had the fellow not been thoroughly from twentieth century he might even have entertained thoughts of the old legend of John Flynne. Ah well, whatever the explanation, it was a fisherman's tale he imagined no-one would believe.

'Do you mean to tell me,' William demanded, 'that you didn't ask him what his business was?'

'I've told you,' Angus said. 'He didn't give me the chance. Did you really expect me to stand making polite enquiries while I lost my fish? Did you ever see such a beauty?'

Dorothy ran her finger pensively along the impressive length of it and said, 'He wasn't by any chance a foreigner, was he?'

'How should I know?'

'Well, surely he must have said something.'

'Not much. You can't carry on a conversation at a moment like that.'

William sighed. 'Someone out for some poaching most likely.'

'Oh, I don't think so. He had nothing with him to suggest that. A tourist I would say.'

'What? There – and that hour?'

'I can assure you that it was extremely pleasant down by the river at that hour.'

William shrugged. 'Ah well, I suppose most people consider a riverbank to be public property. As you know I've never particularly objected to the village people using the path. It is a pleasant enough short cut from our gates to the Whittingham. But on the other hand I haven't particularly encouraged it either. I must say I'm less than keen to have people prowling around the place at night.'

The subject was closed. Only Dorothy continued to wonder about the stranger who had chosen to take a short cut between the lodge gates and the village at such an unlikely hour – and to entertain increasing doubts over her own hasty judgment. But it was too late for questions. Her decision had been made – and now there was no going back.

* * *

Rain was just beginning to set in as Matt made his way along the drive. The evening had become oppressively humid, and as the house was left behind, a heavy, almost tangible darkness closed in about him. The sky was densely black, electrically charged and fathomless. To Matt it appeared to reduce worldly matters to insignificance by its sheer power and magnitude. And it was only a question of time before the mother and father of a storm broke.

In his personal world matters of concern largely amounted to no more than a sudden lack of resolve. The decision he had reached some days before was to leave Anya to the business that had brought her to Foxsteads, and forget the unsettling emotions that her presence had aroused. But this afternoon at the garden party all that had changed. As he had drawn her into the midst of the party, without so much as a word being spoken or even the touching of fingers he had felt the magnetism of mutual attraction passing between them. This alternating current was both new and electrifying. Of course it did not answer any of the questions that plagued him. It explained nothing of what he longed to know – beyond the fact that apparently she was not entirely immune to human susceptibilities. There had to be something more complex than that causing Anya Paris to shy away from the merest gesture of affection - seeing any sign of friendship as some kind of a threat. And suddenly he needed to find out for himself just what it was.

He reached the lodge as the first huge drops of rain began to fall, accompanied by a vivid flash of lightning. A clap of thunder followed closely. Anya's voice invited him to enter – and as he stepped inside he saw her sitting in near darkness on the window seat beside a wide-open casement. A gentle breeze stirred the curtain, and as though in response to another rumble of thunder, she turned to greet him. Nothing in her manner suggested surprise at seeing him, even at so late an hour. She did not ask why he had not been visiting her of late – or why he had chosen this moment to return, but patted the seat beside her and returned to gazing in fascination from the window.

'I adore storms,' she told him. 'I've been here for hours watching the darkness roll in and waiting for this one to break.'

'I thought most women were afraid of thunder.'

She laughed. 'Did you think to come and protect me?'

'No – and I can see that the only protection you need is from pneumonia while you sit here getting wet.'

'I'm not wet – nor cold – and the air smells wonderful.'

He watched her with brooding eyes. A flash of lightning, closer now, lit up her face and he saw a look of almost wild elation in her eyes. 'I came,' he said unevenly, 'because I thought you wanted me to.'

'Why should you think that?'

'Well don't you then?'

'Of course I do. Is that a big deal?'

'I rather thought it was,' he replied. 'But then I'm afraid I can't claim to be able to read your mind.'

She began tracing an imaginary picture with her finger on the cover of the window seat in a silent moment of thought. Then she said, 'My mind is such a confusing mess at times that I can't read it myself.'

'That doesn't surprise me. You are unfathomably deep.'

'Oh no!' she protested with a little laugh. 'I'm not deep at all. I'm shamefully shallow. My confusion is only a floundering attempt to keep afloat to avoid deep situations. You see, all too often the things I really want are at odds with the very things that trouble me most. So I just keep moving on.' And with a deliberate finger she erased the imaginary picture from the window seat with a sweeping gesture.

There came the musical hissing sound of rain beyond the open window. The storm was approaching steadily and the next flash of lightning, reflected from a thousand rain-soaked leaves, was as dazzling as a shaft of light through a crystal glass. 'This promises to be one hell of a storm,' he said.

'Yes, yes it does. My goodness, you didn't get here a moment too soon.'

'I think you should close the window, Anya.'

A crash of thunder obliterated her reply, so in a gesture of defiance she stretched her arms over the sill into the rain as her answer. When the sound had died away, she said in a light tone, 'Well at least it spared the garden party.'

Matt, clutching at the straws of platitude, nodded. 'Thank goodness. It all went better than we'd dared hope. Actually my mother had been rather dreading it – relinquishing her small place in the village community. But it had a good feel in the event.'

'It did. And seeing your father's response was revealing also - a little insight into his character.'

'Was it?'

'Oh yes. Your parents are very close, very united, aren't they?'

'Of course.'

'Good God, Matt, there's no "of course" in marriage,' she said fiercely. 'The whole damned thing's a mine-field.'

A great roll of thunder filled the ensuing silence, louder, closer and more threatening than before. As it receded she added in a more conciliatory tone, 'Anyway, I'm glad I was there and didn't quite miss the moment.'

'You almost did.'

'I know. It couldn't be helped. I was practically ready to leave when a friend dropped by and there was nothing I could do about it.'

'I see.' He said, thinking that on the face of things this sounded unlikely. It was hard to imagine the elusive Anya having friends who dropped by unannounced – a woman who claimed to need no friends. But she did not offer to expand on the subject – and for some reason he did not doubt her.

Something in the atmosphere of the lodge that evening suggested that she had not long been alone. It was hard to explain. Maybe there was just the faintest lingering smell of coffee and cigarette smoke, although Matt fancied that it was something less tangible than that – as though the echo of a conversation still lingered in the room. It gave him the feeling that this unknown friend had not only interrupted the garden party, but had not long since departed. The stimulated look in Anya's eyes, the air of excitement in her manner, might well have been evoked by the storm – but on the other hand maybe not.

And now the storm was coming closer. A flickering shaft of blue light illuminated every detail of the garden and woodland, even reaching into the corners of the room, exposing them in their strange isolation. Then as quickly it plunged them back into anonymous darkness. Moments later a crash of thunder shook the little lodge to its foundations. Anya's eyes were alive and excited as she turned to him. 'All that untamed power! Don't you think it's the most terrifying and thrilling thing?'

He returned the look with a rueful smile. 'I agree – but I still think you should close the window.'

She withdrew her dripping hand from the sill and lightly touched his cheek with it. 'Feel that. Fresh beautiful rain! What a fuddy-duddy you are Matt!'

The contact, as though somehow charged with the primitive elements from whence it came, sent a physical shock through his nerves. As though in a reflex action he took the rain soaked fingers and drew them to his lips. They were cold and sweet smelling. 'Am I really such a dull dog?'

She laughed. 'Oh no, not dull. That's a different thing altogether. I think underneath all your inhibitions you – and your whole family – are intriguing.'

'I protest. Inhibited? I'm quite sure no-one has ever accused us of that. To the contrary I fancy that amongst ourselves we can be brutally free and outspoken.'

'Ah yes, amongst yourselves. But with you it's always "amongst yourselves". You are such a close-knit family that that in itself is inhibiting to other people – which for someone like me is hard to comprehend.'

He eyed her quizzically. 'I wonder why. You of all people shouldn't feel like that. Haven't you been made welcome here?'

'Yes, of course. You've all been kind beyond the call of courtesy. I didn't mean that either. I meant that I can't imagine how it must feel to be that close and intimate.'

Now it was his turn to laugh. 'Christ Anya! You of all people make an art form out of being close-knit all on your own! Just think about it. Your tight little fence keeps everyone at a distance – and if you'd just step outside for a minute you find you'd find a door with welcome written across it into our so-called tight-knit circle – and it would be standing wide open!'

To his surprise Anya did not laugh in response, but cast her eyes into her lap and waited for a great peal of thunder to settle uneasily into silence. Then she said unevenly, 'I do know that - but somehow I seem to have lost the way out.'

'Try talking about it,' he ventured.

She shook her head fiercely. 'You know I can't – and you know I don't want to – and for very good reasons that you wouldn't begin to understand. That's why I can't and don't want to. Doesn't that make any kind of sense to you?'

'Not a grain,' he replied following her gaze to where their hands lay on the window seat still lightly linked.

'Then please try,' she said. And suddenly he felt her fingers tightening on his. 'I mean, isn't that why you came?'

For a moment Matt's response to her was uncertain. A sharp shock seemed to quicken his heart-rate. His hand closed about hers and he wondered in astonishment how it was possible for so powerful a sensation to be aroused by so slight a gesture from so small a hand. He sensed rather than saw the questioning in her eyes, and in the moments that followed, silent but for the drumming of the rain, he tried to fathom the answer for himself. Then he said, 'I came because I believed you wanted me to.'

'Why did you think that?'

'Was I wrong then?'

'No. You weren't wrong.'

'So tell me what it is you're so afraid of.'

In the silence that ensued a little shudder was conveyed to him through the lightest of contact, and he saw that he had touched a tender spot, and that her eyes glittered brightly. 'I'm afraid of nothing,' she answered fiercely. 'And nobody.'

He shook his head. 'I don't believe that,' he persisted. 'I think you're afraid simply because you wanted me to come - and that's not how your text book ought to read for you. Okay, so my book reads differently. I want to be here because you intrigue me - and because I want to know more about you – and because you're lovely and desirable…'

'Please don't,' she begged. 'I don't want to hear any of this.'

A huge crash of thunder precluded a reply, echoing through the night in a series of violent after-shocks. 'Deny it then,' he said at last.

Solemnly she looked down at their hands, still lightly linked, then slowly up into his face. 'I can't. You know I can't.' He sensed rather than saw her expression of quiet resignation.

Then suddenly the storm was not just overhead but all about them. A blue explosion split the darkness and crazed the sky into fragments, and before the last crackling trails had died away, came a thunderous crash that reverberated through the little house until the doors and windows shook on their hinges. For incalculable moments they seemed to be drawn into the very nucleus of its force. Then the darkness and silence returned to find them locked closely together in each other's arms.

CHAPTER TWELVE

Dorothy slept little that night, and as dawn broke she lay restless and unhappy. Of course her planned visit to London should have filled her with nothing but pleasure, but somehow it did not. All that had gone so terribly wrong now weighed heavily against even such a welcome outlook. Faced with a grey, unpromising morning that echoed her mood, Dorothy flung on oilskins and wellingtons and set out to walk off her blues.

Angus's tale the night before had also raised hackles of alarm – she was not sure why – and retracing his steps she made her way down the river. The night's torrential rain had made the going heavy and she clambered cautiously along the bank until she reached the place where Angus had been fishing the night before. It was his favourite spot where the river widened into a deep sheltered pool, and she guessed it to be the place even before she saw the grass well-trodden in evidence. There she sank down onto the broad slab of rock where he had sat tying his casts, and gazed pensively, as he had done, into the slow moving current. It was beginning to rain again. A pattern of expanding circles ruffled the surface of the water. Dorothy gazed into it, half mesmerised by its rhythmic patterns, and lost in a personal mist of contemplation.

For a while she sat thinking of Angus's strange encounter of the night before. Somehow it seemed to connect in Dorothy's mind with all that had happened in the last few days – from the moment when she had first stepped over the threshold of the lodge to the reckless decision she had reached as a result. The stranger on the riverbank appeared to form part of an indistinct picture that at this moment lacked all focus. Yet somehow it evoked inexplicable disquiet. She gave a little shudder. Imagination was a powerful thing when it ran riot.

She rose to her feet, a shower of rainwater spilling from her oilskin, and began to wander along the river path in the direction of the lodge. It was beginning to rain heavily now. Dorothy pulled up her collar and bent her head. The path was muddy and slippery and she kept her eyes carefully downcast. Just a short distance further on her attention was caught and held by something lying in the mud. Wet, but still recognisable, she saw a battered cigarette packet. Its familiar shade of blue struck into her subconscious with a startling shock. She drew to an abrupt halt and stared down at it in disbelief. The blue face of its trademark, the Gaul with his horned helmet, stared tauntingly back. For a moment Dorothy did not move; she did not even breathe; but stood gazing down at the blue oblong in a paralysis of dismay.

In that one moment all her preconceived ideas were blown to pieces. The feeling that somehow these apparently unconnected events had a common denominator gained in credibility. The discovery not only conjured the image of Luke himself, but also Angus's stranger on the path, and the 'fancy foreigner' she had been so quick to dismiss, and even the Frenchman who supplied Luke with his cigarettes. Her hasty conclusions suddenly did not seem quite so well founded after all. Only the common denominator was beyond question. Anya. Angrily Dorothy ground the packet into the path with her boot. She was close to hating Anya Paris and the conflict of loyalties she had caused.

Doggedly she pressed on, her mind turbulent. Thoughts of Luke and her hasty accusations, of Angus and his words of warning, of her father's very apparent attachment for Anya, became a melange of jealousy and mistrust. And by the time she reached the lodge, the only hope of shelter, the rain was becoming heavier, and she was muddy, cold and thoroughly soaked to the skin. She was also very close to tears.

Of course she had not intended to burst in unannounced. But suddenly the heavens opened, so that there was not even time to pause and contemplate what she should say to explain her peremptory arrival at such an uncivilised hour. She simply bent her head, braced herself against the stinging onslaught of the storm and flung herself against the door. Of course she had intended to knock and wait politely before entering. But the door had been carelessly fastened and yielding to her weight it admitted her without any preliminaries whatsoever. Pursued by a saturated gust of wind, Dorothy found herself struggling to regain her balance right in the middle of the little sitting room with a pool of water gathering round her feet.

For a moment she paused in uncertainty, quickly ashamed of her undignified arrival. The silence of the little house after the noise and wildness of the rain outside seemed to settle around her, isolating her in her guilty situation like a stunned silence greeting a social blunder.

Furtively she tiptoed back to the door, closed it against the weather and called out. There was no response. Dorothy tried again and waited. Could Anya still be asleep? Could she possibly be asleep after all this? Still no answer.

Slowly she looked about her. The room looked much as before - the same clutter, the same smell of linseed oil and turpentine, nothing else. Small details held and intrigued her. The table held a pile of letters addressed in Anya's neat hand, gathering dust as they awaited the post. Beside them were some sad-looking flowers in a glass jar wilting from lack of water, together with two unwashed mugs and a well-thumbed magazine. Beyond she saw that the door of the bedroom stood ajar. With guilt dogging every step, she crept across the room until she could see inside. The bed was unmade but empty. There was no sign of Anya there, nor in the kitchen, which echoed with the same silence. She returned towards the front door, ashamed and suddenly wishing to be anywhere else, despite the rain, which now hammered down more heavily than ever, despite increasing curiosity over Anya's whereabouts. Trespassing seemed somehow exaggerated by the inexplicable absence of life.

It was then that she noticed the attic door also standing ajar. It was usually locked and barred – Anya's private domain – and a place guarded jealously. Dorothy drew in a sharp breath and turned on her heel, for this of course could explain everything. Passing through it she paused at the foot of the stairs and called yet again. 'Anya. Are you about?' Still no reply.

Dorothy eased her way up the stairs and went into the attic. Curiosity had now taken hold. No-one, as far as she could tell, had yet been permitted entry into this piece of carefully-guarded privacy – and here was she, apparently quite alone, with the fruits of Anya's labours strewn about her.

The little studio appeared to be a clutter of industry. One of the Victorian paintings stood on the easel, half cleaned. Dorothy examined it with interest, seeing how the sharpness and detail of the finished portions shone against the dark yellowing gloom of the original. Perhaps this was proof of the revelation for which they had all been praying. She looked further about her. There was no sign of the portrait, except evidence that a great deal of painting was being done, judging from the litter of paint tubes and brushes on the untidy table. A small box-room leading from the studio was locked.

Dorothy's eyes strayed along the rows of canvases arranged on the floor about the walls. The still life which had interested them was protruding from behind another yellowed canvas. She withdrew it and studied it for a moment. Then she stiffened. From first noticing it she had felt that it looked somehow different – darker, less detailed than before – and now she examined it more closely with a questioning frown. This was not the same picture at all. It must be its partner –

for this was the work of the same unskilled hand – with everything matching from the tarnished frame with its little iron brackets to the actual size and shape of it. But this picture depicted a wine jug and a silver dish of black grapes. Intrinsically it was no more exceptional than the other, apart from the fact of its existence, and that in itself was extraordinary. Dorothy knew for certain that she had not seen it before.

She withdrew its partner from the pile. Then she stared in perplexity once more. This too appeared mysteriously different. She was pressed to decide why – except perhaps that a greater density of blackness in the background appeared to give it a depth unnoticed before. Maybe this had been achieved by some cleaning procedure. She stood back and looked at it - remembering how her father had been afraid of it as a child, imagining a face lurking amongst the fruit. She rather fancied that this strange illusion had now vanished for ever in the process. For some reason a little shudder ran up her spine.

Then the sound of a car followed by the slamming of a door cut into the silence and brought her sharply back to reality. Of course! She had not thought to check whether or not the little red car was in its place, and now its return explained a great deal. She all but threw herself down the stairs and stood in the centre of the room flushed with embarrassment and heavy with guilt. As the door opened she called out, 'Anya, you've got an invader. I'm really sorry, but I'm afraid I got caught in the storm.'

Anya swept in and stopped in her tracks. 'Good God Dorothy, what on earth are you doing here?'

'It's as I said. I simply got caught out. I'm really sorry.'

'It's okay,' Anya said in a flat tone, her green eyes veiled, guarded. Then quickly recovering herself, added more kindly, 'Hadn't you better take off that coat?'

'No - no I must be getting along now.' Dorothy was suddenly aware of a trail of water around the room which seemed to proclaim her guilt. She fervently hoped that Anya had not noticed. 'I must be getting back.'

'You can't possibly leave in this. It's teeming down. Look, I've got some coffee on the stove. You'd better sit down for a bit.'

She swept up the mugs, disappeared into the kitchen and returned moments later with coffee that had been hastily reheated. 'Okay then, so what on earth brought you here at this unearthly hour?' She did not volunteer to explain why she herself had been out and about at the same unearthly hour and Dorothy did not ask.

'I couldn't sleep. I went for a walk.'

'On a morning like this? Whatever possessed you?'

'It wasn't raining when I started. Besides a bit of rain doesn't matter – not when you have the feeling that you've got to get away from everybody.'

Anya's brows shot up into her fiery hair. 'That surprises me.'

'Why?'

'I simply didn't imagine that the Chevenings ever felt the need to escape from one another. You all seem so – so interdependent and happy to be in each other's pocket.'

'And you can't imagine wanting to get away from that?'

Anya gave a curt little laugh, and perching herself on the arm of the sofa said, 'I can. But then I'm not one of you.'

Dorothy sipped her coffee and frowned. 'I know you consider yourself a solitary person...'

'I am solitary. Do you doubt it?

'No – of course not – but then I don't really understand it either. Solitary just sounds horribly lonely to me.'

'Simply because you of all people couldn't begin to understand the meaning of the word,' Anya said dismissively. 'Believe me, I know all there is to know about being lonely and just how thoroughly different it is. For me, lonely was when my mother walked out on me for a man half her age. Solitary was when I came to terms with it and saw it in a new light - as freedom. So there you have it.'

Dorothy shook her head with a brittle laugh. 'That's far too simplistic for me. It still doesn't make sense. What about friends? For someone like you there must have been plenty of them.'

'Yes, of course there were. I had some inspirational friends – like my self-styled godmother - and the one schoolmistress who believed in me – my wonderful college lecturer - and Jean-Paul.' She smiled, her face reflecting some distant memories. 'We met in the Uffizi you know – when I was trekking round Europe on my own. I adored Florence! And Italy.'

'So who was Jean-Paul?'

The smile faded, and as Anya looked down into her lap the familiar veil descended once more, closing the briefly opened page on her thoughts. 'A memory,' she said abruptly. 'From a very long time ago.' And she rose to her feet, scooped up the empty mugs and added briskly. 'Come on – I'll run you home in the car.'

'No need Anya. I can easily walk. The rain's gone through.'

Anya shrugged. 'Please yourself.'

It appeared that the brief moment of intimacy had passed. Dorothy pulled on her coat and hurried to the door. 'Well thanks for the coffee anyway,' she said. 'And the loan of your roof.'

'You're welcome.'

And the food for thought, she added silently to herself, as she set off along the drive in the dampness and drizzle of the grey morning – aware that her quest had succeeded only in producing rather more questions than answers.

* * *

Dorothy's foray left her feeling restless and disturbed. The mystery of her discovery in Anya's studio preyed increasingly on her mind, and she knew that she would not feel easy until she had mentioned it to her father, even though she sensed that he would not want to listen.

She found him in the library, seated at a littered desk, fighting his way through an untidy pile of household accounts. It represented another task recently inherited from his father, and invariably made him irritable. His tendency to put off the evil moment generally made things worse, so that by the time he got around to settling the debts, they had become overdue demands. This occupied his attention when she found him, and as he glanced up his eyes told her that the interruption was both ill-timed and unwelcome.

'If you must bring your coffee in here, Dorothy, please do it quietly, or you'll throw my whole morning's accounting awry.'

Dorothy uttered an apology, then slid past and settled herself on the window seat. She eyed his preoccupied back as he bent to his task, then ventured, 'Can't I fetch some coffee for you, Daddy?'

'Not now.'

'Any help then?'

'Hush, please Dorothy.'

She shrank back into her private thoughts, rebuffed. And when eventually he spun the chair of the desk towards her, she had more or less decided that the moment was no longer right for approaching the delicate a subject of Anya. Instead she asked non-committally, 'If our accounts are in such turmoil, why don't you let me act as secretary for you? I'm really very efficient, you know.'

He gave a bark of laughter. 'The turmoil is only in my mind, Dorothy. Signing cheques always upsets my equilibrium – and I'm afraid there's nothing you can do about that.'

She frowned in response. 'It worries me to hear you talk like that. Are we so hard up?'

'We are about to be – when the builder's accounts begin to arrive.'

'What about our sale? Haven't you seen the splendid job Anya's making of our so-called rubbish?' Resolve had crumbled. Dorothy uttered Anya's name in a faltering tone, wondering how to guide the conversation along the delicate line of her thoughts.

'Yes, yes, she's doing fine – but there's not a really good painting amongst the whole damned lot. You know that as well as I do. Even Anya can't make a silk purse out of a sow's ear.' His tone was light, but Dorothy detected a false note, and watched him as he swung his chair back to the desk in a gesture of disinterest, suggesting that he did not intend to be led along any conversational lines that included Anya.

'Daddy,' she persisted ruthlessly, 'things are not always what they seem. Anya may not be all that she outwardly appears for a start.'

'Oh? What's that supposed to mean?'

Dorothy's courage began to falter. 'I think she could be hiding something.'

'What sort of thing?'

'A great deal of knowledge about painting that we can't begin to question.'

'Well, doesn't that go without saying? Of course she knows more than we do. It's her profession. It's why we asked her to come here.

But don't try to weave fantasies about it. There's nothing in our art collection worth hiding I'm afraid.'

'I wouldn't be so sure. Take that pair of still life studies.'

'Which pair?'

'The ones depicting our old pewter fruit bowl and the grapes.'

'Was it a pair?'

'Well, wasn't it?'

'Forty years ago perhaps it was. But it's been one on its own ever since – and something of a monstrosity.'

Dorothy looked away. Her mind was beginning to spin. So he did not know about the mysterious canvas in the studio.'

Dorothy,' Matt said, eying her shrewdly. 'Things are what they appear. That's the whole trouble. Stop trying to fool yourself. There are no wonderful secrets waiting to unfold.'

'No secrets?' Dorothy began to clutch at the straws of her suspicion. 'Did you ever explain the five-foot canvas that disappeared then?'

'The one Philip put his foot through?'

'Well did you?'

Matt laughed. 'No, I didn't explain it. No doubt it disappeared in the rubbish cart. A pity. It was probably a Goya.'

Dorothy rose to her feel in irritation. 'All right then, have it your own way. I'm in no position to argue the case, but if I were you, I'd want to ask a few questions. I wouldn't sit here bemoaning my poverty while people carried my property away in the dust cart.' And angrily she left the room and slammed the door behind her.

Matt, in a determined effort to remain unperturbed, braced himself against the resounding crash that marked his daughter's departure, shrugged his broad shoulders in perplexity and returned to his columns of figures. He would not allow himself to be upset by her tantrums this morning – and he would not be drawn into a discussion about anything connected with Anya – not while the memory of the night before was still so graphically etched in his thoughts.

Matt's cool blue eyes took on a veiled look as he remembered the passion which had passed between them. At the time it had seemed so natural, so right, that now he wondered why shreds of doubts should cloud the joy of such a memory. She was sensational.

He closed his eyes tightly, perhaps to prolong the image, perhaps to obliterate the sight of the desk before him. Matt could not be sure. And for a few futile moments he continued to juggle with his columns of figures. Eventually he gave up. Dorothy and her outburst had shaken his concentration, finally destroying what remained. Rising from the desk, he crossed the room to where the Sunday paper lay awaiting him on the table, and gathering it up, he followed her from the room.

* * *

In the drawing room his parents were enjoying a drink before lunch with the Crisps, who had called unexpectedly. They were passing the little vase between them.

'Such a happy occasion Katherine. You must have been delighted,' Henry was saying.

'Of course. It was all very touching if not entirely unexpected – and altogether undeserved.'

'Nonsense,' Amanda protested. 'You've done more than your share of giving over the years.'

Matt entered quietly into this circle of pleasantries, pouring a drink for himself from the side table as he passed. 'Something to hold onto when the rest has gone under the hammer,' he said, eyeing the little vase with a rueful smile.

'Don't be foolish Matt. It's just charming little gesture.'

'Besides,' Henry said. 'You've already relinquished enough to create quite a bit of interest in the sale. I know you don't believe me, William, but it's perfectly true.' Then sitting forward in his chair, he paused, weighing his thoughts for a moment, before adding, 'Do you remember we were talking about the Longhirst sale a while back?'

'Yes I do. Not that I recall just what was said – although of course I've also read about it. It's been in the news quite a bit these past weeks. And good luck to them I say. I understand they expect to raise a small fortune.'

'Yes and no,' Henry said. 'As you know, the Hazelwood collection has always been considered one the most important in private hands. So now what happens? Suddenly everything changes. In the event it seems that you can't even be sure of such an apparent certainty.'

'In what way?'

'Extraordinary though it is – I've been told that now there are doubts of provenance over some of the better works.'

'Good Lord. Really?'

'Well I'm not sure yet. But it rather looks as though some of the so-called masters may not be up to scratch – in a word, not genuine.'

'Fakes, do you mean?'

'Excellent and convincing reproductions of dubious origin was actually how it was put. What that implies we've yet to learn.'

'I can't believe it. Where did you hear all this?'

'Well, that was the strangest part of it. A fellow from the fraud squad turned up in the auction rooms a couple of days ago, ostensibly to alert me to the possibility of further fakes turning up.'

William gave a bark of laughter. 'Not in our collection I trust!'

'I think not! But you know, Hazelwood too is a man of integrity.'

'And he's suspected of foul play?'

'That wasn't said of course. There may have been fakes on the walls of Longhirst for years. Who's to say? But the implication that there's to be a serious investigation was the gist of the conversation. At best, William, it's an ill wind that could bring an agitated art world to your door – which is why I'm telling you about it.'

'Surely not,' William said. 'Surely no-one in his right mind could imagine the unexpected materialising out of our bucolic collection.'

'Well, as they say in theatrical circles, bad publicity is better than no publicity. So we'll just have to wait and see. I imagine the papers will have got hold of it by now.'

They exchanged incredulous glances. Only Matt averted his gaze and lapsed into silence. For some reason his heart went out to Hazelwood, who probably had maintenance problems of his own at Longhirst. Perhaps he also sought to raise capital from his sale. Maybe he too had a Robson breathing down his neck. At least Matt had the satisfaction of knowing that their own small plans to save their comparatively minor heritage did not have the potential to cause a headline disaster. It was almost reassuring to know that there were degrees in all things.

Nevertheless it made an ironic comparison. And the bills he had abandoned on the desk next door seemed to loom ominously in the background, and his thoughts of the intrusive upheaval of even a small auction sale to cast a gloom of its own. Even his thoughts of Anya and the pretext which had thrown her into his life, with the result of stirring it into such turmoil, spun more wildly than ever in his mind.

He was no longer part of the conversation. Somehow he could not chase from his thoughts the bizarre suggestion that someone had just carried away a Goya in the dustcart.

CHAPTER THIRTEEN

'Did you say Longhirst?' Edward asked Elizabeth. Over breakfast she had purloined the centre of the newspaper, leaving him to browse through the business sections, and had stumbled on a story that soon would be occupying the front pages.

'Yes, I feel I've heard of it somehow.'

'Of course you have. It's Hazelwood's place. Don't you remember discussing the art sale they're having at the end of the month? We talked about it over dinner that night at Foxsteads.'

'Yes,' Philip said, suddenly returning to the real world from the planet on which he'd been daydreaming. 'And Anya told us about the restoration she'd been involved with. You must remember that.'

'Of course, I do now. I knew it was familiar.'

'She's very proud of what she did there,' Philip added. 'It was very prestigious.'

Elizabeth raised an eyebrow and handed the page to Edward who read it slowly and emitted a low whistle. 'Heavens above. She won't like this then.'

'Why not?'

'Because it seems as if all of a sudden there's the suspicion of fraud hanging over the entire collection.'

'Fraud? At Longhirst?'

'Surely not.'

'Well, that's what I'm reading. God, what a scandal.'

'Unbelievable. In a place like that.'

'Gosh,' Philip said in dismay. 'Anya will be devastated. Oh hell, she's going to be really shocked.'

'And she'll not be the only one.' Edward said, reading the article again and shaking his head. 'There'll be shock waves passing through the heart of the art world. If this turns out to have substance there will be an awful lot of questions being asked, raising doubts in an awful lot of minds.' He folded the newspaper, reached for another slice of toast and buttered it thinly. 'These days art represents a huge investment you know, and this could cause a rapid loss of confidence in the market.'

Elizabeth passed him the marmalade and said, 'Could that include our sale also?'

'I wouldn't imagine so. Had your father had the good sense to include some of his better works, then maybe it would have made a difference – one way or another.'

'I thought at the time he should have done – we've so much of everything at Foxsteads – and so many bills to settle.'

'You're probably right – but it would need a very expert assessment I'm afraid.'

Philip regarded them solemnly. 'But we have a captive expert. Shouldn't we be asking Anya for advice.'

Edward's face lengthened to its most pessimistic. 'I'm sorry Philip – but in my opinion she of all people should be kept out of it altogether.'

'Oh? Why?'

'Use a little nous. A woman like Anya, connected, however loosely, with the scandal at Longhirst, is the last person on earth who should be allowed within range of the collection at Foxsteads.'

'Good God Father – what on earth are you implying?' Philip demanded, his eyes blazing. 'I hope you're not suggesting what I think you are – because if so you're getting it badly wrong.'

Elizabeth looked from father to son in confusion. 'What exactly is being implied?'

Edward shrugged. 'Nothing beyond the fact that Anya is a stranger in our midst – that we know nothing about her apart from her association with a famous art collection that is now under suspicion.'

Philip rose from the table, paced the length of the kitchen and back, then flinging himself back into his chair, exclaimed angrily, 'But that's ridiculous father. It's absurd. Anya is a distinguished restorer.'

'Then what's she doing in a place like this? It never has made sense to me. What's more, from the little I've seen of her, not only would I question her right to an opinion, but I wouldn't trust her an inch either.'

'That's just it. You don't know her. Ask anyone who does and you'll get the same answer. She's straight as a die.'

'She also has everyone bewitched,' Edward said, giving his son a withering look. 'You included. In my view you spend far too much time in her company. Not healthy in a chap of your age to be glassy-eyed over a woman like that – a woman who's seen too much of world to be good for her.'

Philip turned scarlet and rose from the table toppling his chair with a resounding crash. 'That's just plain stupid!' he shouted. 'You simply don't understand – and you've got it all wrong.' And in a vain attempt to preserve his dignity, he strode, incandescent with rage, from the room.

* * *

Edward wasted no time hastening to Foxsteads on the pretext of borrowing a book. In the library his parents-in-law were relaxing after lunch, and for a while he browsed amongst the dusty shelves, thinking how ironic it was that such a remarkable collection was so largely unappreciated and in need of a good librarian. One day he resolved to sort through it all.

'Strange business, the art fraud at Longhirst, don't you think?' he remarked as William came over to join him.

'Yes,' William agreed. 'Extraordinary business. Most unlikely. I met Hazelwood some years ago. I must say he didn't strike me as the kind of chap to try anything underhand. But there it is. It looks rather as though he's trying to pass off copies as the real thing – unless the family has been fooling itself for generations.'

'Or,' Edward added, 'there has been a bit of clever manipulation on someone's part.'

'Surely you don't think so.'

'Why not? It wouldn't be that difficult to switch originals for fakes – not for the clever fraudster – and as you know the whole collection has just been cleaned and restored.'

'I didn't know that.'

Edward frowned impatiently. 'We all know it has. Surely I'm not the only member of the family who remembers Anya Paris telling us how she herself was personally involved there.'

'Ah, yes, I do remember something of the sort.'

'And doesn't that strike any kind of a chord with you?'

'Should it?'

'Well I would say that it raises a number of questions.'

Slowly the gist of Edwards's implication began to dawn on William. He frowned contemplatively, then shifting the weight from his game leg in an impatient gesture, he said, 'You're surely not suggesting, Edward, that Anya or the entirely reputable firm that employed her could know anything about the Hazelwood scandal, are you?'

'Well, I would be interested to know her reaction.'

'Then perhaps you should ask her.'

'I thought it might be more in your interest to do the asking,' Edward said. 'After all, it's your art collection that she's working on right now.'

William gave a brisk little laugh as Edward's seeds of doubt took root. 'Scarcely in the same league,' he said, 'Nevertheless I certainly shall.'

In the event it fell to Katherine to do the asking. She and Anya had become good friends over the weeks of their acquaintance, occasionally finding time to sit and talk together, usually to discuss London and the fascinating changes that had taken place since Katherine's own fondly remembered girlhood. She looked forward to these pleasant conversations, to be transported back to where a small part of her heart had remained and where memories were sweet.

The following day was just such an occasion. The clouds and rain had at last lifted, leaving a clean and shimmering afternoon. The garden had emerged damp and sweet smelling. Like the Phoenix of Summer itself the flowers beside the sunlit terrace had risen from the ashes of battered leaves and fallen petals that the storm had left in its wake – and now bloomed in undefeated glory.

Katherine carried the wicker chair onto the terrace, assisted Aunt Florence into it and settled herself beside her on the swing seat with her tapestry to occupy her. Oh, how good it was to feel the sun on her face. Yet how sad also, she thought, to have to count the sunny days in this northern clime so preciously.

She closed her eyes and found herself remembering another sunlit terrace far away in a quiet corner of London where she had once sat sewing with her mother, listening to the distant hum of the London traffic and the singing of birds that had ventured from the heath to invade their little garden. It seemed that then long sunny day had followed long sunny day in sweet unbroken succession - that summer had always kept its promises. Of course it could not have been so,

Katherine reasoned, but she emitted a nostalgic little sigh.

Somehow the years of battling with the cruel elements, that at times ravaged this stark uncompromising corner of England, had softened every memory of her gentle youth. Besides it was pleasant to cling to such illusions. She smiled a little ruefully. Perhaps the sounds that assailed her in this country garden were not so very different; the same bird song, the hum of insects and even the gentle snoring of the old lady in the wicker chair curiously reminding her of the traffic noise she had always missed so painfully.

She was still smiling to herself when Anya, stepping lightly onto the terrace, jogged her from her daydream. 'Oh dear, I've woken you,' she said contritely. 'I'm so sorry. And you were having such a lovely dream.'

'I wasn't asleep, my dear.'

'But you were dreaming.'

'Yes – yes, perhaps I was.'

'And it must have been a lovely dream. You were smiling so contentedly. I shouldn't have disturbed you.'

Katherine patted the seat beside her. 'Sit down, my dear. You're not disturbing me. I'm delighted to have company – and you of all people will perhaps understand an old lady who occasionally has dreams about a little garden far away in Hampstead.'

Anya sat down beside her. She was herself a little reminiscent of the past, Katherine thought, with her flower sprigged dress and her old straw hat, which made her seem strangely out of place at Foxsteads where the young tended to live in breeches and allow the sun to tan their faces. Anya's porcelain skin beneath the shady brim of the hat was the texture of magnolia, in dramatic contrast to the vivid tendrils of amber hair and the lively sparkle of those intriguing eyes. She was, Katherine decided, altogether an antithesis – in some ways almost comical – in others uniquely beautiful.

'You would have loved it, Anya,' she said. 'It was only a little garden of course, surrounded by a high red brick wall. There was a wonderful wisteria on the south side. I imagine if I returned now it would seem smaller than ever – but it was very pretty.'

'Town gardens do have a certain charm,' Anya agreed. 'But surely there is nothing to compare with the wonderful views and the glorious sense of space you find in a country garden like this.'

'Yes, it is a beautiful garden. I have spent my happiest days at Foxsteads planning and improving and working in it. When I came here, it was a maze of fussy old-fashioned flowerbeds. It needed half a dozen full-time gardeners to tend it all. Between us Hodges and I have completely remodelled it. Now we can cope with it together. Ah, Anya, you should see it in spring! Up here, just when we begin to give up hope of the arrival of spring, suddenly it explodes upon us and the view from here is a golden sea of daffodils.'

'I would love to see it,' Anya said.

Florence stirred in her chair, and struggling to awaken at the welcome sight of Anya, muttered, 'There were never more than three gardeners employed at Foxsteads, Katherine, and you can't claim all credit for yourself. My father planted the rhododendrons – and they are the real glory of this garden.'

Katherine smiled tolerantly. 'I do agree, dear. I was coming to the rhododendrons next. And of course I don't take credit for more than the tiniest part of the landscape.'

'I should hope not. The credit for that,' Florence asserted, trying to focus her failing sight upon the distant scene, 'is God's.' When this met with no response, she demanded, 'Don't you agree, Anya, that this is the finest landscape you ever clapped eyes on? The finest in England. How I wish I could still see it with eyes as young as yours.'

Anya smiled kindly at the old lady. 'Yes, it is a most beautiful scene. I shall never forget it.' For a moment silence engulfed them. Florence's chin sank into her collar again, and after a few futile attempts to keep awake, she succumbed once more to her gentle snoring. Anya turned to Katherine. 'I am a restless creature, Mrs Chevening,' she said. 'And it astonishes me to believe that I could never tire of this place. But that's how it makes me feel.'

'That's the nicest compliment you could pay Northumberland.'

'It is a compliment to you all actually.'

'And to one of us in particular, perhaps,' Katherine said shrewdly. Her tone was light, her

216

smile teasing as she spoke, but Anya's gaze at once dropped into her lap as though lost for a reply. This Katherine had not expected. She had not expected Anya to blush either, and pleasantly encouraged she said, 'It would give me so much pleasure to think so.'

Anya's moment of confusion passed quickly. The gaze she returned was perfectly direct as she answered carefully. 'Then I wish I could say it were so. But I'm afraid I can't. You have all been kindness itself. There's not one of you I could single out from the rest. And it's better that way, Mrs Chevening, believe me. That is the greatest compliment I can pay. You see personal attachments are not for me. I'm a rolling stone, consciously gathering no moss, and when people close in on me I know it's time to move on. That's simply the way it is.'

Katherine returned the gaze uncomprehendingly. 'That sounds to me awfully like running away from the very things most people run after.'

'It's freedom. I have to be free. It's as important to me as the air I breathe.'

'Then I fancy that you have left a trail behind you of disappointed people.'

'I don't think so,' Anya said with a little laugh. 'I don't plant very heavy footsteps as I go.'

Katherine lapsed into a perplexed silence for a moment or two. Anya puzzled her. There were things about her that simply did not add up, as though the radiance that surrounded her was only an aura to hide some sadness or insecurity - as though secrets of her past somehow clouded her vision of the future. 'Freedom,' she said gently, 'can tend to turn into loneliness when one gets older. I cannot believe, Anya, that you haven't parted with little bits of your heart along the way.'

'Hearts mend,' Anya said briskly. 'I'm devoted only to my work. If I have left anything of myself behind they are only the kind that are found on canvas. That's the way I like people to remember me.'

Katherine drew in a long breath and held it bated while she gathered her thoughts. Then she said in a matter-of-fact tone, 'In that case you will be very saddened by what is happening at Longhirst at the moment.'

Despite doubting the wisdom of her remark, she was shocked by its reception. Anya's green eyes became momentarily fixed and glassy. The pupils seemed to dilate, giving Katherine a brief, but incomprehensible insight into the mysterious depths of the mind beyond. She did not understand what she saw – only that Anya was shocked and afraid – and she knew to her chagrin that her anticipation of a lively discussion between them on this controversial subject was not to be.

Anya regained her composure almost at once, but the green eyes were carefully averted as with a hollow little laugh she said, 'The pictures I encountered at Longhirst were the most genuine and beautiful works of art I've ever seen. To have handled such treasures was a privilege I shall cherish always. And if they are proven to be fakes, then I shall never trust my own judgement again.'

After that she lingered for a short while – just long enough to exchange a few careful platitudes with the old lady, who chose that moment to reawaken. Then she took her leave. Katherine watched with a sad and puzzled little sigh as the retreating figure disappeared behind the bank of rhododendron. With deep regret she wondered whether she herself had unwittingly stretched the hand of friendship beyond the invisible line that Anya drew between the love of her work and the restless need to move on.

* * *

'I do hope I haven't offended Anya,' she said later to Matt, when the two them were enjoying a rare moment of quiet together in the library. 'Perhaps I shouldn't have mentioned the Longhirst affair quite so abruptly.'

Matt smiled at her kindly. 'I can't imagine your upsetting anyone. I think the emphasis everyone is trying to put on the poor girl's connection with that ill-fated collection is getting to you.'

'Of course it isn't, Matt.'

'Then stop worrying about it.'

Restlessly Katherine rose to her feet and crossed the room, then stood straightening the ornaments on the mantelpiece, as though precision of the arrangement were of some particular importance. 'Really Matt, she is very difficult to understand in many ways. I begin to wonder if she understands herself.'

'I know. I've been down the same road, believe me!'

'She seems so insecure.' Katherine picked up a Staffordshire figure and examined it minutely. 'I can't help wondering why.'

Watching her thoughtfully, Matt waited until she had replaced the ornament to her satisfaction, then said, 'So why are you telling me this?'

'Because I sense you are fond of Anya.'

'I am.'

'And about to be hurt.'

He laughed. 'Heavens mother! Maybe there's no fool like an old fool, but I'm too old and seasoned to cause you that kind of anxiety!'

'I've become fond of Anya too, you know.'

'Yes, I do know. We all have. But as for me, I'm past chasing rainbows, so you can tick that worry off your list.'

Katherine watched as he turned away, in no way convinced, and saddened that in all these years he had not found the right woman for himself. Plenty had thrown themselves at him, heaven knew, for he was both eligible and attractive, possibly more so now that wind, weather and the passing of time had taken their natural toll. Then she smiled. He was so like his handsome father had been at the same age! It was such a waste.

Matt wandered over to the window, afraid that his face would betray him. Truth was that he was still young and ardent enough to make a fool of himself. The years had only taught him to recognise the folly of his desires. He gazed into the garden in an uneasy silence.

From here he could see Angus crossing the lawn - a jaunty figure in green oilskins, his rod and basket broadcasting his intentions for the evening. Doubtless he would forget to return for dinner, forget everything in his absorption by the river. Matt envied him. How simple it must be, he thought, to be able to lose oneself in so undemanding a pursuit – one which needed no soul-searching, and in which hope was eternal, not to be dashed by one false move, its mood invariably one of sweet tranquillity. Angus bore a mark of contentment that evoked in Matt's turbulent mind echoes of how he had once been – before that fateful lunch at the White Hart just a few weeks before. Yes, the price of his father's portrait had seemed reasonable then. Not so now. Immeasurable was the expense of all the emotion that had shaken the very foundations of his peaceful existence – and at such cost.

It was almost indecently late when Matt at last succumbed to the need to set things straight with Anya. He had to know her views on events – but more than that, he needed to be with her. He wondered whether she would even be up and about, but the atmosphere at the lodge was very much wide awake and charged with energy.

Anya clattered downstairs from the studio attic looking flushed and dishevelled. 'Oh Matt, what are you doing here?'

'Interrupting something important it seems'

'Only the most important moment of my career,' she declared in a theatrical tone.

For a moment he stood motionless, astonished rather than dismayed. But she was laughing. Then his eyes strayed between the clock, about to begin running on midnight oil, and the flushed figure in the paint-stained smock. 'I'm sorry, Anya. I know it's indecently late to be calling.'

'No more indecently late than for me to be still working in my studio – I know that too.'

'Do you want to be left to it?'

'No – no – really I don't. I need to be saved from myself – or I shall end up painting all night. I'm like that when I find my brush obeying my heart so obligingly, even though I know my body is disobeying my brain! I want to get it all onto the canvas at once. Madness of course.'

He stared at her irresolutely. 'Then you'll hardly welcome my company. I'm enough to dampen the most ardent inspiration tonight.'

'Not mine. I'm not easily dampened – and I am most dreadfully hungry. I shan't have the energy to squeeze another tube of paint if I don't eat something soon.'

'You haven't eaten?'

'I've been painting since tea time.'

He gave in with a little shrug of resignation, then stood watching through the open door of the kitchen as she began to hack a loaf of bread to pieces and smother it with butter and honey. 'What has brought on this surge of inspiration?' he asked as she returned with her laden plate and two mugs of coffee. 'You look positively feverish.'

'It happens sometimes. I suppose it's the happy fact that the work's going well – and the realisation that probably I've been at Foxsteads far too long already – and that I have to be thinking of moving on.'

'I see,' he said slowly. 'I suppose you have another commission to go to.'

She shook her head. 'Nothing specific – but the future, whatever it is, has to be pursued. I have nothing in particular but everything in the world to go to.'

'And your work here?'

'In a week or two it will be finished – if all goes well – and it is going really well at the moment. Tonight I feel special and wonderfully gifted – so close to being a genius that I'm afraid to stop working in case tomorrow I awaken as an ordinary human being again!' Her green eyes sparkled with mirth.

He laughed at her extravagance. 'So when can I judge your genius for myself?'

'For as long as the picture pleases you.' Then she grew solemn. 'With all my heart I hope you'll remember me kindly when you look at it.'

Slowly the reality of the situation sank in. Matt felt a constriction in his throat as he recognised this feverish activity for what it was – the need to be away from Foxsteads as soon as possible. 'I'll hardly need a picture to remember you by, Anya. You'll not be so easy to forget.'

She shrugged. 'That's how it is now. Time changes things.'

'But doesn't necessarily obliterate them.'

Nonchalantly she continued to tuck into her supper with apparent relish, finally licking the last remnants of honey from her fingers like a careless child. Then thoughtfully stirring her coffee she said, 'I'm always suspicious when I start to throw out roots. I told your mother this afternoon how easy it is to love this beautiful place – but for me that doesn't work. I need the pressure of seeing beyond the present to achieve the best from myself – and if it's any consolation to you, it is very important to me that this portrait ranks amongst my finest achievements.'

'So important that you can't wait to escape from us all?'

Suddenly the bravado crumbled and she looked bereft. She hung her head until the fiery tendrils hid her face from him and said unevenly, 'No, it isn't like that at all. Actually you have to take it as a compliment, Matt, that I'm afraid to stay.'

His heart seemed to miss a beat or two. Until this moment he had not had the courage to believe that the bitter-sweetness of their brief affair could have touched so fiercely guarded a heart. But now for the very first time he discerned the slenderest chink in its armour. He saw the shadowy reflection of his own longings in the veiled depths of her green eyes. And this just at the moment when she had decided that time was running out. 'Have the walls of Foxsteads begun to close in so oppressively?'

She smiled. 'No, I think perhaps it is the wall I've built around myself that's starting to crumble.'

He took hold of her hands and drew them to his lips. They smelled curiously of turpentine, linseed oil and honey, a strange combination that seemed to sum up Anya herself. 'And you're afraid because you know that I'm in love with you.'

'No, it isn't that.'

'Then it's because you are in love with me.'

Anya's face contorted in anguish. 'Don't Matt – please don't. You know I'm not - that I can't.'

'I understand that you think you can't.'

She bristled. 'In actual fact you know very little about me.'

'Then isn't it time to talk about it? Aren't I allowed to know what it is that isolates you and refuses to let the world come close? I need to know.'

'It's all too complicated to explain.'

'Then try. I have all night to listen. And I'm pretty sure it has to be some story.'

She drew a very deep breath and exhaled it in a shuddering sigh. 'All lives are stories, aren't they? Dramas dictated by circumstances and decisions and by the way we relate to one another. Mine just happens to have been a catalogue of mistakes.'

'What kind of mistakes?'

'Oh, so many I've lost count. I suppose it comes down to trusting the wrong people - or believing in fairy tales – although I suppose everyone does that at some time – or worst of all, failing to tell the difference between being needed and being used. It's endless.'

Matt, still holding her fingers gently shook his head and smiled. 'People are meant to learn from mistakes, aren't they?'

She nodded sagely. 'Exactly. So that's precisely why I am the way I am.'

For a long time Matt watched as she gazed through the window into the darkness, as though projecting transparent images from a chequered past into an unfocussed future. The bravado had evaporated. An air of melancholy now prevailed. He had not intended to dampen her spirits, but it seemed as though he had.

'But that's giving in,' he said. 'And I don't subscribe to giving in. Life is also a game. There are winners and losers and I don't intend to lose you that easily. I want to make you smile – to believe in the power of two – for one reason alone. That I've fallen in love with you and I want every bit of you.' It was, Matt decided in retrospect, one of the shortest but most significant speeches he'd ever delivered, for even as she shook her head in denial, he read the hungry longing in her eyes.

'Oh Matt – you can't and you mustn't – please don't try to change things that can't be changed.'

'I have to,' he replied, and taking her face in his hands he kissed her very gently on the lips. 'If I want to win.'

He knew from her response that she could no longer help herself any more than he could. It was as if the simplicity of a gentle kiss had released some powerful force and primitive longing that had been there all along.

Already she had begun to unfasten the buttons of her paint-stained shirt. In moments they were stepping from their clothes with almost indecent speed, no longer conscious of the rights and wrongs or the wisdom and folly of wanting each other with such longing and such urgency.

It was a moment that changed everything. She slid into his arms so easily that it was as though they had been destined to form a perfect fit. She was amazing, her skin almost translucently white, her body smooth and firm, reminiscent of Giorgioni's Venus. She was sensational. And with her extravagant vitality and desire matching his own, he forgot all resolve, all better judgement, and banished the haunting spectre of the Longhirst affair into thinnest air.

Possibly for each of them their different lives were pale images of what might have been had circumstances not dictated otherwise. But together, in anyone's language, they were a masterpiece.

CHAPTER FOURTEEN

Dorothy having been brought up on Giles's own tales of impending success and the Chevenings' natural scepticism, had never been quite sure what to make of her uncle. She was well aware that the family mistrusted anything it did not understand – and it understood neither his desire to live in London, nor any ambition without roots in the soil – leaving her unresolved. At his most profound he could reduce her to the uncertainty of the proverbial country cousin - at his most charming, to the sweet confidence of sophisticated womanhood. And of course he had never been in the least like an uncle. Anything but. He was fun and amusing and unpredictable. Being with him was never dull.

A kind of palpitating excitement, a pleasant tingle of anticipation, accompanied Dorothy past the porticoed entrance of number forty-three and down the basement steps to the front door. Suddenly she felt foolishly nervous. But there was no time to reflect upon it. She had scarcely put down her case, was still scanning the door for an elusive bell, when the door itself was flung wide and Giles, dishevelled, handsome as ever, his brown eyes alive with welcome, burst upon her.

'Dorothy! I wasn't sure if it was you on the stairs. I really wasn't. How you've changed!'

Apprehension fell from Dorothy like the shedding of heavy coat. She abandoned herself to being hugged and hugged him tightly in return.

'Since Christmas? Of course I haven't. And neither have you.'

No, he had not changed. He was the same as ever, warm and spontaneous and as excited as she. 'Come in, come in. So how was the journey?'

'Fine.'

'I should have come to the station.'

'Nonsense. Of course you shouldn't. There was no need. You haven't a car – and Dad paid for the taxi. I got the driver to take me past some of the sights. Don't tell Dad that.'

'Lips are sealed.' He beamed at her as he carried the case inside and drew her into the sitting room. 'Anyway, for a start I'll make coffee – then you must tell me everything – all the news – every detail – from home.'

'I won't know where to start – although in many ways nothing really changes of course. Grandfather is getting on fine – Aunt Florence is more trying than ever – and I'm sinking into something of rut, I'm afraid.'

'I don't believe that. You have blossomed, Dorothy. What a metamorphosis!'

She smiled a little ruefully at his extravagance. It was mere months since she and Giles had last seen each other, but at that time she had been scarcely out of school, and she supposed that the past eventful months had changed her more than she realised. Besides, Giles's visit to Foxsteads at Christmas had been brief and fraught with anxiety - a visit undertaken while his father was lying seriously ill in hospital. It had not been an occasion for happy reunions as they waited and watched, fearing that he might lose the injured leg or suffer permanent paralysis. Giles's journey north had been made in utmost haste, even before Imogen could find time to come with him. Dorothy remembered the occasion with a sad little sigh. But the shadow quickly passed. All that was now long ago, and her grandfather had recovered splendidly. All the same it was little wonder, she supposed, that she herself had cast off her schoolgirl mantle so abruptly, after such a winter. And if Giles's visit at that time was not to be counted, then it was getting on for two years since the last real get-together. It would be especially strange to see Imogen again after so long.

As she waited for Giles to make coffee she wandered across the room. Standing on tip-toe peering between the dusty leaves of the plane trees she could see the glitter of parked cars - and beyond these the worn pavements, white pillars and painted railings of the street. It was all so London, and to Dorothy strange and exciting. Giles had placed his desk in front of the window, making use of the room's limited light, and one glance at the battered typewriter and the litter of paper spilling onto the floor told her that a great deal of work was in progress.

It was, he told her, the script of a play that was nearing completion. Dorothy listened wide-eyed. She had heard it all before of course, but was still moved by the fervour and the optimism with which he faced an always-rosy future, quickly forgetting the struggles of a disappointing past. She did not understand the complex, symbolic nature of the plot, but fascinated by Giles's own confidence in its depth and potential, she could only marvel that Foxsteads had produced so remarkable a son.

'Being recognised is the hardest part of the work I do,' he told her. 'And I couldn't do it at all if Imogen didn't work so hard to keep us both.'

'But she believes in you. You know she does.'

'Yes, though I scarcely know why. I'm a fortunate chap. But rewards will be reaped one of these days. You'll see.' And he beamed at her.

'Of course.'

'So enough of me. Tell me all about the family.'

'You mean all the trivia?'

'Nothing will be too trivial.' Suddenly he was hungry for news of everyone up north – from his irascible great aunt to the adolescent Philip. He wanted to hear about the horses and the dogs, the crops, the building project, the garden, the neighbours. And he wanted above all to hear about Anya.

He was surprised to perceive a shadow passing across the brightness of Dorothy's conversation as Anya entered into it. All at once she became matter-of-fact and obtuse. 'We still don't know whether she's as brilliant as she thinks,' she said. 'She hasn't allowed any of us to see the great work yet.'

'She is remarkably talented,' Giles assured her. 'I've been told so on the very best authority.'

'Well, certain of her talents are more apparent than others.'

He eyed her shrewdly. 'I see. Then perhaps I was wrong to imagine that the two of you would become good friends.'

Dorothy gave a brittle little laugh. 'Oh, I dare say we might have been – had the queue for Anya's attentions not been quite so long.'

Giles's eyes lit up with laughter. 'I did also think that she might cause something of a stir amongst you all. Is there perhaps a story behind that reproachful look?'

'I think there is the beginning of a long story,' Dorothy admitted. 'But I'm not going to be drawn into any discussion about Anya Paris at this moment. I've come here to escape from all that.'

His look became circumspect. 'Escape? Is that why you're here?'

'Oh no, of course not. You know that's not why I came. It was to see you and Imogen and London…'

'And perhaps also to mend a broken heart?'

Dorothy looked away, dismayed, and hanging her head, focussed uncertainly on the carpet. 'If that's what father told you then be assured he was only guessing.'

'He told me nothing. I'm the one who's doing the guessing. Am I wrong then?'

She stared at the floor. She noticed that what once had been a fine Turkey carpet was now living on borrowed time – and that someone had taken the trouble to disguise the bare threads of it with coloured inks. This discovery strangely stirred her. No wonder Giles was so adept at probing beneath the apparent. Perhaps even his own air of optimism was no more than a good touching-up job to hide the worn out wishes and aspirations of his threadbare hopes. How ashamed she was to be despairing over her own first disappointment in life. The reds and blues and greens of the carpet merged into a bright blur as she answered unevenly, 'You are right and wrong. There is a boy and I was fond of him. But it didn't work out – and it doesn't matter really. My heart certainly isn't broken – only a bit bruised.' And she raised her eyes with a wavering little smile.

No more was said, and shortly afterwards Imogen returned. Clearly she had run every inch of the way from the bus stop, for she was flushed and excited. 'How dreadful not to have been here to greet you!' she exclaimed. 'I do hope Giles has looked after you properly.' She was laden with shopping. Life was pretty hard for Imogen, Dorothy thought sadly, but it did not show.

She had not changed either. She still looked about twenty, despite having been married to Giles for longer than that. She was naïve and uncomplicated as ever, with wide brown eyes that took in the world at face value, and an elfin face that wore an expression of sublime acquiescence. Of course she accepted Giles's exaggerated opinion of himself without question, and not once was Dorothy to hear a discordant note or vindictive word spoken between them.

What fun that first evening was. They ate spaghetti and drank cheap red wine – fare that would never have been on the menu at Foxsteads! - then sat talking until the small hours about the world at large and themselves in particular. And late though it was, when Dorothy at last dropped into bed she was too stimulated and excited to sleep. She lay awake for a long time, pleasantly digesting all that had been said and wondering, as she would often wonder, just why her family so misunderstood Giles, and why it was unable to accept Imogen.

Of course their lifestyle did not match the Chevenings' idea of respectability, and Dorothy knew that because it had begun as a runaway affair her grandmother had always questioned whether they were actually married at all. But even the sceptics were bound to acknowledge that the union, whether or not blessed by the church, had worked. And Dorothy was convinced that if kindness and empathy were the things that truly mattered, then the battling, destructive nature of so many marriages could only stand in deep shadow when all was said and done. She knew also, with a little pang of bitterness, that she and Luke could only have spent life together destroying each other in just this way. Nevertheless, as sleep at last claimed her, she was dreaming of the bitter-sweetness of just such a fiery future.

* * *

Being in London was the panacea - a perfect tonic and an inspiration. Mostly Dorothy was left to her own devices while Imogen worked and Giles slept, having burnt midnight oil at his typewriter the night before. And it suited her that way. Her itinerary consisted of museums and art galleries and shops recommended by Imogen - or sometimes the arty little coffee houses that Giles himself liked to frequent. There were many such places mushrooming in the back streets of theatre-land, serving cappuccino with a plethora of fiery talk designed to set a brave new world to rights. She enjoyed riding on buses and trains, and the challenge of getting from A to B without losing her way, which sometimes went wrong but did not seem to matter too much. It was fun just to observe the passing scene without being observed. The anonymity of London was what made it such a comfortable place to be lost in.

The much-heralded visit to the theatre came at the end of the week. It was to be a gathering of the elite, she was told, mostly by invitation, and clearly stirring Giles and Imogen into a fever of expectation. Dorothy pleasantly anticipated the gilt and glitz and glamour of the West End stage, echoes of which she had known all her life from Newcastle's illustrious Theatre Royal, where her vigilant grandmother had overseen her progress from pantomime to ballet. She had hoped that they would be seeing My Fair Lady, London's latest hit. But Giles assured her that the choice he had made would be even better than that. This was to be theatrical art - and a debut in every sense of the word.

They set out in high spirits, first taking the tube, then a bus, alighting at the door of an austere building into which streams of people poured. The entrance bore no sign of anything happening within and no resemblance to any theatre ever seen by Dorothy. For a moment she hesitated and cast a questioning look towards Imogen who simply nodded reassurance and followed Giles into the door.

Such was the disappointment of this reality that Dorothy could scarcely believe her eyes. Then she was struck by the funny side of it. Suddenly she dared not look at Imogen again for fear of bursting into laughter and letting the side down. For this, it seemed, was the revered theatre, a dingy hall in the back-streets of Bloomsbury, with a meagre stage set in the centre of rows of wooden seats, ten deep. There was no curtain, and the visible scenery consisted of one solitary chair and a table bearing a potted palm, lit by a glaring spotlight.

'Isn't this just fantastic?' Giles said, looking about him in palpitating appraisal. 'This is the latest kind of production in the footsteps of the famed Theatre in the Round. Which you've heard of I'm sure.'

She shook her head. ''Fraid not.'

'The latest innovation. Which is why you can expect to see everyone worth seeing. In theatrical terms this is the elite.'

Her eyes answered him in questioning silence. He squeezed her arm, as his gaze guided her amongst the audience. 'The chap over there in the velvet jacket is Robert Morgan the writer. Have you read "The Way of an Ill Wind?"'

She shook her head again.

'It was quite controversial but much admired in certain quarters. And see the fellow behind... the one with the beard. That's Gifford Warner, the TV director. They say he's brilliant and quickly up and coming. And the blonde with him. You must recognise her.'

'Is it who I think it is then?'

'Delia Pride. She's married to Warner.'

'I saw her in "the Gentle Alliance". Gosh Giles, isn't she beautiful!'

He smiled at her. 'A beautiful bitch, I'm told.' And his gaze continued to sweep the auditorium.

Slowly Dorothy's mirth and scepticism evaporated into the smoke scented atmosphere. Giles's sense of excitement became curiously infectious as she looked wide-eyed about her. She chastised herself. How indeed could she have found it risible, when clearly this was rarefied theatre that she was privileged to see?

The company was indeed remarkable in its variety. The long hair and flamboyant shabbiness of the aspiring blended in surprising harmony with the sobriety of success. There were also several well-known faces evoking frissons of recognition. 'And that man over there, Dorothy,' Giles said, the pressure of his hand on her arm suggesting that at last he had found the face he sought, 'is Marco Bellini.'

She found herself looking at a tall distinguished man with greying wavy hair that reached his collar. 'I've heard of him. Who is he?'

'A producer with one of the new ITV companies. I've been trying to make his acquaintance for ages.'

'Ah yes, Marco Bellini. Of course I've heard of him.'

'I doubt whether you have. He's not well known beyond inner circles.'

'He is to me, Giles. Believe me, I know all about him - because he's Luke's brother.'

'Luke?'

'You know. Luke Robson. My friend from home.'

'But that's not possible.'

'I couldn't be more sure. With a name like that and a career in television. It has to be.'

Giles gave an uncomprehending little laugh. 'Come on, Dorothy, you've lost me somewhere here.'

'Well, Bellini is just a stage name, a soubriquet if you like.' And a pretension by the look of things, she decided to herself, but added, 'It's their mother's maiden name.'

'Well, well, well,' Giles said slowly, as the reality began to assemble itself in his mind. 'So you're quite sure.'

'Absolutely.'

He slid his arm round her and squeezed her in a joyful embrace. 'Dorothy, that's perfectly wonderful! It's so exactly the break I've been hoping for that I can hardly believe it. And just as I'm reaching the final pages of my play. Somehow I knew you'd bring me luck.'

From that moment the performance on the open stage – so acclaimed by the rest of the audience – was as lost on Giles as it was on Dorothy herself. She sensed that his expectant mood had now found its focus. Not even the actors, who with the chair, potted palm and a solitary saxophonist, held the entire theatre in thrall for nearly three hours, could quite claim any of his attention.

As soon as it was over he was fighting his way through the crowds, urging Dorothy and Imogen to follow closely. His timing was a credit to his preoccupation. They reached the foyer at precisely the same moment as Marco Bellini.

'Good evening.' Giles stepped into his path smiling engagingly.

Bellini responded with a frown. 'Good evening.'

'Remember, we met at the T.W.A. Conference. Giles Chevening.'

'I'm afraid I don't recall.'

'I'm a playwright. You showed interest in my work.' A lie of course, but these were desperate times. Bellini, clearly irritated, made to move on, and Giles added swiftly, 'My niece Dorothy from the north is staying with me and tells me she's a friend of your brother Luke.'

Bellini paused and looked Dorothy up and down. 'Luke? Well, well.'

Dorothy smiled prettily. 'We're close neighbours in Northumberland.'

'Then I trust the family's well.'

Your family, Mr Bellini, she thought to herself. Surely you know. Then said, 'Yes, very well thank you.'

'And the new house?' He cast an apologetic glance towards his companion who hovered impatiently alongside - a dark imposing figure, in fact looking more foreign than Bellini himself. 'I've heard it's some edifice?'

'It's certainly big.'

'You must send my regards.'

During this chilly exchange Dorothy was uncomfortably aware of the other man's eyes upon here. It was the scrutiny of a serial womaniser, denuding and unnerving her. The man's look was brooding, his eyes dark and unfathomable, his very good looks making him curiously threatening. 'Taxi's here Marco,' he said abruptly.

Bellini gave a curt little bow towards Dorothy and stepped forward. 'Okay - I'm with you.'

Adroitly Giles moved alongside. 'Actually I was hoping to use this opportunity to arrange a meeting to discuss my play with you.'

'Then you're welcome to submit it in the usual way.'

Giles persisted. 'I'd rather hoped to avoid starting at the bottom of the slush pile.'

Bellini shrugged impassively. 'Cream always rises to the top, doesn't it? You should know that. Now if you'll excuse me…'

'My apologies, but you gave the impression that you found my work of some interest,' Giles persevered. Another massive lie of course, and a serious error of judgement.

Bellini stopped in his tracks. His look was vitriolic as he said, 'I recall no meeting Mr Chevening. In fact I don't remember ever having seen you before in my life. And furthermore, as a so-called professional writer you should know better than to expect to discuss business out of the office. A very good night to you.'

The two men departed, discussing the exchange in disparaging terms, audible to all who still lingered in the foyer. The atmosphere was brittle with derision.

Giles's face turned ashen. He could not speak as he shepherded his little flock from the hall. Imogen, who thankfully had remained invisible throughout the dialogue, was clearly close to tears. Dorothy herself was incandescent. They hurried along the pavement in dismayed silence.

There was a small late-night café at the corner of the street near the bus stop – a shabby place, ill lit, practically empty and smelling of chips, but they were grateful to find it open. Since it raised few hopes of a decent cup of coffee, they ordered tea and sat looking at each other over a plastic table.

'Such a rude, objectionable man,' Dorothy said. 'Was there any need to be that arrogant?'

'Probably there was.' Giles said, shaking his head despondently. 'It was all entirely my own fault. I should have known better.'

'But you had to take your chance.'

'I know. But if I'd had the sense to sleep on your info first, I would have done things differently. I suppose I got what I deserved.'

'Nonsense Giles. There is never an excuse for discourtesy. Just wait until I tell Luke.'

He grinned at her. 'Well, that's progress anyway. At least you're planning to get back on speaking terms with him again!'

She shook a derisive head. 'Oh Giles, what a mess we are, the pair of us.'

She could tell how disappointed he was and could sense his deep regret at having laid waste what should have been the perfect opportunity. It had quite demolished all that was good about the evening - from seeing of all those extraordinary people who clambered to be part of such an incomprehensible piece of theatre – to putting names to faces and faces to names.

'Who,' she asked, 'was the man Bellini was with? Did you know him?'

'Oh yes – mostly by repute. He has a well-known gallery in Chelsea – and is something of an expert in early English painting. He's also one of the top interior designers in Town. It's quite an emporium he has. I came across him briefly while I helped research a programme about The National Gallery for an ITV company – the same one that employs Bellini as it happens. So you see the crossing of paths wasn't entirely fictitious!'

'But almost?'

'Well yes, almost.'

The tea arrived on a tin tray. Imogen poured from a thick brown pot into thick white cups. The tea was strong and homely, bringing them thankfully down to earth from the rarefied planet of thespians.

'Isn't that how you met Anya Paris?' Imogen said, passing the cups round.

'Yes. She was advising on restoration. I was doing the journalistic bit – the research that the so-call experts didn't want to do. You know, the bread and butter stuff. Jean-Paul Castaletz was the kingpin – or acted that way.'

Dorothy, who had been stirring her tea in a desultory way, looked up sharply. 'I know that name too. Why have I heard of Castaletz?'

'You could have - easily. He's big in the art world.'

'Wouldn't mean a thing to me – unless of course Henry has mentioned him – or … wait a minute … Anya perhaps.'

Giles laughed. 'I'm not entirely sure that Anya likes talking about Castaletz.'

'Oh? Why's that?'

'She's an ex I believe.'

'An ex. An ex what?'

'Not sure of that either. Although someone told me that they thought they'd been married at some time.'

'*Married?*' Dorothy's eyebrows shot up into her hair. 'Married? Anya and Castaletz? Are you being serious – or is this some kind of a joke? You didn't tell us that Anya was married.'

'I don't know for sure. It was little more than a rumour and I remember thinking at the time that they were on pretty good terms for a couple who apparently couldn't live together.'

Dorothy shook her head in utter bemusement. The drama of reality was beginning to outstrip the world of make-believe that she had just been at such odds to understand. It all fitted into a pattern, but the pattern made no sense. Her eyes questioned him as she said, 'Is this possible? I simply can't believe it.'

'Why not? How much do we know about her past?'

'Well, nothing I suppose.'

'So?'

'But it's bizarre, Giles. You must see that.' She sipped her tea while the wheels continued to go round in her head. 'It's the coincidence of it all – Bellini being Luke's brother and Anya being his friend's 'ex' as you put it – now living at Foxsteads, supposedly knowing none of this. It's all a bit uncanny, isn't it?'

'Coincidence usually is – it's more or less the meaning of the word. But not that unreasonable if you think about it. It's a pretty small world when it comes to the narrow confines of art.'

'So that's where you met Anya.'

'Then later at a party.'

'The one we gate-crashed,' Imogen said.

'Did she suggest coming to Foxsteads? Or was it the other way about?'

'I don't know. It just sort of – seemed to fit.'

'And that's coincidence too?'

'Dorothy, what are you getting at? So it was a coincidence. So what?'

'Giles, I think it's rather more than that. Because you see I've just remembered where I've heard the name Castaletz.' She watched in silence as the only other customer rose to leave the café. The waitress emerged from the kitchen, fastened the door behind him, turning the open sign to closed. Then having eyed the rest of them wearily, disappeared again. Dorothy said unevenly, 'I'm beginning to wonder just how closely involved they all are. Because you see Castaletz was the name on the delivery crates containing Arthur Robson's pictures. He's the famous guru - the J.P. of interior design and cigarettes from France. Furthermore I think there's more to all this than we know - and a whole lot more than meets the eye.'

* * *

Dorothy slept little that night. Images of the theatre, the so-called elite in all its manifestations, Bellini, Castaletz and a crestfallen Giles, robbed her of all but minutes here and there. She awoke incredibly tired - weary of excitement, of London even, and of being torn apart by events that were not just beyond control, but beyond comprehension.

She rose early and dressed carefully, choosing her prettiest dress and smartest shoes. If she planned to confront Jean-Paul Castaletz – and she did – she needed to look her best. Thankfully Imogen had already left for work and Giles was still asleep, so scooping up her street map of London she set off for the tube bound for Sloane Square.

It was a beautiful morning. Above the rooftops of London arched a pale luminous sky. Sunshine spilled through the plane trees and glittered on the cars streaming along the Kings Road. Yet paradoxically Dorothy felt suddenly stifled and homesick. A longing to be in the wide-open spaces of Northumberland assailed her - to be breathing clean country air and listening to gentle country sounds, instead of engulfed in the relentless grind of the city. In all this mayhem it was almost impossible to put any thoughts in order.

A side street café had already spilled onto the pavement, tables and chairs parked under parasols. Dorothy sat down and ordered coffee. She would study the map and gather herself before seeking her destination. She was almost alone. A solitary businessman sat nearby, his newspaper folded on the table before him, which he quietly perused.

As she waited she watched the world of Chelsea passing by. London people were so self-confident; all apparently knowing where they were bound and what they were after. There was that inexplicable something that set them apart; an aloofness that made Dorothy feel very provincial and vulnerable and strangely conspicuous. She began to study the map. Suddenly London seemed such an unfriendly place.

She was still thinking her uncharitable thoughts when the businessman rose, folded his paper into his briefcase and came over to her side. 'Forgive me for interrupting,' he said. 'But I can see you are searching for somewhere, and if I can be of any assistance.'

She looked up astonished. 'That's very kind, but I'm sure I can manage thank you.'

'What are you looking for? I know the area well.'

She looked at him again. It was not an unfriendly face after all, nor threatening. The man clearly just wanted to help. For some reason

Dorothy felt relieved. 'Elmbury Street,' she told him. 'I'm trying to find the Castaletz Gallery.'

He looked interested. 'I know it well. It's a good step away from here though.'

'I don't mind. I'm used to walking and it's a lovely day.'

He traced the route on the map with his finger. 'Keep going straight down here as far as you can until the road forks. Elmbury Street is the second – no third – on the left and Elmbury Mews is on the right about half way down.'

'That looks straightforward enough.'

'Yes, it isn't complicated at all. The Castaletz Gallery is in that courtyard just off the road. You can't miss it.'

She thanked him warmly and set off. He was right. It was not difficult to find, and it was a very long way. But she did not mind. He had restored her faith in the basic kindness of people, and felt better already.

He was right also about the gallery being impossible to miss. It stretched half the length of the mews in an expanse of plate glass, polished brass and dark green blinds. Visible within was the glitter of crystal chandeliers and the gleam of gilt-wood furniture. A wide entrance, flanked by ornamental trees in white tubs, divided the building into two distinct halves.

Dorothy paused across the road and gazed fascinated. The closer half of the property bore the name Castaletz Interiors. In its window was a Persian carpet on which stood a Louis Quinze chair. A selection of silk brocades had been draped over it in a jewel coloured cascade. The further side was clearly the gallery, for a mahogany easel bearing an enormous gilt framed painting occupied the centre of the window in solitary splendour. Nothing else. It all tacitly proclaimed that genuine intention, backed by serious money, was an essential requirement for venturing across its intimidating threshold.

Already Dorothy's courage was beginning to fail. She was not even sure why she had decided to come and what she hoped to achieve. It seemed that her suspicions were based on very little but a sequence of coincidences and flashes of intuition. The rest had all the substance of fresh air. And at this moment she regretted it all.

Then as she watched a taxi drew up across the road. The passenger, a man, probably in his forties, dressed in brown corduroy trousers and a tweed jacket, began to unload a number of hefty parcels from inside. He carried them in three trips into the showroom, clearly with some difficulty, for she noticed that he limped badly. No-one came to help. He climbed back in to the taxi which immediately drove off. The small insignificant episode at least brought a breath of normality into the rarefied atmosphere of the street, giving Dorothy a moment's respite in which to gather together her courage to cross over. She had not come all this way to turn back now.

Once again quiet returned to the mews. Traffic sounds were muffled, mingling with just the faintest strains of classical music from an unseen source. The absence of activity was strangely unnerving. Moments later Dorothy discerned rather than heard the opening of a door. Aware that she was no longer alone, she spun round and to her dismay found herself face to face with Castaletz. Pausing in the doorway of the shop, he stood eying her curiously. 'So it is you. I thought so. Miss Chevening.'

Dorothy drew another deep breath and tried to regain her composure. He must have been watching her, and wondering why she was loitering across the road. She felt disadvantaged and foolish. 'Clever of you to recognise me Mr Castaletz,' she said unevenly.

'After so short a time? Not really.'

'But to remember my name.'

He smiled complacently. 'I am a businessman.'

She considered this, then said, 'And of course I almost forgot, my name isn't so unfamiliar to you I imagine.' His eyes questioned her. She braced herself for a moment before adding, 'I meant that of my family – because of course you know Anya Paris, don't you?'

An almost imperceptible emotion flickered in the dark, otherwise unfathomable, eyes. Dorothy had not intended to come quite so quickly or abruptly to the point and felt the blood rising to her cheeks. 'You do know Anya, I understand.'

'My dear young lady,' Castaletz said, at once recovering himself. 'I'm afraid I don't know Anya Paris at all.' She was conscious of a noticeable foreign inflection in his voice.

'But I thought…'

'I know what you thought. Yes, I was once committed to the young woman, Miss Chevening, deeply committed, but I certainly never knew her. Nobody has ever really known Anya.'

Dorothy was not sure whether or not she was meant to laugh at this, and Castaletz himself betrayed nothing. 'I agree she's not easy to understand,' she ventured. 'But of course she's an artist – so I wouldn't expect to. And a very talented one too, I believe.'

'She's also the cleverest restorer we ever had at Castaletz. But then so she should be. I taught her all she knows.'

This time Dorothy detected a spark of irony in his eye. Maybe he was being obtuse on purpose. Maybe not. But one thing was certain, she could not quite reconcile herself to the concept of a liaison between this cool customer and Anya. For one thing Castaletz was considerably older. Also there was something distinctly effete in his manner, an extravagance of articulation and gesticulation that might or might not have been down to his artistic persona. Somehow it did not conjure images of a torrid love affair between two such different people. But then of course all this was new territory for Dorothy – coming as she did from a place where men were not ashamed to dirty their hands for a living – and art was appreciated in purely objective terms. Only Giles had broken that mould in her family – as indeed Bellini had in Robson's. Close friends, Giles had said they were, and until this moment she had not questioned his meaning. Besides, none of it quite added up, and possibly did not matter anyway. Beyond recognition that what once had been seen by Dorothy in terms of black or white, in these circles apparently could be varying shades of grey, it was probably best not to wonder.

'So what can I do for you, Miss Chevening?' he now asked. 'Have you come to see me – or the gallery – or were you just passing by?'

'A bit of each, I suppose,' she replied, suddenly feeling very naïve and rather self-conscious. 'But of course I would love to look round.'

Airily he waved his arm towards the door with a sweeping gesture. 'Then be my guest.'

Inside the atmosphere was rarefied. The last remnants of sounds from the city were silenced as the doors swung behind them, enclosing them in a breathless – for Dorothy, stifling – world in which she at once felt uncomfortably out of her depth. She was thankful when he left her to wander on her own, seating himself a huge mahogany desk, littered with tasteful paraphernalia which she felt was probably never used. He took a cigarette from a silver box and lit it. The familiar French aroma from it filled the air, evoking a painful pang of recognition.

She wandered into the labyrinth of the gallery. The paintings on show were mostly modern, many by one artist, a D. Goring, whose work she found curiously uncomfortable and wholly incomprehensible. They were wreathed in symbolism, surreal, evoking erotic overtones. Some she found perversely fascinating, with naked bodies entwined into weird designs. Some she could scarcely bear to study at all.

She was relieved at last to come across a section devoted to the seventeenth and eighteenth century art for which she understood Castaletz to be renowned; bucolic scenes of old England which drew her back to a reality she recognised. These were reminiscent of some of the paintings at Foxsteads, she thought. She wondered what Henry Crisp would make of Castaletz's prices when it came to estimating the value of the Chevening collection.

She paused now and then as some image arrested her. She did not wish to be thought hurried or uninterested. Then for a long time she stood before a small dark painting that struck chords of nostalgia. It was a scene so reminiscent of home that it might almost have been Foxsteads itself - a windswept northern sky silhouetting rugged hills, the crenulated edifice of an old castle half hidden by trees. 'I feel I know this place,' she said quietly to herself, and again the longing to be home, safe in familiar pastures, assailed her.

She turned to the door. Someone else had entered the gallery, a tall suited gentleman, who was engaging the attention of Castaletz at the desk. Gratefully she saw her chance to escape. The man was taking files from a briefcase. Castaletz was deep in concentration. He lit another of his French cigarettes. Dorothy paused by the desk until he looked up. 'Thank you for letting me see your wonderful collection, Mr Castaletz,' she said. 'It was immensely interesting.'

'My pleasure.' He stood, his courtesy now something of a formality, his mind clearly preoccupied.

The man stood also. As he turned Dorothy drew in a deep breath of astonishment. She knew at once that she had seen him before. With a stab of recognition she met his eyes and saw the recognition reflected there. Then she stood rooted to the spot. She did not know why she knew him, only that she did, and that he knew her too. Plainly he did not intend to acknowledge it. Probably he too wondered where and when.

Dorothy took two small steps backwards, then hesitantly took her leave, suddenly wanting badly to be on her way.

Outside the air hit her. She exhaled in a long, long sigh of relief. All at once the pavements of London seemed less unfriendly, the long walk to the station profoundly welcome. Her thoughts, coloured by artistic images and unfamiliar faces, were jumbled and confused. That it all had nothing to do with her somehow did not seem possible. Instinctively she knew it had everything to do with her. An uneasy weight pressed down on her.

Halfway along the Kings Road she went into a florist shop and bought a bunch of yellow roses. A goodbye gesture for Imogen and Giles. All at once she knew that she had been away from home long enough, and an intuitive feeling that she was needed there was fast lodging itself in her brain.

Then the reason for the shock of recognition revealed itself. Even the long arm of coincidence could not stretch to this extent. For she realised that the man in the gallery had been none other than Mr Smith.

CHAPTER FIFTEEN

Matt awoke as the sun was creeping over the treetops, casting the first strands of light through the narrow bedroom window of the lodge. It was half past five. And he had overslept. He eased himself from the pillow, and resting on an elbow, looked down at her. She was sleeping peacefully beside him, her naked body elegantly curved, her face tranquil, and her abundant red hair a fiery corona on the pillow. He felt a constriction in his throat. How extraordinary it was that so small and slender a being could exert such power to move him. But he was utterly captivated and he knew it.

Matt slid from the bed. She stirred but did not wake. He went through to the living room. Here the debris of the night before confronted him. It had been quite an evening. Anya had at last decided to unveil the portrait. And there it was, in all its glory, displayed on the makeshift easel of a chair. Alongside, strewn over the table, was evidence of their celebration – the empty bottle, glasses and remnants of a hastily assembled snack. It had been a jubilant occasion.

Matt paused before the painting, now in the sober light of dawn looking paradoxically more impressive than ever. Although it was not large it was remarkable. Anya had captured his father to the very essence. She had depicted him standing at Mazurka's head against a backdrop of the Stud. It was not what he had expected. He had thought to see a horseman, mounted, formal, set in the Northumbrian landscape she had studied so closely. But he would not have changed it by as much as a brushstroke. This picture was strangely intimate. The kindly side of his father's character, his empathy with his beloved horses, was what it portrayed. In the background she had achieved a minor masterpiece in subtle light and shade that made it Northumbrian to the detail. Perfect. He wondered how the family would react when they were shown the painting later that day.

'Do you still like it?'

He turned. She was beside him, still tousled from sleep, a thin wrap carelessly clasped around her shoulders. 'Yes, I still like it very much.' He paused and stood looking at her pensively for a moment, then said, 'And do you still intend to leave?'

'You know I must.'

'Must? Or want to?'

'Matt, please don't go down that path again.'

'I have to. I love you. You know that. The whole family loves you. You fit in here.'

'I know all that.'

'And you love me. Look me straight in the eye and tell me that you don't.'

'I can't.'

'Then why?'

Her glance slid to the floor. Her face was lost to him under a cascade of red hair. He could only feel her desolation. And how his heart echoed it. With a sigh he dropped a kiss onto her head, then disappeared to get ready to leave.

Back at Foxsteads he found his parents still at the dining table. He had rather hoped to breakfast alone, not wishing to risk his integrity or exchange platitudes, but it was not to be. Avoiding eye contact, he helped himself from the sideboard and took his place at the table.

William gave him a penetrating look. 'Dorothy 'phoned last night.'

Matt reached for the butter. 'Oh good. Having a nice time, is she?'

'She's coming home today.'

'Surely not. I thought she was staying until Thursday next.'

'We all did. But apparently she has something important on her mind and needs to be back.'

Slowly Matt spread the butter onto his toast. 'What sort of thing?'

'I've no idea. She sounded anxious, I thought, a little urgent. Anyway I said you'd meet the train in Newcastle.'

'Newcastle? Good Lord. What time?'

'She offered to get a connection to Hexham, but it seemed a bit rotten to let her do that – so I said you, or someone, would go. Is there much pressing today then?'

Matt shook his head, at the same time thinking of his plans for the great unveiling. Then he realised that this meant Dorothy would be there too, which would be splendid. At least, he hoped so. Dorothy, even in her absence, concerned him. He wondered what was so urgent that it had shortened her holiday in London. Then he shrugged. Probably it was no more than Luke Robson's magnetism exerting its force once more.

Meeting Dorothy at Newcastle Central was thoroughly nostalgic. It transported him back to countless times when he had stood amongst a gaggle of straining mothers, all waiting to catch first glimpses of returning schoolgirls. To Matt, Dorothy had always looked smaller, more vulnerable, than the others. He pictured her striding resolutely towards him, that ridiculous brown felt hat squashed down on her fair hair, her arms so laden with bags of books and the inevitable hockey stick, that she had had to drop them all in order to fling herself into his arms. He felt a lump in his throat at the thought.

Then he spotted her in the distance as the crowd from the London train surged down the platform. How different she looked now; so grown up and sophisticated, and very smart. The neat blue suit she was wearing was new. She must have been shopping in Town. Then she caught sight of him. And it was almost as though the years had rolled away. She fought her way through the throng, smiling with delight at seeing him, impatient to hug and be hugged.

'I'm so pleased it was you who came,' she told him when they were safely under way and driving west from the city. 'I had a sinking feeling you would send Hodges or something.'

'Would that have been so terrible then?'

'Absolutely the last straw! Can we stop in Corbridge and have tea at the Spinning Wheel?'

'What on earth for?'

'Old time's sake?'

'I thought you'd want to get home as quickly as possible.'

'Of course I do. But I want to talk to you first.'

'Can't we talk in the car?'

'Please, Daddy, it's important.'

Something in her tone provoked pangs of disquiet. Without further argument he drove to the little tea-room in Corbridge, which was another little part of that coming-home tradition. On the way she chattered about Giles and Imogen and how fantastic London was but how she had missed home.

The Spinning Wheel was a wonderfully archaic little place close to the village square, where two elderly ladies baked scones and cakes and served tea on lace tablecloths. Coffee houses had yet to reach rural Northumberland.

Tea came. She poured it while he waited for her to begin to talk. He tried to guess what was on her mind and sensed that she was far from happy. Even so he was shocked when at length she set down the tea pot, looked at him with startling directness and said, 'Daddy, I honestly think you ought to question whether Anya should be allowed to stay at Foxsteads any longer.'

This was certainly unexpected. He returned her look in astonishment. 'Good heavens, Dorothy, whatever has provoked that idea?'

'Just that I've suspected for a long time that she isn't what you all seem to think she is. Now I'm pretty sure.'

'I can't imagine what you mean. I realise you don't like her very much. I've never understood quite why, when everyone else feels differently. But in any case she will not be with us much longer – and I can assure you that most of us will be very sad to see her go.'

'You may be sadder than you think.'

Matt eyed her curiously. 'Come on Dorothy, just what are you getting at?'

She rested her elbows on the table, lifted her cup with both hands and eyed him over the rim, reminding him sharply of the schoolgirl he had once brought here for tea. At that time he would have scolded her for her lack of manners. Now he merely regarded her in silent contemplation.

'What do you know of Mr Smith?' she asked him.

'Little enough.'

'He's a policeman or a detective or something, isn't he?'

'Something of the kind.'

'Or fraud squad?'

'Maybe.'

'Then why was he sloping around here?'

'He was 'sloping around' Robson's place as I read it.'

'And Robson's buying paintings as fast as he can stick them on his walls.'

'Yes, I'm with you so far.'

Dorothy sipped her tea. 'There's a lot of missing art in circulation at the moment, Daddy. The discoveries at Longhirst have opened up a can of worms.'

'And you're thinking that because Anya worked at Longhirst that two and two make five. What nonsense.'

Dorothy set down her cup and shot her father a penetrating look. 'Daddy, I haven't started yet. That's only the beginning of it.'

Suitably chastened, he passed the plate of cakes to her. She took a piece of sponge cake oozing with cream, almost without looking, and continued. 'Robson employs a firm called Castaletz to do his décor and supply him with paintings. It's a pretty flashy set up. I went there and had a look. Jean-Paul Castaletz is a very close friend of Robson's son.'

Luke do you mean?'

'No, no. His elder brother, the television director who goes by the name of Marco Bellini.'

'Hold on Dorothy, you're losing me already. I can't take all this in.'

Dorothy looked apologetic. 'I know, I'm sorry, it does sound complicated, but it isn't. Robson has an elder son in television. He uses Stella Robson's maiden name, which is Italian, so I suppose she is. Bellini. Giles knows him a bit – or tries to know him actually – but that's another story. Anyway, I met him and this man Castaletz was with him. Now are you with me?'

'Yes, I'm just about with you so far. But I still don't see any problem in that. It all sounds perfectly logical.'

'Because there's rather more than this to come. For one thing I understand Giles met Anya in the company of Bellini and Castaletz.'

Matt eyed her thoughtfully. 'I see…' He reached for the teapot in which Dorothy seemed to have lost all interest, and poured second cups for them both. The elderly owner of the tea-shop hovered for a moment, asked whether they needed more of anything, which he politely declined, then retreated once again. He shook his head. 'Even so, I still can't think that it has much to do with us. Our collection isn't even valuable.'

'We don't know that.'

'Dorothy. We do know that. You are trying to read something into nothing. And I really can't fathom your reason for trying to make this big deal of it.'

'Because I've still not reached the point. Besides you must agree that coincidence is following coincidence.'

'Yes, I agree it all seems rather circumstantial.'

'It's more than circumstantial, Daddy, it's extraordinary,' Dorothy said, drawing a spiral in the sugar with her teaspoon, then smoothing it out again. She put down the spoon resolutely. 'You see, Smith came into the Castaletz gallery while I was there. I recognised him at once, although it was hard to place him at first. He was so out of context. He looked pretty business-like too – you know, suit, briefcase, that government official look. I was fairly sure that it was serious talk between them. You have to agree it was an amazing coincidence. But then I thought to myself, 'Was it?' Daddy, I know there's something going on. I just know it all ties up.'

'But what has it to do with Anya?'

Dorothy looked at her father for a long time. She felt a sudden sadness tearing at her heart; an unexpected reluctance to continue. She had known almost from the beginning that he had fallen for Anya more deeply than any of the others had realised. She had watched it happening, unable to prevent it – yet wanting to prevent it so much. Even now she was not sure why she hated to see her father falling under Anya's spell; only that she did. And now, acutely aware that her final revelation would cast a shadow over all his hopes, she supposed she should have welcomed it. But she didn't. Suddenly her special love for him meant very much more than her irrational dislike of Anya Paris. She paused, hesitant and unaccountably just a little ashamed, aware that the last link in this chain of coincidence would hurt him very much. She looked at him sadly.

'It has everything to do with Anya,' she said quietly, 'because you see, she used to work for the firm as a restorer. It is where she learnt her craft. And it does look as though it is this firm that is under investigation by Smith.'

'I'm beginning to understand.'

'But, darling, I'm afraid that's not all. You see she was – and very possibly still is – married to Jean-Paul Castaletz.'

* * *

Matt felt as though he had received a body blow. It was almost impossible to take in what he was being told - even harder to believe it. But

263

Dorothy's sudden revelation, based on such a string of coincidences, was not easily dismissed. The flimsy substance of his hopes and feelings for Anya seemed to fall into disarray as he tried to unravel the facts. Clearly Dorothy had jumped to conclusions. It was hardly surprising in the light of what she had discovered and how she had felt about Anya in the first place. Grimly he tried to dismiss it. The implication was just too incomprehensible.

In silence he finished his tea, paid the bill, and escorted Dorothy back to the car. The rest of the journey was superficially bright. Remorsefully Dorothy attempted to whitewash over her revelations with cheerful anecdotes of Giles and Imogen and life as a London tourist. Matt responded manfully, telling her how work on the pele tower and plans for the auction progressed. Both were outwardly as before, but inwardly churning over inexpressible thoughts. As the car crunched to a standstill on the gravel before the house, a thin wall of restraint seemed to rise between them. Dorothy felt none of the expected uplifting of spirits, nor joy at the longed-for sight of home - only a wretched stab of impending gloom.

Outwardly the house greeted her with a familiar face. It was bathed in late afternoon sunshine, bright reflections turning its many paned windows to polished copper. The doves on the roof cooed softly, sunning themselves, their gentle voices mingling with the hum of bees in the lavender that skirted the driveway. It was all so familiar and painfully beautiful. Dorothy stepped from the car onto the gravel just as the dogs hurled themselves from the front door and down the steps towards her, almost flattening her in their joyous haste. She knelt down and allowed herself to be licked from ear to ear, while she hugged them. 'Darling, darling dogs! Have you missed me?' Their ecstatic welcome assured her that they had.

In stark contrast, inside it was cool and dark as they entered. Slowly her senses adjusted, as first she breathed in the age-old smell of wax polish and wood smoke, then focussed on the sight of the timbered hall with its towering stair well. The image of her father following behind with her luggage once more evoked that schoolgirl feeling, and with it an inexplicable pang of guilt – which briskly she dismissed as she looked about her.

'Daddy, where are the pictures?'

He set down the cases and eyed her wearily. 'Pictures?'

'Yes, the sporting paintings of the fishermen and the shooters.'

'They're being cleaned.'

'Surely we're not thinking of selling those.'

'No, of course not. It's because they're darkened and smoke damaged. They are quite valuable we're told.'

'By whom? Anya?'

'Yes, Anya – and Henry. Surely, Dorothy, you don't have a problem with that.'

She remained staring at the blank spaces on the panelling where the two paintings had hung, frowning and suspicious. 'Did Anya suggest cleaning them?'

Abruptly he took up the cases again and marched towards the stairs with them. 'Probably,' he snapped, now thoroughly angry and upset. In silence he mounted the stairs. In silence she followed.

The triumphant unveiling of the portrait quite simply did not happen. Matt could scarcely quell his sense of disappointment. On Anya's behalf he was so proud of her achievement, knowing that it would delight the family and vindicate all their plans. But somehow it no longer seemed appropriate. Briefly he called at the lodge to explain that Dorothy's return meant postponing the event. She merely shrugged. He could not tell whether or not she minded. Of course she said she did not. 'I shall have an early night which I seriously need,' she told him. He read into this that he would not be welcome to return.

Instead he saw through dinner as best he could, then slipped away to telephone Henry Crisp. 'I could do with a word or two of advice,' he told him. 'Any chance of seeing you tomorrow?'

'Come over now if you like,' Henry said without hesitation. 'Amanda's at a church meeting. I'm here with nothing in particular to do.' Matt had the impression that perhaps his request was not unexpected.

He was glad of the invitation. Hillhead was a tranquil place and Henry's erudite company just what was needed. He sank into the comfort of the Crisps' drawing room with the relieved sigh of one who has made a great leap and happened upon a soft landing. A large glass of scotch was put into his hand.

He came straight to the point. 'I'm in a bit of a quandary, Henry. Dorothy has a bee in her bonnet about Anya. She seems to think that she's not all we think she is.'

Henry registered mild surprise, sat staring into his glass for a bit, then he said, 'I'm afraid there are a number of things that don't quite add up at the moment.'

'In connection with Anya, do you mean?'

'Not exactly. But I understand that questions are being asked – requiring a great many answers.'

'What sort of things?' Matt asked, scarcely wishing to know. 'What questions?'

'Mostly matters connected with the art world at large. You know, the kind of things that come up from time to time – questions of authenticity – of integrity, or lack of it – matters that more often than not turn out to be small, but occasionally are the tip of a bigger iceberg.'

'I see. And are the questions being asked just now of iceberg proportions?'

Henry shrugged. 'Could be.'

They were both silent for a bit. Matt wondered how he could expect the minor concerns of his own insignificant art collection to rate at all in the fine art world which apparently concerned Henry in his business affairs. He supposed that in provincial North East England the firm of Wise and Crisp steered a careful course between what was important to small collectors like himself, and what was important in the grand halls of artistic magnitude. There was a certain skill, he imagined, in treading such a path. And just sometimes perhaps the two collided. Then the tip of an iceberg might be detected. He took a large slug of scotch and a deep breath before asking, 'Does it by any chance have anything to do with that man Smith?'

Henry raised an eyebrow and nodded. 'Yes, as a matter of fact it does. As you probably remember, he first came to see me about a month ago.'

Matt frowned, and pensively tracing the engraving on his glass, ventured, 'Who is he, Henry? What is he doing here?'

'He's a detective – fraud.'

'Yes, yes, I realise that. But why is he here? Has it something to do with Anya?'

'It's never actually been said,' Henry assured him. 'It's the Robson collection that's being investigated – and the source of some of his recent acquisitions.'

'I see. And don't you find that just a little strange?'

Henry shrugged. 'Not really. Hardly surprising at all in my view. The man's buying paintings and antiques as fast as he can fill his house and I rather imagine he knows next to nothing on the subject. A sitting duck, you might say. There's a lot of dubious so-called fine art in circulation at the moment. And the Longhirst affair has thrown something of a spanner into the works.'

Matt became pensive. Perhaps Dorothy was right. Henry might well not yet recognise it, but the Longhirst affair possibly had all too much to do with Anya. It was already known that she had been involved in its restoration, and now it was also clear that through her connection with Castaletz she was linked to Robson in the most curious circumstance. Certainly it posed a great many questions. His heart sank as the evidence against her multiplied. He shook his head in dismay. Thus far Henry might largely be missing the point, but for how long? Matt longed to unburden himself. Henry was, after all, one of the family's oldest and closest friends. And besides why else had he come?

But Henry continued. 'It all harks back to when the Longhirst collection was restored last year,' he said. 'Copies – fakes - could have been produced and switches made at the time when the paintings were in the hands of the restorers.'

'Not in the hands of a reputable firm, surely.'

'True, it seems unlikely. But a clever restorer is an intelligent person and determined forger is a force to be reckoned with. You wouldn't believe the skill and wasted talent that lies behind the most notorious frauds.'

'But what has it to do with Robson, bearing in mind that the Longhirst collection never actually reached the market?'

'Longhirst is only one of many such collections. That could be the very tip of the iceberg.'

'Then it is some iceberg, isn't it?'

Henry rose to refill their glasses. He did not speak as he attended to the task, but Matt detected a mind working overtime. Henry, he decided, was a misleading fellow, giving the impression of a dusty academic in an ivory tower, when actually he had both feet firmly on the ground and was pretty astute.

Evidence of this was all about him. The Crisps' home was something of a treasure house - always immaculate, everything in impeccable taste. Amanda had a liking for old Meissen, Chinese jade and flower paintings. In dramatic contrast an immense painting of Tristram and Isolde dominated most of the far wall. Henry saw Matt's eyes upon it and smiled. 'Sublime, isn't it?'

'Yes, yes, it is.' It was indeed extraordinary, Matt thought, trying to match this lusty work to its sober owner. 'It has a certain magnetism, doesn't it?'

'I bought it almost thirty years ago,' Henry told him, 'from a dealer in Paris. It caught my eye as no other painting has before or since, and I have loved it ever after. It is by a French painter called Auguste Lescure – not well known, but so remarkable. The strange thing is that I understand Robson also has a Lescure. They are not so very rare, but it is quite a coincidence, isn't it? I would be most interested to see it.'

'Where did Robson acquire his?'

'A London firm has supplied most of the furniture, furnishings and paintings for Fallowfell Hall.'

'Yes, that must be Castaletz.'

Henry registered surprise. 'Yes, Castaletz. So you know of them.'

'I have just heard of them today – from Dorothy. She visited the gallery while she was in London.'

'On Luke Robson's instigation?'

'I don't think so. Dorothy seems to have been doing a bit of investigating of her own. Furthermore, she saw Smith there.'

Henry raised his eyebrows. 'Well, well. I had certainly expected Smith to be asking Castaletz some questions – although that in itself is extraordinary. The firm is so prestigious and well-established. But there it is.'

'And that's not all. The coincidence doesn't end there, Henry, I'm afraid. Jean-Paul Castaletz is an intimate of Robson's elder son.'

'That would add up I suppose.'

'And so I'm afraid does this.' His heart sank as he spoke. The words seemed to stick in his throat. 'You see, according to Dorothy, he has been – and quite possibly still is – married to Anya.'

The silence that now stretched between them became palpable. Henry's gaze was so incredulous that Matt could not bear to meet it. Suddenly he was aware of every minute sound about him; the tapping on the pane of a solitary leaf - the anguish of a fly caught in a web; the ticking of the ormolu clock on the mantelpiece. Then the clock struck the hour in a melodious carillon. Echoes of half a dozen clocks about the house immediately followed. It was typical of the Crisps that all the clocks in this house were synchronised. At Foxsteads it was in the lap of the gods whether they actually rang out the same hour. Matt looked up, his smile rueful at the irrelevance of his thoughts.

Henry's eyes were upon him. His gaze was sad when at last he said, 'My dear fellow. No wonder you look so torn apart.'

Matt volunteered a philosophical smile, 'Do I?'

'You are fond of her, aren't you?'

'Do I really wear my heart so plainly on my sleeve?'

Henry shook his head. 'Probably not – but I'm an observant old bird – and I've known you for a very long time.'

The silence returned. Matt twisted the glass in his hand. Bright patterns of light shifted through the engraving. He downed what was left of the scotch and replaced it on the table. Then he said, 'I am well aware, Henry, that two and two make four.'

'And I think you're going to have to look quickly and thoroughly into your family's affairs.'

'Surely not. Surely our property is not worthy of that kind of fraud.'

Henry shrugged. 'Maybe. Maybe not. But of course Smith needs to be told all this.'

'Yes, I know that.' Matt drooped in his chair and shook his head in dismay. 'Dear God, what am I doing to her?'

There was no answer.

In truth it seemed that there was nothing more to be said. Henry offered another drink, but it was declined, and as Matt rose to leave, he said, 'Henry, may I ask a favour of you?'

'Of course.'

'Will you keep all this to yourself for just one more day? I want to be the first to ask the questions.'

It was granted without demur.

CHAPTER SIXTEEN

Work on the pele tower had progressed remarkably during Dorothy's absence. She went alone on a tour of inspection and was astonished to find the new roof in place and the old attics looking very much as they always had. Miraculously the new rafters had blended with the old in an almost seamless way, and with the darkness restored to the ill-lit rooms, something of the original atmosphere had also returned. Dorothy drew a deep breath of relief and laid a caressing hand on the ancient stones. In a mysterious way she seemed to draw strength from its familiarity. Somehow she had to find the determination to persevere with the controversy she had stirred. And somehow she had to find the courage to face Luke again. 'Help me,' she said aloud. The house answered her with the sound of footsteps on the stone stairs.

Moments later she and Luke were facing each other across the seeming immensity of the attic floor. Neither spoke for what felt like minutes. Then he stepped irresolutely towards her and sadly looked down into her face. 'Am I forgiven?'

'Do you need to be forgiven?'

'You seemed to think so.'

'Not any more.'

'I'm glad. You did get it all wrong, you know.'

'Yes, I do know. Luke, I'm sorry.'

In the final steps the gap between them closed. She slipped into his arms so easily that she wondered at having felt such apprehension. Far from being a difficult moment, it was very, very sweet.

For a long time they remained locked in a silent embrace. Dorothy felt as though her heart would burst - that the tacit promise in those tender moments provided the answer to everything. Afterwards they sat together on the broad shelf of an oak purlin and talked for a long time in the darkness.

She found herself voicing her anxieties – diffidently at first, then in an outpouring. Everything that had been bottled up inside now exploded in a torrent of words. It was extraordinary. If only she had had courage enough to speak her mind before, instead of jumping to all those wrong conclusions.

One by one facts were shuffled between them as she told him of her discoveries in London, and he tried to explain his family's involvement.

'As you know, Castaletz is a friend of my brother – and my father has done a lot of business with him over the years – but I have no reason to think that he'd ever met Anya before.'

Dorothy remembered something that Philip had once said about Robson and Anya, but could not quite remember what it was, so she said nothing.

'The firm is very reputable,' Luke told her. 'Or so we'd always believed.'

'And now?'

'Who knows? That man Smith has been probing and making my father's life a misery for some time. I think you know that.'

'What does he want from your father?'

'Details of everything Castaletz has supplied – delving into its origins, demanding provenance which I'm afraid has not always been easy to provide. I'd always thought my father was pretty astute, but is does seem as though he might have been taken for a bit of a ride.'

Dorothy wondered uncharitably whether Robson had perhaps chosen to be naïve in this instance, but she said, 'Do you mean that your pictures are not genuine – that Castaletz is passing on fakes?'

Luke shrugged. 'Dad uses the word 'reproduction', which according to him makes all the difference. I'm afraid I wouldn't know.'

'And Anya. Does she have the answers do you think?'

'Possibly. Her and her foreign friends – the ones who leave French cigarettes all over the place – and...'

'Oh Luke – stop – I'm so ashamed.'

He pressed his finger to her lips to silence her. Then he drew her towards him and kissed her very gently. 'Let's not think about Anya any more. Let's just think about us.' His kisses became more urgent. She had almost forgotten how wonderful that felt and just how much she had missed him – and how badly she needed and wanted him now. In the darkness of the old pele tower they clung together in a moment of rediscovery, marvelling at how easy it was, and how right it felt and how this sensation was all the sweeter in its renaissance.

At last she drew away from him and rose to her feet. Then tugging him by the hand, she said,

'Luke, let's get out of here. Let's go somewhere in the car.'

'Somewhere?'

'Anywhere. Let's just drive and drive.'

He gave her a bemused smile and scrambled to his feet. 'Okay. Anywhere you like. To the ends of the earth if you want.'

'Or the top of the world. We could go up to the moors – into the heather.'

'Why there?'

'I challenge you to a race.'

'I'm in no mood to beaten by a little mountain goat.' Their eyes met in a provocative exchange.

'But you might win.'

'And the prize?' Suddenly his smile vanished and he took her hands and looked hard into her face. 'Dorothy, what are you trying to say?'

'That I'm sorry.'

'For what?'

'For getting everything so terribly wrong.'

He looked at her, hesitant, uncertain. 'Dorothy, you don't have to prove anything to me you know.'

Staring down at their hands, still entwined together, she said unevenly, 'I know that. But I've got everything to prove to myself.'

The weight of silence was his reply.

Within minutes they were speeding between the stone walls of a narrow lane, winding upwards towards the hills. The road passed through the close ranks of a spruce plantation, became level for a mile or two, then eventually petered out altogether and became no more than a rutted track.

They drove as far as they could, then parked in the shelter of the trees.

A beaten sheep track led through the heather, winding ever upwards. With joyous zeal they raced along it and at last flung themselves onto the warm springy turf of a sheltered hollow bordered with furze. In the lee of the hill it was suddenly calm. Only the gentlest of breezes stirred the air, carrying with it the heady scents of the moors - of ripening gorse, newly flowering heather and damp peat. Far overhead curlews were circling. Dorothy knew that never again would she hear that plaintive cry without remembering this extraordinary moment.

They slipped into each other's arms like two halves of a perfect dovetail. She closed her eyes and wondered how such a day could have materialized so miraculously from the blue. No wonder she trembled from head to toe. Fiercely she tried to convince herself that it was not the chill of cold feet, or that she was afraid of what was happening, or doubting the wisdom of it all. Perhaps she feared disappointing him and losing his respect – just as her grandmother had predicted in her few words on the subject. It was all such a muddle of emotions. And she wanted him so very badly.

Gently he unfastened her blouse and slipped it from her shoulders. He saw the apprehension on her face. 'Darling Dorothy, it doesn't have to be like this if you don't want it to be,' he said.

'I do want it to be.'

'But perhaps it shouldn't be this way for us.'

278

'For me I think it has to be. You see I'm through with saving myself for what might never be.'

'Never be?'

'Luke, I've done a lot thinking and a lot of learning – and sometimes I wonder whether I'm really the marrying kind at all.'

'You an old maid? Of course not. I for one would be disappointed if I thought so!'

'Would you?'

'You must know that.' He looked earnestly into her solemn little face. 'Or do you really think I'm such a rake?'

Her grey eyes softened in response. 'And do you really think I'm so proper and such a prude?' And with her eyes tightly closed and face up-tilted, she said, 'So please, please kiss me, Luke, before I lose my courage.'

* * *

A lifetime later Dorothy lay on her back in the long grass and looked at the sky. Surprisingly it was still the same shade of blue, and she fancied that even the self-same white puffs of cloud drifted across it in their ever changing shapes and patterns. The same curlews still described idle circles overhead and filled the fragrant air with their distinctive cries. Nothing had changed at all.

Nothing and everything.

For a long time she lay there gazing heavenward, as though searching for some sign to mark the significance of the moment. Or was this where heaven was? A little smile tugged at her lips, for the fanciful notion did not really match her irreverent inner thoughts.

Beside her Luke reclined with his eyes tightly closed, looking primitively handsome. She knew he was awake and that he watched her surreptitiously. But she did not wish to talk. She felt suddenly embarrassed and shy. Slowly she reached out for her clothes, and still conscious of his eyes upon her, she dressed herself. Then when the last button was safely fastened she sat hugging her knees to her chest and allowed herself to contemplate what had happened, and the commitment she had made. She felt strangely at peace with herself.

It was as though the future lay unravelled before her. Looking down into the valley she could see her grandfather's land spread out before her in its entirety, the house and its towering pele clearly visible between the trees, and the long curving stripe of the drive leading towards the road. Following the course of the land she could also see the stark Victorian edifice of Fallowfell Hall with its sloping lawns. Only the winding course of the burn divided one from the other. Together they presented a fertile green crescent of land set amidst the grey hills of Northumberland. Together. Dorothy closed her eyes very, very tightly. Together. That was the way she suddenly saw it – the way it could be in a shared future. Slowly she opened her eyes again and scanned the distant landscape. For an instant she found herself focussing on the small grey square that was the lodge with its Gothic gables. An immense shadow passed across the brightness of her vision, reminding her that even the most promising future could not be achieved without unravelling one more knotty problem, thus surmounting the biggest obstacle of all.

'A penny for your thoughts.'

She turned, startled, as Luke sank down beside her and slipped his arm about her shoulders. 'They're worth much, much more than that,' she told him.

'But no regrets?'

'No regrets.'

'I'm glad of that,' he said. 'You're amazing, Dorothy. No really, I mean it. You are lovely.'

She blushed in a moment of retrospect and looked away. 'No-one, Luke, could really call me that – not with the most rose-coloured of glasses!'

'That's what makes it all the more amazing – the fact that you don't even know how lovely you are.'

'What nonsense!'

'Well, that's how it is and how I feel, so now you can reveal your very costly thoughts.'

She rested her head against his chest and closed her eyes. 'I was looking into the future, trying to see it all through my own rose-tinted glasses.'

'So how did it look?'

'At this moment it's never looked better. That's the crazy thing about it, because in truth things actually have never been worse! It's all such a mess.'

'Surely not.'

She fell silent, thinking of just how uncertain everything was - her father's infatuation – his disbelief in what was staring him in the face - and Grandfather's dogged hopes for an auction which would probably turn out to be a fiasco, and insufficient anyhow to meet the debts piling up over the pele tower. Furthermore, the commitment she had made that very afternoon, and the recklessness of those sublime moments, well could be the biggest mistake and cause the greatest upset of all. But at this moment it did not seem to matter. She had never been happier in her life.

As they made their way down from the moor she felt curiously light-headed. The turf was unnaturally springy beneath her feet and the air soft with fragrance. A cloud of meadow pipits rose like stardust from the heather and swept noisily into the air. She watched until they had settled back to earth like falling leaves. Then there was stillness. Suddenly the sky had become ineffably blue, and thick yellow sunlight was spread with impasto strokes over the landscape. The anxious clouds had mysteriously evaporated. And in those few brief moments the world was a very beautiful place.

* * *

It was green and silent in the boundary woodland, the stillness broken only by the occasional rustling of bird-life or the cracking of a twig. Here the sunlight, so bright above the canopy of the trees, was curiously diffused, throwing colours and outlines into patterns of sharp contrast.

He had meant to make a small detour on his way to the lodge. He had actually been walking non-stop for over two hours. Almost without thinking he had found himself striding out across the moors towards the crag in time-honoured fashion, to the place that was ever the panacea, where the raw winds cleared the mind and the conscience. Yet today it did not deliver. He paused to find that its uncompromising façade simply reminded him of the unpalatable nature of his errand; that of facing a metaphorical stone wall which he was obliged to scale. Resolutely he turned back, ashamed of his prevarication.

Now, making his way through the woods, he was nearing his destination, reluctance dogging every step. How could he of all people begin to tell Anya that her integrity was in question? How on earth could he cast such doubt when he did not believe it himself - even though the evidence was plain to see? He reached the burn, where silence gave way to the noise and rush of its progress. There beyond the bridge, no more than three hundred yards away, was the lodge and whatever truth he might discover.

She was in her studio. Through the window he saw her descending the stairs, locking the door behind her and slipping the key into the pocket of her man-sized, paint-stained shirt. His heart lurched at the sight of her - dishevelled, her bright hair awry, her elfin face puzzled at the intrusion as she hurried to open the door. Normally he would have let himself in. But today he paused, uncertain and diffident.

'Matt, this is a surprise.'

He wondered briefly why it should be, when he had spent so much time with her in this place. But he said cautiously, 'I was passing – and I wanted a word with you – so I thought – although of course if I'm intruding at a bad moment – if you're busy.' Already he felt himself in retreat.

'Well, I am busy – but of course I can take a break.'

'May I come in then?'

'Yes – yes, of course.'

She did not offer the usual coffee, and as he sat down on the sofa she remained standing for some moments before perching herself on the end of the table. The exchange between them was like that of near strangers – they who had slept together just two nights before and shared such passion. Now he was casting about for reasons to explain his intrusion. He was grateful to have news.

'We now have a date for the auction,' he told her.

'Yes, I heard. You must be glad to have it settled.'

'Very glad.' How had she heard, he wondered? 'The whole thing's beginning to take shape. It's extraordinary what Henry recommends including – things we'd have thought of as mere bric-a-brac – books, even old toys and the like.' The words tumbled out as he struggled to appear relaxed and normal. 'It makes one wonder what valuables have been sent to church jumble sales over the years.'

'There's quite a market these days for things like that.'

'Yes, so it would seem. Anyway it's all coming together nicely. Even my father has warmed to the whole idea and is throwing ideas into the ring.'

'Well, that has to be progress, doesn't it?' she said with a watery smile.

He glanced at her encouragingly, knowing perfectly well that the platitudes were merely a veneer over unspoken thoughts - that there was restraint even in her politeness.

'You've also probably heard about the marquee that's been arranged,' he ventured, manfully soldiering on.

'Yes, yes I have.'

'Makes sense, doesn't it, since the whole thing's threatening to mushroom out of control, and of course we're planning to put on a bit of a show for my father's birthday?'

'Yes, I heard that too.'

'I wish I thought that you'd still be here for it. It will be quite something, you know, with the unveiling of the portrait and half the county here to witness it.'

'But of course I shan't.'

She rose, crossed the room, and stood gazing from the window into what he strongly suspected to be an unfocussed void. It was clear that some kind of intuition had alerted her to the nature of his errand – or that someone had beaten him to it. Dorothy perhaps, although he doubted it. She was not on visiting terms with Anya.

Almost as though in response, she said, 'Philip came to see me yesterday.'

'Philip? Good God – whatever for?'

'He does call from time to time – when he's passing.'

'He's a bit of a pain, I'm afraid.'

'Oh no, I don't mind. As a matter of fact I find him pleasant enough. And interesting.'

Matt frowned and bit back his own opinion that Philip was only fractionally less boring than his father. He supposed the foolish boy had a crush on Anya, for which he hardly blamed him of course. But still it rankled. 'I hope he doesn't make a nuisance of himself.'

'To the contrary, he's a nice kid – who feels completely misunderstood – and he likes to talk.'

Matt eyed her shrewdly. 'And do you open your heart in return?'

'You know me better than that I think'

Matt exhaled in a bitter sigh. 'Christ, Anya, sometimes I think I don't know you at all.'

For the first time she met his gaze with a long cool look. 'That simply isn't true.'

'Well certainly I don't see you in the role of agony aunt to the likes of Philip.'

She shrugged. 'He amuses me. Since everyone else seems to be viewing me in a dubious light all of a sudden, it's nice to have someone to fight my corner for me.'

So that was it. Philip, it seemed, was the one who had marked her card, having overheard snippets from his parents no doubt, from which he had drawn conclusions of his own. Feeling chastened, he shifted uncomfortably on the sofa and looked about him. Everything looked – and was – different that day. Even the room appeared changed - in some way tidier than usual. The clutter of her occupancy seemed to have been curiously sanitised. There was something transitory in the atmosphere. With a stab of alarm, he said, 'So your work here is almost at an end.'

'You know the portrait is finished.'

'The portrait is wonderful'

'Your father was the perfect subject.'

'He will be overjoyed.'

'I hope so.'

'And the restoration work?'

'It will all be done on time.' Again that non-committal shrug. Panic was beginning to seize Matt. He longed to take her hand, to draw her onto the sofa beside him, talk to her - hear from her that all the gossip and innuendo was for nothing. But the cool restraint between them stretched taut and tangible and so brittle that he sensed that one wrong word would destroy it altogether.

She rose to her feet, crossed to the window and stood gazing through it. He watched in silence. A hundred images swept through his mind, reminding him of times they had shared in this room; moments of companionship, exploration, at times with dissent, but always with passion and powerful chemistry. Even now in this long awkward void he felt it smouldering still. He went over to her side. 'Anya, we have to talk.'

'I thought we were talking.'

'You know perfectly well that we're not – not really.'

'What do you want to talk about? Isn't the sale the topic of the moment?'

'Yes, it is – of course – but I'd prefer not to think of it as an ending.'

'Is that what it is then?'

'It seems that way to me.'

'Because I'm leaving?'

'Partly.'

'Okay, so we've been through all that before. I don't want to talk about it anymore. You know that my mind is made up – that I have to go – and why.'

'I don't know why. There are things I have to know – deserve to know – questions I have to ask.'

'Too many people have been asking questions. I'm weary of it, Matt. I don't want any more.' She turned to him briefly and he saw a stricken expression which shocked him. She looked suddenly bereft, despairing. 'What have I to stay for?' she asked. 'More questions and more answers? More fingers pointing? Besides my work here is all but finished.'

'Is that all that keeps you here?'

'You know it is.'

She had turned back to the window. Now without seeing her face he felt the resolve. The stiff little back defied him to touch her or to probe with questions. Her whole being was defensive.

He braced himself. 'If your work is finished, when can we see it?'

'My work was the portrait. I thought you liked it.'

'You know I do. But we're talking about the sale. And you have half the lots here – and we haven't seen any of it yet. Can't we go up to the studio and go through it?'

'No – no – we can't. I'm working up there.'

'Anya, but it's our work too.' He thought of their joyous celebration over the portrait – just two days before. 'Your work is my business. I want to be part of it.' He could no longer keep the impatience from his tone. She did not answer.

Matt turned and retreated across the room. As he looked about him he noticed still further evidence of her impending departure. The mantelpiece had been cleared of clutter. Her own few possessions were piled into a small cardboard box on the hearth, and on the table by the door was a pile of her books, her stationery and a bundle of correspondence. Her personal address book lay open alongside. He determined not to look at it, but somehow the initial 'C' sprang from the page. He knew even as he turned away that the 'C' in this case would stand for Castaletz.

He looked up to find her watching him. Almost as though in answer to his thoughts she said, 'I was going to tell you that I know a good framer in London. I don't know whether you would like me to make enquiries.'

'I see. Henry Crisp said he could arrange to have the portrait framed for us in Newcastle, but if you know someone particularly good…'

She stared at him boldly. 'I know the very best as it happens.'

In an immeasurably long silence he returned her look. Then he said unevenly, 'I think you mean Castaletz.'

The moment he had spoken he regretted it. Despite his very best intentions, and against every instinct, he had uttered the one word which could snap the last thread of restraint between them. He saw her pupils dilate, and a fearful, trapped look dull the brightness of her eyes - those expressive green eyes that were always a perfect mirror of her thoughts. How fervently he wished that he could snatch back the word and start again, and tread more gently through the minefield of this fragile conversation.

'Don't say another word,' she breathed, fear turning to anger. 'Just let me finish my work and go.'

'First let me see your work.'

She shook her red head fiercely. 'It's not yours to see.'

'Anya, it is.'

'Not this. I'm painting a last canvas for myself. If it gives you any satisfaction, you may as well know that I wished for a reminder of this place to take with me. I really don't know why. I'm beginning to think that the memory will give me nothing but pain'

'Anya don't. Sit down. Let's try to talk this through. Tell me about Castaletz. I need to know.'

Fiercely she shook her head. Then she unfastened the buttons of the overall-shirt and tugged it off, snatching the keys from the pocket before tossing the paint-stained garment wildly onto the floor. 'I don't really know what I'm supposed to have done. I have no idea why everyone is sloping around me, suspicious and hostile.' Dressed now in close-fitting jeans and a neat blue sweater she looked five years younger and suddenly very vulnerable. He felt unaccountably sad. 'That's why we have to talk.' He saw that her eyes now glittered with angry tears.

'I don't want to talk. Whatever it's all about, I really don't think I want to know.' She had begun to shout. 'Take the portrait to Henry Crisp if that's what you want. It really doesn't matter to me anymore. And take your precious, undistinguished family art collection with you too.'

'Anya, stop it!' He tried to take her hands, to meet her face to face, but she snatched herself away. Then she tossed the keys onto floor at his feet.

'Help yourself! It's all yours.'

Like a small tornado she swept from the lodge, slamming the door behind her. A moment later came the roar of the MG as it burst into action. He stood listening, motionless and stunned, until the sound faded into the distance and the realisation dawned upon him that she had gone.

For a long time Matt sat staring at the carpet and the keys lying by his feet. He listened for sounds of her return, but there was nothing. He even wondered whether to accept the invitation to explore the studio alone, but knew that he could not. At last he scooped the keys into his pocket and left the lodge, closing the door quietly behind him.

CHAPTER SEVENTEEN

Back at the house he was at once aware that something was astir. The family had not yet assembled for lunch. He could hear Aunt Florence complaining bitterly that meals ought to be on time and that her digestion would suffer for the rest of the day. His mother's usual gentle tones of patient appeasement were to be sensed rather than heard. Then she came bustling into the hall.

'Thank goodness you're back.'

'There was no need to wait for me surely.'

'No, no, it's not that. Your father is tied up with that man Smith – a ridiculous time to arrive, I thought – and he's been looking for you.'

'Where are they?'

'In the library. I have no idea what it's all about – but they've been in there for nearly half an hour. I invited him to stay for lunch in the hope of breaking things up – but he declined. It really is too bad.'

Matt responded briskly. 'You'd better start lunch without us. I'll go and see if I can help.'

He made his way into the library where his father and Smith were seated together at the desk in the window, a sheaf of paper spread between them. They both rose as he entered.

'I'm glad you've come, Matt. Mr Smith and I are having an extraordinary discussion, and you certainly should be in on it.' He gestured towards his visitor. 'I believe you know each other.' They shook hands. Strictly speaking their acquaintance so far had been purely superficial. But now, apparently, circumstances were set to change.

Matt drew up a chair and listened in silence as his father delivered a summary of what already had been said. None of it came as surprise. It merely confirmed his very worst fears - that Anya was suspected of fraud and misconduct, and that the tenuous threads of coincidence connecting Robson's art collection with his elder son's closest friend in London, and Anya's own association with him and the Longhirst affair, were probably rather more than circumstantial.

As he waited patiently for his father to finish speaking, he studied Smith with interest, seeing a man quite unlike the expected image of a detective. He was remarkable only for being so ordinary - soberly dressed, the kind of fellow passed unnoticed in the street. Matt wondered whether this perhaps was the secret of his success.

'So you see,' William concluded, 'it looks as though we have been failing to recognise the obvious all this time.'

'But that just seems incredible,' Matt said, shaking his head in dismay. 'Besides, it simply doesn't make sense to try to equate what happened at Longhirst to what is, or might be, happening here. We don't have that kind of art collection.'

'There are degrees in all things, Mr Chevening. It's too early to say for sure.'

'And Robson? Are you trying to tell us that he is acting as some kind of receiver – and that he has been buying a load of fakes?'

'I think you would find that he uses the word 'reproduction'.'

'Which makes it different and legal, I suppose.'

'Exactly. But it doesn't end there. You see it takes the same skill to paint a reproduction as it does to produce a fake. And that's where the questions start.' Smith leafed through the pages on the desk, selected the one he sought and quickly scanned it. 'To an expert, not only the style, but the choice and composition of the paint itself are indications pointing to the hand of the artist. All kinds of tiny details provide 'fingerprints' of the work. Actually it's fascinating science. You see we need to establish a link between the Longhirst fakes and Robson's collection. Your own pictures could well be something of a catalyst – which is why we are investigating.'

'I see,' Matt said slowly.

Smith continued. 'You yourself are aware of a link between the young artist and Castaletz.'

'I understand they were married.'

Smith shook his head. 'Oh I don't think so. At least, not in the eyes of the church – or the law. They possibly co-habited at one time, but our records to not show that Miss Brown was ever married.'

'Miss Brown?' William said. 'Is that Anya's name?'

'You didn't know?'

'She is known to us only as Anya Paris. Something to do with her French connections, we understood.'

'Then I'm sorry to let her down.' Smith gave a mirthless little bark of laughter.

'Brown is not a name she chooses to use,' Matt said.

'Agreed. But her mother was married for a short while to a man called Brown. Her natural father is unknown, so that is her official identity.'

'But unofficially Anya is something of a wartime refugee,' Matt said. 'Truth is that her background is veiled in mystery that she only half understands. Paris is the only word she brought with her as a young child escaping from Nazi occupation.'

'Quite so,' Smith said, looking curiously at Matt who suddenly appeared to be taking sides. 'We are aware of all that.'

'So what is the next move?' William prompted, suddenly remembering that lunchtime was passing and that he was uncommonly hungry. 'Do you have a schedule?'

'Yes, and I also have a warrant to search the lodge – which is what I have come to explain. I didn't wish to exercise this option until I'd spoken to you and put you in the picture.'

'I see.'

'Purely routine, I assure you.'

'It sounds suspiciously to me like a police raid.'

'Hardly that, Mr Chevening, although it will be necessary to have back up from the local police of course.'

William and Matt looked at each other incredulously. It all reeked of the most far-fetched of fiction, at best the kind of thing that happened to other people. 'So is it permission you need?'

'I'm afraid not, Mr Chevening. A warrant doesn't require permission. But I would like to think that it has your backing, and that you'll exercise discretion until we have completed the mission. I am here largely as a courtesy to you.'

William nodded and glanced sadly at Matt. 'Then of course we will comply.'

At this point the interview appeared to be over. As William escorted Smith to the door, Matt heard the invitation to lunch being reiterated and once more declined. But he himself had quite lost his appetite. He remained where he was for a long time, his head in his hands, his mind turbulent. It was all such an appalling mess. Suddenly he did not know which way to turn. And yet in the midst of it all, like the proverbial ill wind, came one pervading and strangely uplifting thought.

Anya Paris was single.

* * *

Evening came and the family went its various ways. The house was unusually quiet. Standing alone in the hall he was conscious of its stillness. Only the ticking of the clock on the stairs and gentle snoring of the sleeping dogs broke the silence. It was as though the house itself held its breath waiting for something to happen.

For some time Matt wandered from room to room, unable to settle. His parents were dining with the Crisps, Florence had retired to her room with supper on a tray, while Angus was fishing, he supposed, or calling on Millie Carter. He was not too concerned. And Dorothy – Dorothy was heaven-knew-where. This also raised only the mildest pangs of concern.

He was glad that he had telephoned Elizabeth, suggesting he might call round later in the evening. At first she had sounded anxious at the thought of an extra mouth to feed. 'We're only having left-overs and salad,' she told him regretfully, but he assured her that he would have supper at home and call later. Only afterwards he remembered that lunch had been missed that day and he was suddenly hungry.

The pantry at home revealed that left-overs would have to be on the menu here as well, so he made himself a doorstep of a sandwich – beef laced with mustard and chutney – which he devoured indecently quickly at the scrubbed kitchen table, only grateful that there was no-one else to witness it. Then, with a beer and a packet of crisps, he returned to the library to fill in yet another half hour with his unwelcome thoughts.

The dogs were awoken by the rattle of the crisp packet and eagerly joined him by the hearth. He shared the crisps with them, and sat fondling their velvety ears. 'Dear dogs, if only you could tell me the solution to all this.' Two velvet muzzles rested on his knees, brown eyes soft with sympathy. But of course there was no solution.

Slowly the clock ticked the minutes away. If Dorothy did not return soon it would be too late for him to go over to Larch Hill, for it was a family rule that Florence should not be left alone in the house. He was once more engulfed by a sense of hopeless frustration.

Then all at once the dogs shifted, eyes became alert, ears picked. He heard the front door creaking on its hinges, followed by brisk footsteps across the hall. 'Daddy. Good gracious. Are you all on your own?'

Suddenly Matt could not decide whether to be pleased or sorry to see her. 'You're awfully late,' he said.

'It isn't late. It isn't even nine o'clock.'

'But you've been out since this morning.'

She ignored this and sank down onto the floor beside him like a little girl. 'I'm glad you're here on your own anyway. There's so much I want to talk about. I don't even know where to start.'

'Dorothy, I've arranged to go round to the Birketts' tonight. I'm already woefully late. Can it all wait until another time?'

She looked hurt. 'Is it so important then to go round there?'

'Only in as much as I arranged it and they're expecting me. And is it indeed so urgent for you to have my undivided attention?'

'When I've just had the best day of my life? I think so.'

'That good?' Despite himself he gave her a teasing smile.

'Yes – that good.' She gazed at him with a rapturous smile. 'The best ever.'

For several moments Matt could find no reply. That this could be the best day of anyone's life, a

299

day close to being one of the worst of his, was the ultimate irony. At last he said unevenly. 'I suppose that means you and your young man have patched up your quarrel.'

'Yes, it does. But don't make it sound so trivial.'

'I didn't mean to. It's just that I've had a hell of a day.' Instinctively he knew that she would not really understand, or be in the deepest sympathy when she heard the reason. In truth their thoughts were not in any kind of harmony at that moment. 'I'm sorry darling,' he said. 'I know you don't want to hear my woes.'

'Of course I don't. I want to talk about cheerful things.'

'Are there any cheerful things then?'

'I think so.'

'Then cheer me.'

She smiled up at him. 'All right. Because you see, Daddy, today I saw a very clear picture of the future. And it was pretty cheery. I looked at Luke's family and ours – and we're all striving for things we haven't got, aren't we? – when between us we've got absolutely everything. And don't you see – Luke and I together can be the perfect answer.'

He laughed at her gravity. 'You're probably right – but there's an awful lot of water to pass under an awful lot of bridges before that can happen.'

'Is there?'

'Of course. Visions of the future, however rosy, need to have substance to make them work.'

'Substance? Dreams don't have substance.'

'Exactly. And things are never that simple.'

She looked disappointed. 'I thought you'd see what sense it makes.'

'Maybe it does. Given time.'

'Time for what?'

'For starters, your time at university. I trust you haven't forgotten that.'

She shrugged. 'I'm beginning to feel that it's no longer appropriate.'

'For heaven's sake, of course it is. You worked hard – night and day - for your place. Would you waste that?'

'Waste? I thought you told me that learning was never wasted. Anyway, that's how it is. I've moved on. I know now what I want.'

'Dorothy, you've got an awful lot of living to do before you know that for sure.'

'I am sure.' For a moment she sat looking up at him, reading the scepticism in his face, feeling his sadness. Then she said, 'Darling Dad, you have to understand. If you can find what you want, instinct tells you when it's right. Surely you can relate to that.'

'I can relate to it only too well,' he said. 'Call me an old cynic if you like, but you'll probably fall in and out of love a dozen or more times before you can be that sure. Give yourself time. It's too soon to commit yourself.'

'I already have committed myself.'

He looked at her sharply. 'Meaning?'

She hung her fair head and stared down at the floor, and at the end of an uneasy silence, she said almost inaudibly, 'that I couldn't be more committed or more sure.'

An arrow of alarm pierced his heart. Yet another arrow, today of all days. Suddenly he could bear it no longer. He rose unsteadily to his feet. 'Go to bed Dorothy. I have to go to Larch Hill. Perhaps we can talk about all this in the morning.'

He looked at her sadly. How dearly he loved her. How fervently he wished he could turn back the clock and be the wise counselling parent he should have been. But now the little girl in her had vanished - the dependent child who had once painstakingly made a card for him on Mothering Sunday! – and now all the gems of wisdom in the world would only fall on deaf ears.

He dropped a light kiss on her head, ashamed to feel the sharp stab of tears and a great constriction in his throat. Then despondently he left her there, unable even to utter goodnight.

* * *

By the time he set out for the Birketts' the light had long faded and evening had drawn its welcome veil over a day he was glad to see ending. The breeze had dropped to a mere breath, and the great beeches along the drive towered dark and still, their silent outlines silhouetted against a purple afterglow. It was as though the whole world hung in limbo as he did.

He glanced uneasily at the lodge as he reached the gate. Clearly there was no-one at home.

Halfway along the lane he drew to a standstill and paused thoughtfully. Possibly Anya had not returned all day - in which case the door was still unlocked and her possessions, together with their pictures, were there for the taking. Perhaps he should at least check that the attic door itself was safely locked, and then leave the key for her to find on her return.

He reversed the car along the lane and approached the lodge in some trepidation. A knock on the little gothic door brought no response, so he pushed it open and entered warily. Everything was just as it had been that morning. A last shaft of weak evening light cruelly illuminated the shabby furnishings of the little house, now stripped of its few adornments. The soulless boxes containing these few possessions were just as they had been left. The paint-stained smock lay where she had carelessly tossed it. He stood looking about him, the memory of their bitter altercation flooding back. He wondered how she would feel towards him when Smith descended in the morning, guessing that probably she would hold him responsible. Then the unthinkable came to him. Perhaps she would not return.

He tried the attic door. It was still locked. He produced the bunch of keys from his pocket and stared at it for a long time. Still he could not persuade himself to open it. Somehow it would be the final violation of her privacy - the one thing she seemed to value above all else.

Instead he replaced the keys where she had tossed them and pushed them out of sight under the sofa. Then as a small concession to her invitation to help himself, he lifted the precious portrait from the chair where it still stood, a sheet covering it. He carried it to the car, leaving the door on the latch behind him. Then he continued on his way.

The portrait caused the expected sensation at Larch Hill. 'It's wonderful – so much more wonderful than I dared hope.' Elizabeth's blue eyes glittered with delight.

'She really is talented, isn't she?' Edward said, impressed, his tone reflecting his surprise at such a revelation.

'Which is why the things that are happening are so terribly sad.'

'Yes, of course it's sad if real talent is put to dishonest use. It is a tragic waste.'

'I'm still hoping there's been some kind of mistake. I simply cannot believe it.'

'Matt, you only have to hear the evidence. You know that.' Elizabeth and Edward exchanged glances. To see Matt looking so dejected, his broad shoulders drooping under the weight of despair, was perhaps the saddest part of the whole sorry business.

Matt poured forth an account of the day's events; Smith's visit, the impending police intervention, Anya's disappearance. They did their best to cheer him. Elizabeth chattered about the auction and the new foal and how hard it was to keep an adolescent occupied during the long recess. Then, as though in response, Philip himself appeared – possibly for the first time in his life at the right moment – and managed to persuade his uncle to help with his holiday project. Elizabeth disappeared to make cocoa. All was comfortably normal.

Edward shifted the painting to his desk and trained his lamp on it. 'I'm afraid I'm a disappointment to my son because I can't relate a first-hand account of World War Two,' he said. 'Pity. I could tell him a great deal about the Roman Invasion if he'd listen.'

'I'm not doing the Romans, Father.'

'But why the Blitz?'

Matt settled at the table with his nephew. 'Yes it does seem a strange subject to have set you.'

'They didn't specify that in particular. Any great battle was what they set us. I s'pose they hoped for something like Agincourt. But I chose the Blitz.'

'Why? It wasn't strictly speaking a battle anyway. You should have gone for the Battle of Britain.'

He shrugged. 'It interests me. I think it must have been incredible, all those people sleeping in tube stations, waiting for the sirens to go off, and then waves of bombers coming over. It must have been amazing.'

'It was hell. But then that goes for most battles I guess.' What an extraordinary young fellow he was, Matt thought, always interested in the darker side of things and the macabre. 'When I was your age,' he told him, 'it was the Jacobites who fired my imagination. And they were here, in this very place. You couldn't have a better subject than the battles that raged in these wild border counties.'

'Not to mention the Romans,' Edward said coldly.

Matt looked from father to son. 'Listen Philip,' he said persuasively. 'I do have some old diaries from 1940 – before I was called up – life on the Northumbrian Home Front – no don't smile – they are quite revealing actually. You could use those, then do a piece about the Forty-five Rising – Northumberland past and present. How about that?' He felt rather proud of the suggestion.

'Hey!' Philip said. 'Great balls of fire! That's really cool.'

Edward muttered 'genius', although whether in response to this or in respect of the portrait still under scrutiny, was not clear. Elizabeth returned with steaming mugs of cocoa, reminding Matt that it was getting late. He left shortly afterwards. As he reached the door young Philip appeared by his side and whispered, 'I believe in her too, you know. What's more they won't find any evidence against her. I'm perfectly sure of that.'

Matt gave him a sharp look, but Philip merely smiled. 'She's quite innocent you see.' And for some reason this cheered him more than he would have dreamt possible.

The lodge was still in complete darkness as he passed - no sign of the red MG. And back at home all was quiet, the family already retired for the night. Even the dogs merely thumped their tails once on the floor before returning to sleep.

For a long time he paused in the empty hall. Its silence settled around him, and he had the overwhelming sense that others before him had stood as he stood now trying to draw comfort from its familiarity. Most likely the old house had seen it all before. The squabbles, the intrigues, the interweaving of human lives that took place within it were as much a part of its fabric as the stones of the pele tower itself – and this lofty hall – and the great staircase, its banisters dark with age and only the oaken rail still pale and smooth from the countless hands that had worn and polished it. It was somehow heartening to feel that fresh waters still flowed between the well-worn banks of tradition. Pausing there he felt a strange communion with the silent house, and his soul reached out to it for strength and guidance.

And suddenly its gentle voice was all about him – in the creaking of the stairs as he ascended them, in the dogged tick of the grandfather clock on the landing, in the stirring of a breeze through the old creeper outside – and in a prolonged sigh that seemed to come from its very heart.

CHAPTER EIGHTEEN

It was already late before Angus realised that evening was giving way to night. He had been fishing his favourite pool for some hours - with little success as fishing went. The trout simply weren't biting and the midges certainly were. But the tranquillity and calm of the riverbank did not disappoint. Even as darkness defeated him he remained for a while in his pleasant solitude. Later as he gathered up his paraphernalia and prepared to leave, a figure came towards him along the path from the direction of the lodge. Angus watched for a while unnoticed, then realised with a surge of excitement that it was the same man he had encountered there all those weeks before. Resolutely he stepped into his path, determined that this time he would get to the bottom of the minor mystery surrounding the stranger.

'Good evening. So we meet again.'

'Yes indeed.' The man looked startled. 'I'm trespassing once more I'm afraid. Forgive me.'

'Paths are fair game,' Angus replied equably. 'But why this way at this hour?'

The man shrugged. 'It's a pleasant path, isn't it?'

'In daylight it is. And if you've somewhere to go.'

'I was visiting the lodge down there as a matter of fact.'

Angus eyed him in interest. 'Visiting Anya? I didn't know she had friends in the area - although of course you're not from this neck of the woods, are you?' Again he detected the trace of a foreign accent, French possibly, but almost unnoticeable.

'No. No, I'm up from London.'

'I see.'

Angus did not see. In fact it made the whole thing even more unlikely - that anyone visiting from London should either know of the path or choose to use it at this hour and in preference to a perfectly serviceable road - unless, that was, he did not wish to be seen. 'Why should you come this way to the lodge?' he asked.

'Why not?' the man replied. 'I'm staying at the inn in Whittingham. I have no transport and it's a short cut.'

Angus continued to gather up his fishing gear still curious and dissatisfied. Already the man was beginning to wander on. 'Please wait a minute. I admit I'm still puzzled... meeting you twice on our property like this...I mean, is Anya a close friend of yours?'

The man stopped, withdrew a packet of French cigarettes, and hesitated. Then he said, 'We go back a long way, if that's anything to go by.' He gave a little laugh. 'I'm her guardian angel actually.'

Angus scowled. 'Is that so?' He declined the offer of a cigarette, shaking his head, more in perplexity than anything else. 'Whatever that's supposed to mean.'

'Someone who watches over her.'

'A minder do you mean?'

'Lord no. Nothing like that. Just as an old friend - a once-tutor - a colleague - someone who taught her a little of what we both do.'

'So you are also a restorer.'

The man nodded, lit his cigarette and exhaled in a thin stream of fragrant smoke. 'Yes, for my sins.'

'Then why are you here now - like this?'

'I keep in touch. There are times when an exchange of views can be helpful. Restoring isn't always the exact science it's meant to be, you know.'

Angus considered this for a moment or two while he weighed up his companion. He was a man of about his own age, or perhaps a little more, he gauged - certainly older than Anya. Briefly he wondered about such a relationship, and decided that on face value it probably didn't amount to anything as explainable as a clandestine affair, for this man was no match for Anya. 'Is she in need of advice at the moment then?' he ventured. When a reply was not forthcoming, he added, 'It's our art collection that's being renovated, and if there are problems I think we deserve to know. It must be of some importance to have brought you here from London...'

'Most old pictures have question marks hanging over them, when two heads are better than one. I make use of my few visits - a bit of fetching and carrying - you know. I help out now and then.'

Angus's mind began to work overtime. Fetching and carrying what, he wondered? He was reluctant to ask. Of course it was all too easy to make wild guesses about why this mysterious stranger could not present himself at Anya's door in the usual way, or why Anya, who had herself been treated in every way like a guest of the family, had not told them that she had an old friend and colleague who stayed at the inn in Whittingham and advised her on the restoration of their own collection of pictures. 'I suppose she needs supplies and art materials from time to time,' he volunteered a little lamely, knowing full well that this beggared belief.

'Yes, that sort of thing,' the man replied non-committally. 'But anyhow, tonight it as a wasted journey. Somehow we must have misunderstood each other.'

'You mean there was no-one there?'

'Well certainly Anya wasn't. Some crazy looking teenage kid was wandering about the place, peering through the windows. I didn't like the look of him much.'

'What was he like?'

'Tall – lanky – nondescript.'

He shrugged. 'It was probably only my nephew.' Then turning to his companion with an apologetic little smile, he added, 'The name's Angus Chevening, by the way.'

'Mine's Jacques.'

'Jacques what?'

'That is name enough. You are welcome to call me Jacques.'

'Perhaps I can keep you company to the end of the path then?'

'Of course. It's your path, isn't it?'

They set out in the darkness, in silent single-file for a hundred yards or so, until the path widened and they were able to draw abreast. He noticed that the fellow limped quite badly. So why choose a path like this? Angus mulled over what he had been told, instinctively uneasy and suspicious. Who was he? And just how well did he know Anya?

Drawing abreast of him, he asked, 'if you are such an old friend then maybe you know what it is about Anya. Just what is it that makes her tick? We are mystified. Is she running away from something?'

The man seemed taken aback by this bluntness. 'I doubt whether anyone knows what 'makes her tick', as you put it.' He gave an airy gesture with his hand and a little Gallic shrug. 'I rather think she's been running away all her life.'

'Why? From what?'

'It would take longer than the length of this path for me to tell you the little I know. And then you wouldn't understand.'

'Try me. I promise I'll do my best.'

'You'd have to have known her childhood I think.'

'And did you? Do you go back that far?'

'No. But I do know that she's had to fend for herself all her life, and that she has reached this point in her career in the most unconventional way.'

'It would help us to understand if we knew.'

'I've already said that if we walked from here to Land's End I'd not be finished telling you. You ask what she's running from. Mostly, I think, she's running from herself.' He turned and faced Angus in the darkness, his expression sombre. 'She has more talent and imagination than anyone you'll ever meet. She has every right to be proud of what she has achieved, largely off her own bat and because she has some magic going for her. But it's mostly wasted, because she refuses to let people see it for themselves. Now you understand?'

'Clearly you do,' Angus said.

'The people she allows to come close always do. My brother for example. He was the first to recognise her talent and he taught her practically all she knows. For a while they were very close. But then he made the fatal mistake of trying to take control of her life. Anya is very much her own person and he was domineering, forceful, perhaps even brutal at times. Yes, when she was younger I think she was quite afraid of him.'

'So what happened?'

'She grew up.'

'And?'

'She tried to distance herself as best she could. But in a strange way they continued to need each other. He came to rely on her exceptional talent and finesse, just as she needed his distinguished connections. She loves what she does, you know.'

'I do know.'

'So for a long time he kept his tight hold on her. I'm afraid it does my brother little credit, but I do believe she has been badly-used. And now she simply wants to be free.'

'Of him?'

Jaques responded with a shrug.

'Or you perhaps.'

'Oh no, not me. I'm just what you'd call a trusted go-between!' They had reached the end of the path and stood looking at each other in silence.

Then the strange Jacques held out his hand in acknowledgment of the parting of their ways. 'Take my word - she is very special to me. That is why I am her guardian angel.' Then he gave a low chuckle and began to move on. For a moment Angus could find nothing to say. Jacques bridged the silence. 'She needs to find some happiness for herself you see. And just for short time, it seemed as though she had.' He smiled ruefully. And before Angus could respond, he was limping away into the darkness and Angus was left staring after him with the eerie feeling that although the mystery of Anya persisted, somehow it had taken on a different guise.

* * *

Matt had not expected to sleep. But the grey light of morning filtering into his room told him that he had - and the dream from which he was awakening could only have occurred in the deepest slumber, so unlikely, yet realistic it had been. He had been on an East End street during an air raid. Bombs had been falling all about him, people scurrying for shelter, their frantic figures outlined against the glow of a crimson sky. He awoke shaken and disturbed.

Slowly he got out of bed and crossing to the window, drew aside the curtain. The landscape beyond was grey and still. It was as though a veil had descended over everything. There was no movement of air, no bird song, just an unnatural quiet. The acrid smell of the London blitz still seemed to fill his nostrils. He pushed open the casement and took a deep breath of air, allowing his gaze to drift over the treetops. Then slowly his eyes began to adjust to the light. Rising through the trees in the distance he saw a thick black column of smoke. The blitz returned to history. The present brought with it a sharp stab of alarm. In one flash he knew where it came from. How often lately he had focussed on that very spot. His heart thumped against his ribs and his senses reeled. Dear God, it was the lodge.

Moments later he had dressed and, still pulling his jersey over his head, he sped down the stairs. As he reached the hall there was an urgent hammering on the door. He flung it open to reveal Hodges in a state of panic.

'Quickly, 'phone the fire brigade, Mr Matt. The lodge is going up in smoke!'

'Christ, what happened?'

'Heaven knows.'

'Anya. Where is Anya?'

'I don't know a thing - just that we need help.'

Matt raced to the telephone and demanded 999. 'They'll take for ever to get here of course,' he said when he got back to Hodges. 'Has anyone else been alerted?'

'Morris has taken all the fire equipment from the stables. The lads are with him.'

'Good - good.' They clambered into the garden pick-up, still piled high with hedge cuttings, and rattled off down the drive. Matt found himself praying. Please let her be safe. Please look after her and let her be all right. He had never wanted to believe in God as much as he did at that moment. Every bump of the drive tossed twigs in all directions. The smoke grew dense as they reached the gate. They eyed the scene in horror.

The stable staff battled manfully with what little equipment they had, but the fire had already taken hold at the rear of the lodge. Smoke and flame streamed from the attic windows.

'Where's Anya? Have you seen her?'

'There's nobody here, Mr Matt.'

'Are you sure?'

'Pretty sure.'

He looked about him wildly. The MG was not in its usual place. Perhaps she had never returned. Or perhaps... He did not know what to think.

Long before the fire brigade arrived a crowd had gathered at the lodge - Angus and Dorothy, Elizabeth with Philip, and he in a state of high excitement. Then Rob Wilson, a farmer from across the valley, arrived with a couple of farm hands. But there was precious little any of them could do. The picturesque little house crackled, as the window frames twisted and glass shattered, and the charred timbers emitted acrid choking fumes. They all exchanged hopeless glances. It was unbelievably sad, tragic even, and close to the bitter end in a long and unhappy train of events.

It was almost lunchtime before the fire brigade declared the fire out. By this time the crowd had swelled to include William and Katherine looking on in stunned silence. Matt had never thought his father old, but he looked tired and aged as he stood there seeing yet another piece of his cherished home in ruins. Katherine's concern was entirely for him. Her gentle face was full of sadness.

'Go back, darlings,' Matt said. 'It will not look this bad when it's been sorted a bit.' He knew that they were empty words, but what else was there to say?

Smith had been at the scene for over an hour, with his local police back up. There was no doubting his views and he was already arranging to have the site examined for evidence.

'I suppose we have lost our famous art collection,' Elizabeth said.

'It looks that way. But why, Liz, why?'

'I suppose it must have been an accident. I dare say the wiring in the lodge is pretty out of date.'

'Smith clearly doesn't think so.'

'No, he has it well earmarked 'arson'.'

Matt knew even as he spoke that there were numbers of ways that the finger of suspicion could point. But surely not to Anya, he kept thinking to himself. Surely she would not be capable of destroying all her work. Besides, she had not even known of Smith's impending investigation as far as he knew. None of it made any sense.

Smith was busy cordoning off the area. 'It's too early to know what can be salvaged,' he told them, 'but we can hope that some of the pictures we expect to find up there will be recognisable for identification. 'I'm afraid I'll have to ask you to leave it all to us for the time being.'

'And Anya?'

'We will have to question her at once of course.'

'If you can find her.'

'Mr Chevening, I can assure you that we don't

317

expect the young lady to be missing for long.'

The family began to disperse. Only Matt remained where he was for a while longer. Philip tugged at his sleeve as he passed with his parents. 'Awful sight, isn't it?'

'Yes. Truly dreadful.'

'All her work destroyed. Gone without trace. Now they'll never know. Tragic.'

Matt cast him a questioning look, but Philip merely shook his head and turned away, and followed his parents on their way.

For a while only Matt remained, rooted to the spot, leaning against the staunch stone pillar of the gateway, his eyes tightly closed, as though by blotting everything from view he could somehow remove it altogether. His mind was turbulent. Then gradually he pulled himself together, and allowed himself to gaze once more at the charred outline of the little lodge, where some of the best and worst moments of that extraordinary summer had been spent. Instinctively he knew that all those memories were the dream, and that what he saw before him now was the reality.

* * *

Henry Crisp drove up from Newcastle the moment he heard the news. William had sounded so distraught over the telephone that he had decided to drop everything and get straight on the road. And forewarned though he was, he was still shocked to see the state of the little lodge as he drove in through the gates. Smith and his men were still busy salvaging what they could. It appeared that the attic had taken the brunt of the damage - which of course, Henry knew, included the art collection. The irony of the situation was not lost on him.

'I hardly know what to say to you, William,' he said, his kindly face full of sympathy.

'Simply tell me, Henry, whether it is too late to cancel the plans for the auction.'

'It isn't too late. Of course it isn't. We haven't even gone to press yet - almost, but not quite.' He thought ruefully of the work and expense already incurred in the assembly of the catalogue, and the advertising awaiting the go ahead, but he merely said, 'On the other hand, perhaps you shouldn't be too hasty.'

'Henry, my dear fellow, none of the pictures will survive intact, that's perfectly plain - and the rest, well the rest was being sold merely for the sake of making the sale worthwhile, wasn't it? In the circumstances I think I'd prefer to forget the whole damned business and take the course I should have taken in the first place in order to settle my debts.'

'Which is?'

'To bury my lifelong principles, and face the unpalatable fact that I have to part with the finest and most valuable portions of my pastureland.' He closed his eyes in painful acceptance of the unacceptable.

Henry did not reply. There was nothing to be said.

Later he went with Matt to view the findings of

Smith. As expected little had survived. The charred remnants of frames, bearing scant evidence of what they had once contained, were displayed for their inspection. Most were virtually indistinguishable.

'This is the only one that is still almost recognisable,' Smith said, producing a small unframed canvas. 'This was on the easel, which I suppose is why it nearly survived.'

'I for one don't even recognise it,' Henry said, 'although I dare say you do, Matt.'

'I know what it is,' Matt said, 'even though I've never set eyes on it before in my life. And I certainly know what it means.' He could hardly bear to look at it. Through the blackened paint he saw a picture of the house, glimpsed through the beeches of the drive, its focus the towering edifice of the pele. This was the little bit of Foxsteads that Anya had planned to take with her, the one painting she had done for herself.

Painstakingly they went through the debris, identifying each painting from the scant evidence of the remains. 'You do realise, don't you Henry, that our two wonderful sporting pictures which hung in the hall at Foxsteads are amongst all this? Anya was going to clean them. They are arguably the best of our collection.'

'Lord, that is tragic. They were not even part of the sale.'

'Most certainly they were not. They were part of what we were trying so hard to preserve.'

'Presumably they - and indeed the others - are insured.'

Matt shrugged. 'Not specifically, I'm afraid. The household is insured of course.'

Smith looked from one to the other. 'But I have to remind you that the cause of the fire is not yet known.'

Now Matt and Henry exchanged glances. Both understood that Smith believed he knew. In his mind it was who rather than what had caused it that still remained a mystery.

One by one the paintings were accounted for. 'That at least is satisfactory,' Henry said as they returned to the house, leaving Smith to his unsavoury business.

'Not quite.' Matt said. Together they made their way back along the drive. The greyness of the day had not lifted. Silence seemed to hang from the motionless outlines of the beeches - and the distant view of the house, so reminiscent of the darkened painting they had just seen, emerged through the smoke scented gloom. 'I did not wish to talk any more in front of Smith, but it isn't all quite complete. My mental inventory tells me that there are still two missing.'

'The two sporting pictures in question I suppose. It is certainly to be hoped.'

'Sadly, for some reason I don't think so. I believe you accounted for those. I could be wrong, but some instinct tells me that we saw no evidence of that enormous still life.'

'Why should you think that?'

'Because of the extraordinary frame with its metal brackets. It was very distinctive - and undoubtedly would have survived enough to be recognised. Dorothy seemed to think it was one of pair.' He gave a mirthless little laugh. 'But whatever and why ever, I don't think sleep should be lost over it, do you?'

They continued along the drive in thoughtful silence, their footsteps slackening as they reached the house. Henry paused and turned to Matt as they mounted the steps. 'What about the portrait? Is it safe?'

'Thankfully, yes. I took it over to Larch Hill last night. That is the only blessing I can think of.'

'And is it good?'

'It's stunning. Just stunning.'

Henry laid a kindly hand on Matt's shoulder. 'Good. Good. There has to be some joy in all this for your poor father.'

Matt gave him a grateful look. Only Henry, he decided, dear Henry, could find joy in such a hopeless situation!

CHAPTER NINETEEN

During the next couple of weeks so much happened but so little was resolved that the family felt itself to be in some kind of limbo. Regretfully William cancelled the auction sale. He sanctioned the removal of a few selected items from the house – those already earmarked for sale - and gave instructions for them to be included in Wise and Crisp's next auction in Newcastle. Katherine insisted on this. To think of re-accommodating all the things she had been so glad to relinquish would amount to the very final straw, she assured him, and he had agreed willingly enough. Already the marquee had been cancelled and Katherine, faced with entertaining close on a hundred guests in the house for the birthday celebration, was already at her wits end.

'Why ask so many people?' William said. 'As far as I'm concerned it's just another birthday. It really isn't necessary.'

'Of course it is.'

'Nonsense. And if you really want to know I'd be happier not to have it.'

'It's expected, William.'

He smiled good-naturedly. 'Then keep it simple – a few drinks and canapés – then pray that it's fine enough for them all to go outside.' He was secretly pleased that she had something to occupy her.

Meanwhile he himself was deep in consultation over the price of prime agricultural land, and trying to balance this against the massive account he was soon to have to settle. It was acutely painful. At the end of a year which had seen the failing of his own robust health, the demise of his riding career, when his home had been given a death sentence and his lodge all but destroyed, this final decision to abandon the principle of a lifetime and sell off part of his land – especially to a man like Robson – felt like the bitter, bitter end.

Abandoning Katherine to her endless lists, he ascended the hundred or so steps to the pele tower turret and paused there alone with his thoughts. A crisp wind snapped at his shirt and flattened his hair. He welcomed it. It was cool and bracing, and the air so clear that he could see almost the breadth of England. The land rose behind him towards the Cumberland fells, and before him swept away to Newcastle and the coast.

Suddenly Foxsteads seemed very remote, and he felt as solitary as ever he had in his life. Ostensibly his problems could be shared, but in reality they were his and his alone.

He looked about him. Outwardly nothing had changed. The tower, the turret, it all looked remarkably as it had before. Robson had performed wonders. He had to admit the man had earned his victory. But at what cost? The irony of it pierced William to the heart. Sadly his eyes scanned the pastureland that would shortly no longer be his. Then he closed them tightly as though to obliterate the sight.

For a long time he paused with his thoughts. Then slowly and painfully he made his way back down the stairs. Smith was waiting in the hall.

They talked for nearly an hour - Smith mostly. William listened wearily, feeling that probably he had heard it all before and that there would be nothing new to impart. But there was news of sorts. Smith at least had exonerated Robson from the suspicion of receiving illegal goods. 'I still don't know what to make of Castaletz,' he said. 'Instinctively I don't trust him an inch, I'm afraid. But he has an answer for everything.'

'And provenance for all that art he has supplied?'

'Absolutely. And watertight. A lot of the pictures that Robson has bought might be thought of as fakes or frauds. But there is a third option that goes by the name of 'reproduction' – 'in the style of' – and provided it is sold as such, it doesn't violate the law.'

'No, of course not.'

'But it has been hard to prove, because Robson has been evasive about it, and unwilling to product the necessary documents.'

'Why on earth should he be obstructive?'

'Pride, Mr Chevening. Foolish though it seems, our friend Mr Robson finds it hard to acknowledge that half of his art collection is less than it appears.'

William gave a derisive laugh. 'Good God! He would have some poor unsuspecting dealer under suspicion rather than that?'

Smith looked up sharply. 'Forget the poor and unsuspecting,' he said. 'Jean-Paul Castaletz is anything but.'

William looked perplexed. 'Then is he or is he not implicated in dishonest dealings?'

For a long time Smith considered his response. He opened his brief case, withdrew a sheaf of paper, and sat thumbing through it. William was convinced that he merely stalled for time. 'Creating reproduction paintings, or copies, requires considerable ability, Mr Chevening. I understand that it takes more than an artist to do it skilfully, and that only someone who understands the history and substance of old paintings is qualified to do the job properly. Robson's pictures are of the very highest quality – as were those of Lord Hazelwood – and as I speak we have experts comparing the two. Only then will we know whether or not Castaletz has been entirely honest.'

'I see. But in what way can we help?'

'Very little I fear, Mr Chevening, in the circumstances – now that your own collection is in ruins. But of course it doesn't remove you from the very centre of things.'

'No, of course not. Have you made any progress in the matter of the fire?'

'Yes and no. Anya Paris has a watertight alibi.'

'I'm glad of that. I don't know why I should be, but I am.'

Smith fixed his gaze on the sheaf of papers and studied it in silence. 'She spent the night of the fire in Hexham Hospital,' he said. 'She ran that car of hers off the road and received quite a blow on the head.'

In disbelief William stared at him, shocked and angry. 'Why weren't we told of this before? Is she all right?'

Smith looked uncomfortable as he explained. 'We didn't know ourselves until the hospital informed us. And yes, apparently she is perfectly all right – and the flashy little car. Possibly she did herself a considerable favour.'

'So have you spoken to her?'

'Not yet I'm afraid. She is proving elusive.'

'But she is exonerated.'

Smith folded the papers carefully and stacked them away again in the case. William was convinced that he had not read a word, nor intended to. Smith said, as he clicked the latches closed, 'I'm afraid I didn't say that, Mr Chevening. Anya Paris has done a great deal of work for Castaletz. She is skilled and she is knowledgeable. And I'm afraid that for the time being her involvement cannot be ruled out. I'm truly sorry.'

'I'm sorry too,' William said, his kindly face reflecting a feeling of desolation, which even he was at odds to explain. She was nothing to him. He was also convinced that Matt would fare better without her. Nevertheless the sadness stayed with him, and it was some time before he could bring himself to tell Katherine and Matt of his discoveries.

* * *

Katherine had already written the invitations for the birthday celebration. She had even managed to pare down the list to a manageable size, and with the help of Mrs Hodges was making plans for a buffet supper and a cake, which she determined should bear seventy candles. She smiled as she read through the replies arriving daily – acceptances all of them – and most bearing thoughtful messages to remind her that dark though things had become, there were friends out there who cared greatly about them. She was still smiling when Dorothy came into the room.

'Just look at all those lists,' she exclaimed. 'Do you need any help?'

Katherine shook her head, shuffled the letters into a neat pile and looked up with a smile. 'I was counting the replies actually, and thinking how lucky we are to have such good friends.'

'Yes. Yes, I agree we are.'

'And thank heaven to have something to celebrate amidst all this gloom. Isn't that so?'

Dorothy perched herself on the corner of the desk and eyed her grandmother sagely. 'Things will come right you know – probably sooner than you think. Before we know it we will have forgotten that we ever had dry rot in the roof, and the lodge will be good as new, and Anya will be forgotten.' Well maybe not, she thought, one way and another, but she smiled nevertheless. 'And Grandfather's leg will mend and he'll be rushing around the place again.'

'How I wish that could be true,' Katherine said sadly. 'But I'm afraid we can only hope that it will improve rather than mend.' For a moment she sat rearranging the pile of letters. Then she set them aside. 'If there's one thing that I would like to give your grandfather for his birthday, it is that.'

'What are you going to give him?'

'I really can't make up my mind.'

Dorothy hugged the secret of the portrait to herself. If justice demanded that her grandmother too deserved to be given a present, which truly she did, then this would delight her in equal measure. The excitement was hard to contain. 'You'll think of something. I'm sure you will,' she said.

'For the man who has everything – and nothing?'

'Oh Gran, for shame! He has everything that matters. You must see that.' And she dropped a kiss on Katherine's silver head, then left her to her lists and introspections.

She was still thinking of their conversation when much later that day she stood alone in the drawing room at Fallowfell Hall, waiting for Luke to fetch ice from the kitchen. She supposed she should take her own good advice, and thank her lucky stars that from all the gloom had emerged some good. Well, Anya had gone and that had to be good news. Still no-one knew of her whereabouts - probably London, Dorothy thought – which was far enough. There was always a bright side to everything.

Dorothy looked about her. All at once she saw Fallowfell Hall in a new light also. The French furniture, the pictures, the porcelain even, now bore questions marks. How much of it was what it claimed to be? And how much was fake – or reproduction – or 'in the style of'? In a word spurious? It was strange really, Dorothy thought, gazing into the depths of a picture that was in itself very appealing, drawing the eye into a Pre-Raphaelite landscape that was full of life and colour. Probably it was worth very little, just because it lacked the proper provenance. But it did not make it less appealing, only less valuable. The world was a strange place, she decided.

Luke returned with the ice. They exchanged charged looks. Already she could read the smouldering expression in his eyes and felt a little frisson of excitement. They had the house to themselves. She knew that he could not wait to make love to her – and that even now as he went about the purely practical business of fixing drinks for them both he was mentally undressing her. She watched him thoughtfully. In this same context she suddenly found herself wondering whether he was exactly what she believed him to be. Was he the genuine article, or were the Robsons all as spurious as their surroundings? Bitterly ashamed to have allowed such a thought to enter the brightness of her evening, she gave a little shudder. And when he returned with the drinks, she could not quite bring herself to meet his eyes.

He handed her a glass, gently lifted her chin with this finger and kissed the tip of her nose. 'Little Dorothy, you're most awfully quiet tonight.'

'My head is most awfully full of thoughts actually.'

'Then spill them out. What sort of thoughts?'

'Abut my family mostly, and the way they're struggling along at the moment. And me – trying to do the right thing and probably getting it all wrong as usual.'

'I'm sure you're not – unless – do you mean wrong about me?'

'Of course not Luke. You're the one thing that's right. Although I do wonder sometimes whether perhaps we are rushing into things a bit.' Already he was deftly unfastening her buttons. Half of her desperately wanted him to. But strangely, only half. The other half resisted, suddenly afraid. 'I still have to make up my mind about university, you know,' she said. 'My father is keen for me to go.'

'I thought you had dismissed it altogether.'

'I had.'

'Had?'

'No, of course not. I mean have. But I've got to be sure.'

'And aren't you?' He was so skilful at making her want him. She was weak with longing. He had lifted her skirt and had slid his hand between her thighs. She shuddered rapturously. 'Tell me you are, little Dorothy,' he whispered.

'Luke! We can't make love here in the middle of your parents' drawing room!'

'He pushed her back against the sumptuous cushions of the brocade sofa laughing. 'Give me one good reason why not.'

She could think of none. But something in the back of her mind told her that somewhere there had to be a reason.

* * *

There was a little less than a week to go before the party when father and daughter found themselves alone together at the breakfast table. Matt had the Times folded in front of him and was scanning the headlines. Dorothy was toying with a piece of toast without much enthusiasm. He could see from the corner of his eye that she was fidgety and ill at ease. He eyed her suspiciously. Something was amiss. He was sure of it. At last she met his gaze. 'Dad, there's something I have to tell you.'

His heart descended into the pit of his stomach. He had begun to expect fate to throw problem after crisis into his life, and he did not doubt for a moment that yet another was about to land in his lap. 'Well then, you'd better tell me, hadn't you?'

'I've decided to go to university.'

His mouth dropped open. He stared at her in utter disbelief. 'Dorothy, for heaven's sake, you don't mean it.'

'I thought you'd be pleased.'

'I'm overjoyed! Whatever has prompted this?'

'Oh, not what you think. Nothing's changed you know – nothing at all.'

'Nothing's changed? Everything's changed. It's wonderful news. I can't tell you how much I welcome it.'

'I know Darling. I was sure you would. But I needed to be certain before I said anything. Forms began to arrive and I started to think, and suddenly it seemed absurd to pass up an opportunity like this, when I think how hard I worked for my exams at school. Dear God – it all feels like a lifetime ago.'

'I know. I agree it does.'

She began fiercely to butter the piece of toast. 'Luke and I have all our lives in front of us. I do see that now.'

'And does he?'

'I haven't told him yet.' She sank her teeth into the toast and ate it with almost indecent speed. 'But I know he will.'

'If he doesn't then he isn't the right one for you,' Matt said.

'I know that too. But he will understand. I'm sure he will.'

Matt said nothing, but his heart sang. Suddenly one little corner of his inner self no longer felt quite such a disappointment. For Dorothy at least he could see a bright future and he could have hugged her for joy. Instead he looked straight into her earnest little face and smiled with delight.

Dorothy finished her toast and left, smiling to herself. Now she would find her grandmother and tell her the news. She felt a great sense of lightness and release. Gran too would be overjoyed, Dorothy knew for sure, and it did make a change to be able to impart news that people were pleased to hear – especially people who had rather got out of the habit.

She found Katherine at her desk, speaking to someone on the telephone. 'I can't believe it,' she was saying. 'Are you absolutely sure? Goodness, what an extraordinary thing.' She looked up and

333

saw Dorothy, and covering the mouthpiece with her hand, she whispered, 'Have you seen the paper?'

'Dad's reading it.'

'Please be a dear and ask him to bring it here – as quickly as possible.' Dorothy looked from the telephone to her grandmother in questioning silence. Katherine conveyed the urgency with a frantic nod of her head. 'Henry, that's amazing. I can scarcely take it in. Look, I'll ring off now and will get William to call back shortly.' Dorothy dashed away to find Matt.

They returned with the newspaper in a matter of moments. It was clear that Katherine was in a state of great agitation. 'What's happened?' Matt demanded. Once again he felt half afraid to ask.

'Astonishing news. I can hardly believe it. The Longhirst pictures have turned up.'

Matt and Dorothy exchanged incredulous looks, he still unable to conceal his apprehension. 'Turned up?'

'Been recovered.'

'Recovered from where? How?'

'I don't really know. Henry says it's all over the Times – and that Smith's coming to see him later this morning.'

They spread the paper open on the desk and began to turn the pages. A prominent headline sprang from an inside page, announcing, 'Mystery of Switched Art Treasures Solved'. In silence they read it. It was an astonishing tale.

The entire collection had been discovered in the vaults of a Swiss bank, where apparently it had lain since 1939, when the present Lord Hazelwood's father had deposited it at the outbreak of war. Close on fifty pictures had been recovered, and subsequently it had been discovered that copies were made at the time to replace those at Longhirst.

'Good Lord,' Matt said slowly, when he had read it. 'Does that mean that all that illustrious art has been stashed away in some vault all this time? That no-one knew about it or documented it? I'm sorry – but that defies credibility.'

'Incredible things did happen in the war. This isn't the first such thing to come to light.'

'No – but with all the furore over this particular collection you'd have thought it would have been discovered before now. Apart from anything else, the Longhirst collection has always been famous. Don't tell me that it's taken this for the experts to notice that the place contained nothing but copies. It beggars belief.'

'Yes, I agree it does. Utterly. Something to do with seeing and believing I suppose. But yes, it is astonishing to think that the so-called experts who've handled the paintings over the years have been taken in. Not to mention the scores who've made a pilgrimage to see them - especially the celebrated Rembrandt. How on earth could they have been fooled so easily?'

'It could make anyone cynical, couldn't it? So what was Hazelwood's part in it?'

'Naturally he protests complete innocence,' Katherine said, running her finger down the page. 'As you'd expect. It explains here that he was only

335

a boy at the time and of course his father did not survive the war – so I dare say such a thing could be possible. They were strange and difficult times you know.'

Matt nodded thoughtfully. 'So that lets Hazelwood off the hook.'

'It was always hard to imagine him staging such a scam.'

'And Castaletz. I wonder about him.' He did not dare to utter Anya's name.

Nevertheless it seemed as though the whole picture had changed. It was now the academics under scrutiny – unequivocally in black and white. It had taken a prospective buyer from the Forbes Institute in New York to raise the doubts that had opened up this can of worms. It was a sensation.

Matt's mind began to work overtime. He sensed the clouds over Anya beginning to thin just a little – shedding slender rays of light into the uncompromising darkness of the situation. He was truly able to hope again, and trust his own unswerving belief. From the beginning nothing could have convinced him that the hand that painted the wonderful portrait was that of a criminal, despite all the circumstantial evidence. It was simply the most remarkable piece of work he had ever seen - curiously revealing, full of heart. And if someone of such talent could waste it on deception and fraud, then there could be no sense in anything. Suddenly he felt so choked that he could not speak.

Henry came over later that day, full of the dramatic turn of events. 'Isn't this sensational?' he said. 'It has made the so-called experts in the case look utterly inept - quite incompetent. Smith too, if the truth be known. He is still scarcely able to accept it. I'm sure inwardly he still suspects Hazelwood of duplicity. But that's very unlikely in my opinion – knowing the facts that have come to light – and knowing the man.'

'Who painted the copies?' Matt asked unevenly. 'They must have been pretty convincing. Do they know?'

Henry shrugged. 'It was twenty years ago. Who's to say? Not Castaletz, that's for sure.'

'And not Anya,' Matt thought.

Later he drew Henry aside. 'This puts a very different complexion on everything, doesn't it?'

'Yes, it does of course. For one thing there can no longer be a link between Robson's pictures and the Longhirst affair. Personally I consider Robson a pompous man who puts show before substance, but I would not have thought him dishonest – nor seen him as a fool – nor, to be truthful, wanted to see him taken for this sort of a ride.'

'So does that close the case?'

Henry read Matt's mind and smiled in sympathy. 'I'm afraid it doesn't. For one thing there still has to be a question mark over your pictures and fire in the lodge.'

'Come now, Henry, they were not important pictures.'

'The two sporting oils were more valuable than any of you realised. And you yourself said that there were other paintings missing.'

'But I can't be sure – and besides it was of no consequence. And does Smith know about it?'

'I didn't tell him. I thought it was between ourselves.'

'It was.'

They had wandered together into the hall. The spaces where the sporting pictures had been – two lighter squares on the wall - held their attention, as silently they both considered the situation. Then Matt turned to Henry, with a bleak longing in his eyes. 'I need to see her, you understand. I can't keep guessing like this and wondering. Every day makes me surer that she is totally innocent of it all. But I have to hear for myself.'

Henry drew a clean white handkerchief from his pocket, removed his steel framed spectacles and began to polish them in silence. Then, having finished, he replaced them and looked at Matt as though hoping to see him in a new light. But there was nothing to see but the same utter desolation. He looked at him sadly. In his honest wisdom he would have advised Matt to put Anya out of his mind, to take up the threads of his life again. But he knew it would be pointless. Instead he laid a sympathetic hand on his arm and said, 'I'm afraid I can't help. I have no idea where she is – not even whether Smith knows himself. But things will resolve themselves, you can be sure of that.'

Matt gave an empty little laugh. Dear, kindly, well-meaning Henry. 'I'm afraid,' he said, that I can no longer feel that sure of anything.'

CHAPTER TWENTY

'This week has been a paradox,' Katherine remarked, as she struggled to arrange Florence's chair to her satisfaction beside the library window. 'It has been one of the longest and one of the shortest I've ever known in my life.'

The old lady snorted. 'How can it be both long and short may I ask?'

'Believe me, it can. With all the problems we've had, and new revelations, and questions needing answers that can't be found, it has felt more like a month of Sundays. But at the same time there has been so much to get through and so many things to fit in that time has quite simply run out.'

'And,' Florence added, already looking dazed as she lowered herself into the chair, 'it has never stopped raining.'

Katherine glanced from the window. It was true. For days the weather had battered her precious flowers, and now she was faced with the task of trying to salvage the best of them for the house. She had badly wanted to make a show for the party. Now that too, it seemed, was destined to be thwarted. 'It does appear to have stopped at last,' she said, peering through the glass. 'Although I fancy it's too late to save my plans.' She began to pack Florence into the chair with cushions. 'There now dear. How's that?'

Florence replied with a grunt that passed for a 'yes' and strained her eyes to see. 'I think we'll all be relieved when tomorrow's over, won't we?

What a lot of fuss over reaching a mere seventy. I won't expect this kind of palaver when I make my hundred.'

Katherine smiled tolerantly. 'I'm sure we'll go town anyway,' she said, patting the old lady's hand.

She settled herself at the desk and returned to her endless lists, ticking things off where she could. She would collect the flowers in a moment. Then she must slip into the village for one or two things. Lemons. Yes, she would probably be short of lemons. Katherine sighed. As she worked through her list it was almost as though she could see nothing beyond the next important day; as though after that she would be able to close a chapter of their lives and draw a line under all the events of the recent past that had given them all such grief.

William echoed her sentiments. That morning he himself faced the bitterest of pills, the selling of precious land. Hodges was driving him into Hexham to his lawyer's office, where he and Robson were to exchange contracts for the vast tract of pasture known as Friar's Meadow. After that he would at once settle his debts with the man.

'I cannot face the celebration of my three score years and ten with any lack of integrity,' he told her sadly. 'Then we can begin to go forward again.'

She had seen him on his way a short time before with a heavy heart, knowing that he would never quite come to terms with the hand Fate had dealt him, nor forgive himself for breaking his promise to future generations.

Florence was already gently snoring. Katherine closed her notebook, rose quietly to her feet and went into the hall. Her trug basket and secateurs were in the cupboard by the door with her gardening shoes. She began to prepare herself for a rather damp sortie amongst the flowers. From the corner of her eye she noticed a flash of red beyond the half open door, and heard the crunch of tyres on the gravel. The post, she supposed; more cards probably. People were being wonderfully kind and thoughtful.

She pushed open the door and went out onto the porch. Propped against one of the stone pillars were two immense parcels, a letter attached to them. She was just in time to see the red vehicle disappearing round the sweep of the drive. Since birthday presents had been strictly forbidden the discovery made no apparent sense.

For a long time Katherine stood staring at the packages. Then gingerly she began to tear at the brown paper wrapping from the first of them. Inside she discovered an oil painting – an immense portrait, dark, clearly very old, but quite unknown to her. She stared in astonishment. The man depicted was gloomy and dark with age, an unknown face from unknown origins. As she expected the other package contained another, this one a dark and swarthy man of military bearing. Both were dark and indistinct - their costumes probably Jacobean, Katherine thought. Could these paintings be as old as that? She knew that she had never seen them before, yet somehow they evoked an uncanny stab of recognition. She carried them into the hall, her heart thumping against her ribs, although she was not sure why. It was all so curious, so inexplicable.

Slowly she sank onto a chair and opened the letter. By now she was trembling like a leaf. It was addressed to no-one in particular, so she began to read it.

'I am afraid I have not the courage to return these pictures to you in person,' she read. 'You may not recognise them but they do belong to you, and I discovered them in the course of cleaning and restoring your art collection. I noticed just the hazy reflection of an eye in that ancient still life, and after removing a layer of paint uncovered this face. I am still in awe of what it means, and has made every minute spent at Foxsteads worthwhile. James Edward Stewart is of course the Old Pretender, which experts in London believe dates it back to when your pele tower stood four square in the Jacobite cause. Sir John Flynne of Foxsteads Demesne was his most loyal supporter – and of course the stuff of legend in this very place. Both portraits must have been over-painted in great haste in the face of the Jacobites' defeat. Certainly they are survivors. They only escaped the fire in the lodge because I had taken the liberty of sending them, via a friend, to London for verification. They are, on the best possible authority, indisputably genuine and I understand that The National Portrait Gallery will be contacting you in due course. I am sure you will appreciate that either one of these portraits would pay for your roof twice over. They are of immense value and historic worth. It pleases me very much to be the bearer of such news in the face of the problems you have had, and all your kind hospitality to me. I trust you will remember me kindly. Anya.'

Katherine read the letter again, and then yet again. But somehow she could not wholly assimilate its content, nor come to terms with the enormous significance it conveyed. She was still sitting staring at it when Matt came upon her there. Mutely she handed him the sheet of paper, written in Anya's distinctive rounded hand. Her face was ashen and there were tears in her eyes.

He too read it in silence. Then he turned to the pictures and finished unpacking them, propping them against the hall table. He recognised the old frames with the iron brackets, which suddenly perfectly matched their contents. Two extraordinary faces looked back at him from the distant past. They seemed to return and hold his gaze. A frisson of excitement awakened him to the fact that he was looking at something utterly sensational. 'They are magnificent,' he breathed.

Still Katherine looked stunned. 'I cannot believe this is anything but a dream.'

'I agree, it is wholly unbelievable. When did you discover them? When do you think they came?'

'They have only just arrived – not half an hour ago. I saw the red car disappearing down the drive.'

Matt stared at her incredulously as reality began to dawn. 'As recently as that?' Now his eyes filled with fervour. 'Then don't you see? I must go after her. Dear God – I haven't a minute to spare.'

'Don't be foolish, Matt. She will be miles away by now – and in heaven-knows-which direction.'

'I know. But I have to try.' She shook her head sadly, but already he was at the door. 'You must agree it's worth a try. I need so desperately to see her.'

She looked at him forlornly. Clearly he too had not quite understood the letter. He was still chasing his rainbows and unable to accept what could only be a hopeless cause. It hurt her deeply to see him so wretched.

He came and knelt down on the floor beside her and took her hand. 'Listen carefully, Mother. I have to go. I have to give it one more try. And I want you to do two things while I'm gone. Ring Makepeace and Francis at once and tell them to hold proceedings for the land sale. It must be stopped at once.' He glanced at his watch. 'With luck, Dad won't even be there yet.'

'Very well, I'll do it straight away.'

'Then get Henry to come up from Newcastle as soon as he can. He deserves to see this!' He gave her a hug and a kiss before getting to his feet. 'What a birthday party this could turn out to be. What a celebration! And within minutes he was roaring down the drive, raising a cloud of dust in his wake.

* * *

344

The Military Road traversed the country from coast to coast. It followed the line of the Roman Wall, in places commanding spectacular views of it, in places actually running along its course, shadowed by the deep ditch of the vallum. It dated from the turbulent times following the defeat of the Jacobites. Matt intimately knew every inch of it.

But there were more than twenty tortuous miles between Foxsteads and the Military Road, and the only car at his disposal that day turned out to be his mother's aging Morris Minor, which with the wildest optimism was no match for an MG . Refusing to be daunted, Matt roared through the gears, surprised at how neatly it took the bends and responded when his foot touched the floor. Soon he was cruising down the last steep stretch to Chollerford and joining the Military Road where it crossed the Tyne by a stone bridge. Then it was down into second gear for the long ascent up Brunton Bank.

For the first time Matt's confidence began to fail. His certainty that Anya would head east was less strong, and as the straight expanse of the road stretched before him, quite empty for as far as the eye could see, he acknowledged that this was probably an impossible quest in pursuit of the unattainable.

He opened up the throttle and the little car rattled noisily over a road that now switch-backed its way between the gorse-strewn vallum of the wall to the north and the golden, late summer pastures of the Tyne valley to the south. Ahead lay the metropolis of Newcastle. If Anya had taken this route – and he still believed that probably she had – once in the city his chance would be lost. For a moment he fancied he saw a red dot on the horizon, but it dipped with the road and was lost from sight. In his heart he was beginning to accept defeat.

Perhaps it was too much to hope for a fairy-tale ending to this extraordinary affair. He thought of the two amazing portraits, of the difference they could make to the fortunes of them all. He thought too of the dramatic letter she had written, sensing the loneliness behind it. And in all this she had denied them the opportunity to thank her as she deserved, and to apologise for their misjudgement of her. These thoughts were complex, painful and profoundly sad.

Then all at once he saw her. Rounding one of the few bends on the road he came upon the little car parked in a farm gateway. She was at the wheel, studying her map. For a moment he thought he was dreaming. Slowly he drew in beside her, effectively blocking her exit, turned off the engine and got out. Her response was startled, bleak and unwelcoming.

'Matt, what on earth are you doing here?' She stepped from the car and faced him angrily. 'Are you following me?'

'Of course I'm following you. What do you expect?'

She did not reply.

'For heaven's sake, Anya, how could I let you disappear after what has happened, without so much as a word of thanks?'

'Thanks are unnecessary. I was only returning what's yours.'

He stared at her incredulously. 'How can you say such a thing? You were presenting us with something beyond price – not just something we didn't know we owned – but a future with hope written on it. It is the most unbelievable turn of events imaginable – beyond imagination – beyond fiction – and you can calmly write it off as not worthy of a word of thanks?'

'You misunderstand me. I know perfectly well what a wonderful discovery it has been. I could never write off such a thing. There hasn't been a better moment in my career than when I discovered that incredible face amongst the fruit. It was enough to last a lifetime. I'm the one who's grateful. I don't wish to be given any thanks.'

'Not even for returning them?'

She looked at him sombrely. 'They were yours, weren't they? Of course I returned them. Or did you, Matt, also doubt my integrity?'

He felt colour rising to his face. 'Anya, you know I didn't.'

'Everyone else seemed to.'

'But even you must see perfectly well how hard it was to keep faith in the light of the evidence. You can be sure of one thing, though - my feelings and beliefs were never in doubt for a moment.'

She did not answer, but looked beyond him into the grey distance. Across the valley the hills were sharply defined against a threatening sky. A chill wind carried with it the threat of more rain. It had suddenly become very cold.

'Where are you going now?' he asked unevenly.

'Nowhere and everywhere,'she replied.

'That's no answer.'

'I don't have to answer, Matt.' The wind tossed her hair into a bright unruly halo which angrily she pushed from eyes. 'I don't have to answer to anyone.'

Helplessly he looked at her - at her solemn face, which suddenly looked so pale and wan - at those eyes which could outshine the stars, but which were now dull with unhappiness. She stood there looking fiercely resolute yet strangely and paradoxically bereft. He wanted to reach out and touch her but her look forbade it.

'The family will welcome news of you,' he told her.

'Then tell them that I am truly glad for them – and that I will always remember their kindness to me.'

'They will wonder how you could have come to Foxsteads without seeing them – as I do.'

Her eyes clouded and she looked down at the ground. He saw that her lips trembled just a little as she said, 'If it makes any difference then I will tell you that I couldn't face seeing you all because I couldn't face saying goodbye.'

His heart missed a couple of beats. 'You have been very missed,' he told her.

'I can't believe I have left a very big gap in such a close-knit circle.'

He smiled. 'Then you couldn't be more wrong. There is one lady who longs to talk about the London of yesteryear with someone who understands these things. She is missing you. And another, even older, who is missing the willing ear into which she poured her long memories and endless anecdotes.'

'Is she well?'

'Flourishing.'

'And your father?'

'My father misses you too. Tomorrow he celebrates his birthday. He would have loved you to be there, especially when he sees his wonderful portrait.'

Suddenly her eyes became alive. 'The portrait. Did it survive the fire then?'

'Oh yes, it survived – by some miracle. I had taken it to the Birketts' that evening.'

'I can't tell you how glad I am of that.'

The haunted look in her eyes had begun to fade. He even detected a little smile that tugged at the corners of her mouth. 'Then I have left a little piece of myself behind after all.'

'You truly have. But we want the rest of you back.'

She hung her head. 'You of all people understand my need to move on.'

'That's where you're wrong. I've never understood it. Besides there's someone else who's missed you even more.'

'Please don't say anything else.'

'You have to know. Because his world has stopped turning since you left. He is lost, with all his hopes in ruins. You see, he knows that Foxsteads is where you belong – and he wants you to come back and marry him. He loves you very, very much.'

She stood listening in stunned silence. He could see tears welling up in her eyes.

He returned her look with a gentle smile. 'And who, you ask, is this crazy, mixed up fellow who has his head in the clouds? Even I can't be sure I recognise him.'

'I can,' she said softly. And as she stood looking straight into his eyes, her own became green and sparkling again. Her windswept hair gleamed like amber. The sun had come out from behind the clouds, but her smile outshone it. She slipped into his arms like a slender piece of jigsaw that fitted exactly and kissed him joyously.

'Matthew Chevening, I presume!'

Lightning Source UK Ltd.
Milton Keynes UK
UKOW050655220312

189393UK00001B/2/P